WATER'S EDGE

WATER'S
edge

JENNIFER MCARDLE

Water's Edge
Copyright © 2014 Jennifer McArdle

ISBN-13: 978-1500907235
ISBN-10: 1500907235

Cover design by Jennifer McArdle.
Cover photographs: "View of the Water of the Turnagain Arm Near Hope Alaska in Soft Evening Light with Bright Blue Skies" by M. Cornelius/Shutterstock; "Magenta Coloured Fireweed" by MountainHardcore/Shutterstock; "Red Silk Banner Collection Isolated on White Background" by Elena Schweitzer/Shutterstock; "Old Chapel at the Karwendel in Austria" by FooTToo/Shutterstock.

This is a work of fiction. Names, characters, places, and incidents either are the product of the author's imagination or are used fictitiously, and any resemblance to actual persons, living or dead, business establishments, events, or locales is entirely coincidental.

For my family.
Thank you for your unceasing
encouragement and support.

CHAPTER

1

Shivering, Nora stood on the deck of the M/V LeConte and watched anxiously for her first glimpse of the town of Heron. For hours, the only scenery had been endless water crashing against rocky shores. It was more beautiful than anything Nora had ever seen, the remote wilderness, but since the ferry had departed from Juneau, they had only passed two small towns. Two towns in seven hours. The rest of the time Nora had seen nothing but trees. Forests that seemed to go on forever, rising from the shores of the salty water, up the mountainsides, until they disappeared into the fog.

Nora had spent most of the long ride sitting in the warm lounge watching as the ferry passed by other boats. They were mostly small fishing vessels. Occasionally, large flat vessels carrying cargo containers. When the ferry passed through the major shipping lanes right after leaving Juneau, the waters were teeming with activity. Gradually, they passed by fewer and fewer boats as they made their way toward the more remote areas of Southeast

Alaska.

She'd been on ferries far too long. *It should never take this long to get anywhere*, she thought, itching to get off the water and back on solid ground.

Two and a half days. That's how long the first ferry took to get from Washington to Juneau. Two and a half days of wandering around a ship with nothing to do. She'd spent a fair amount of time in the dining room on the main level of the ferry. With its expanse of wide windows, it afforded a rather nice view of the waters and islands. Once a day, a movie played in the theater, a dark chilly room in the center of the vessel. Nora had only walked by the door to the theater, unsure of whether she wanted to be cooped up in a windowless metal room with a bunch of strangers for two hours. The thought was not appealing. In the evenings, the small bar opened, and people gathered there to get to know one another over a pitcher of beer or a game of cards. There was also a forward lounge. It was lined with rows and rows of plush chairs facing a front wall of windows looking out onto the narrow waterway that wove between islands off the coast of British Columbia. On the upper level, there was a recliner lounge, where many people who hadn't purchased cabins slept the ride away. A few more adventurous folks brought sleeping bags or tents and pitched them outside on the upper deck, sleeping under the stars. Nora wasn't that adventurous. She had purchased a four-berth cabin, a small room on the exterior of the ship's cabin level with a small porthole to look outside and four very basic bunks hanging from the walls. It wasn't much, but it was the largest sized passenger cabin and it included the relative luxury of having a private bathroom.

Within the first day on the ferry to Juneau, Nora knew half of the passengers aboard. Some were Alaskans returning home after living in the Lower 48 for a while. Most were vacationers or people moving to Alaska, excited at the prospect of fulfilling lifelong dreams of seeing one of the most beautiful places on Earth. A few were enlisted men on their way to report for duty. Nora couldn't remember most of their names, but many of them had taken the time to introduce themselves, tell her where they were heading, and ask about her own destination. Of course, they had never heard of Heron. That wasn't much of a surprise because even Nora didn't know much about the town. She could find it on a map, but that was it.

After the longest boat ride of her life, the ship docked in Juneau. But Nora was still only partway to her destination. She had another seven-hour boat ride to endure. So, the next day, she re-boarded the Alaska Marine Highway on a much smaller ferry that served several remote communities on various islands nearby. There were far fewer passengers aboard, all of them local, and all of them tired looking. It was no wonder. Travel had never been so exhausting.

Now, knowing her long journey was coming to a close, Nora refused to sit inside for another minute. She could barely contain her excitement at the prospect of seeing the town she would call home. In spite of the cold, she wanted her first sight of the town to be from the forward deck, not through a streaked window in the lower observation lounge.

Over the loud speaker, the captain announced their impending arrival, adding that the temperature in Heron was a balmy 47 degrees. A joke, Nora assumed, as she walked around the deck of the ship trying to find something to shield her from the cold gust of wind that blew right through the thin sweater she wore, biting at her skin with a ferociousness she'd never experienced before. No, balmy was definitely not the word she would use to describe the weather.

Nora had chosen her favorite outfit for her arrival in Heron, even if it wasn't the most practical. She wanted to start her new life on a good note, looking her best. But she was already regretting the ensemble, a knee-length spring skirt paired with a stylish, low-cut cashmere sweater more for looks than warmth. The tall black boots with stiletto heels completed the outfit, which would have been perfect for a nice spring day in California but proved to be treacherous on the damp deck of a ship headed for a small Alaskan town.

No doubt, Conner would have chosen something else for her to wear. But her ex-boyfriend no longer got to decide what Nora wore and where she went and who she went with. Regardless of how smart the decision was, Nora was going to wear the outfit because she wanted to, not because some prick told her it would be the correct thing to wear for such an occasion.

Thank God that relationship was over. Leaving Conner was the most impulsive thing Nora had ever done in her life. She'd always played it safe, followed the rules. And look where it had gotten her. She'd had a comfortable life with Conner, certainly, but not freedom. Not the ability to be herself.

Conner had just been named the most eligible bachelor in Los Angeles when they'd met. He'd captivated her with his unbelievable good looks, polished charm, and the seemingly unending invitations to exclusive social events. Being with him was like a dream. Before long, Nora found herself receiving invitations to the most important events and more than once she'd been pictured on the social pages alongside the handsome Conner Bradshaw. The men wanted her. The women wanted to be her. And Nora got caught up in the glamorous lifestyle. But the thrill of it all wore off rather quickly when Nora realized Conner put his reputation before everything else in his life. For someone of his social stature, appearance meant everything, which meant Nora had to look, and be, her best at all times. She wasn't given the option to choose her own clothes or hairstyles. Even when they went out, Conner chose where they'd go and what they'd do. Nora couldn't remember the last time she'd been able to choose her own meal off a menu. Two years with a man who had dictated every aspect of Nora's life had proven to be more than enough. She was through with men.

Nora wrapped her arms around herself, trying to ignore the cold greeting of the wind as the ferry eased around a bend and the town finally came into view in the distance. She really should have done at least a little bit of research on the place before spontaneously hopping on a ferry for a three day ride to the middle of nowhere. But she'd been on such an emotional high after finding the courage to leave the security, and the captivity, of her life with Conner that she hadn't given much thought to what she was going to do once she arrived in Alaska. All she cared about was having a home of her own. A place where she could do whatever she wanted, eat whatever she wanted, wear whatever she wanted. She didn't care she was leaving behind a wealthy and successful fiancé, an enormous home, and enough money to buy just about anything a person could ever want. She didn't need much. She already had three times as many clothes as most people. She had a small savings account and if she needed a little cash, she could always sell the car. Nora preferred walking, anyway. And even though Nora didn't really have any job skills, she was sure she'd be able to find a job doing something.

The sight of the cozy little town nestled in along the shore of Chichagof Island brought a hopeful smile to Nora's face. The town was small, as she'd expected, and it had a charming coastal atmosphere. Almost the entire community was built up on pilings over tidal flats. It stretched about a mile along the shore, one long continuous dock connecting the buildings together. Immediately beyond the long strip of houses and buildings, a mountain rose up at a sharp angle, casting a shadow over the town, guarding it the way a mother hen would protect her young.

The weathered buildings and homes looked worn, painted in a variety of colors that were once bright and cheery but had turned dull over the years. The paint on many of the homes was beginning to peel, and some of them were taking on a greenish hue from the mold and mildew of the damp weather. Still, the town looked attractive under the shadow of the tall mountain, with the water lapping at the darkened wooden pillars that suspended the buildings mere feet above the water. It might be pretty far removed from the rest of the world, Nora thought, but the picturesque view just might make up for that one flaw.

Nora pulled the letter out of her pocket and read through it one more time. After she had received it in the mail three weeks earlier, she'd promptly called the attorney to find out if it was real or just some awful joke. The man, a Mr. Marshall Mallow, whose very name sounded made up, assured her she did in fact own the property and the appropriate paperwork would be waiting for her when she arrived in Heron. According to the attorney, the property consisted of 5 acres and improvements that included a house and two storage buildings. Oceanfront property, he had said, left to Nora by her late uncle.

For a week, Nora had kept the letter hidden from Conner as she debated her options. She didn't want Conner's advice on what to do with the property. She wasn't sure she wanted Conner's advice about anything anymore. The more she thought about it, the more Nora realized she didn't want the life Conner had given her. Before she fully thought it through, Nora started packing her bags. She packed up everything important to her, which surprisingly all fit in the back seat of her car, and left the home she'd shared with Conner. Driving up to Bellingham, Washington, from Los Angeles, she had called Conner and left a message on his voice-mail, breaking up with him. Probably not the best way to leave someone, she had to admit, but it had been one of the most liberating acts she'd ever committed. She'd instantly felt free, the weight had lifted off her shoulders. She was setting out on her own, heading to an unknown town, to a house she hadn't even seen a picture of. Every minute, every hour that had passed on the ferry took Nora further away from the only life she'd ever known and closer to her new life in a small bush community, and it felt great.

As the ship passed by the town and made its way toward the dock on the south end of the community, Nora looked at each of the houses, wondering which one of them might be her house. Any one of them would do. Even though Nora had lived in luxury for the past two years, the money had all been Conner's. Aside from her modest savings account, at least modest by Conner's standards, she didn't have much of her own and she couldn't afford to be too picky. A home was all she needed, all she really wanted.

Looking at the seaside homes nestled in closely along the shoreline, Nora smiled contentedly. This quaint community was her new home. It definitely wasn't a large town, but she hadn't expected it to be. After all, it was nothing more than a little dot on the map, a far cry from the city she'd grown up in. But it looked as good as any other place to start fresh.

As the ship approached the dock, Nora folded the letter and tucked it back into her pocket. Then she went to the center stairwell and waited for the crew to open up the car deck. Below, on the lower deck, Nora climbed into her shiny blue Prius, a gift from Conner for her birthday the previous year, and waited for the ferry workers to guide her off the ship.

Apparently Heron was not a highly sought-after destination, Nora realized as a deck hand directed her to pull forward toward the ramp. A few people exited the ferry through the pedestrian ramp and a couple others waited to board the ship, but that was all. In other ports, Nora had watched while dozens of people disembarked the ship on foot and even more by vehicle. But that was not the case here. According to Nora's count, only five people including herself, were getting off in Heron. Even odder, she thought, hers was the only vehicle disembarking the ship. She realized why as soon as she exited the ramp and found herself in a small parking lot that didn't appear to be connected to any roads. Several boats on trailers were parked in the lot, along with only a handful of other vehicles, all of them older, sturdy-looking pick-up trucks.

Simply because she didn't know what else to do or where to go, Nora parked her car and then got out and looked around. *There had to be roads, right?* The only thing Nora saw even resembling a road was a narrow dirt trail leading away from the parking lot and up into the mountains. The trail quickly disappeared from Nora's sight where it entered the forest, and Nora could only assume the trail went inland, further away from the town.

Frustrated, Nora kicked the car's front tire. So the car was completely useless here, she realized bitterly, wishing she'd taken the time to at least do a quick internet search on the town of Heron. If she'd known there were no roads, she could have saved herself hundreds of dollars by walking on the ferry instead of paying to haul a car all the way up to the middle of nowhere. Not to mention, she could have sold the car back in California, or even in Washington before boarding the ferry. It all seemed like such a waste now.

Oh, well. Nora sighed, resigning herself to the fact that she'd brought her car all this way for nothing. At least she had all of her things. She wouldn't have been able to carry all of her stuff onto the ferry as a walk-on, Nora reminded herself, trying to look on the bright side.

Locking the car doors, Nora turned and walked in the direction the other passengers had gone, toward the entrance to a long boardwalk. The others had already disappeared from sight, leaving Nora wondering which direction to follow the boardwalk. To the right, she saw a handful of buildings that looked like houses. To the left, there was a marina and a long line of larger buildings. Left seemed like the logical direction, so that's where Nora went in search of a place called the Pub & Grub. That's where Mallow had directed her to go.

Since the entire town was less than a mile long, it didn't take long for Nora to find a building with a simple wooden sign hanging out over the boardwalk with the words "Pub & Grub" marked in dark blue paint. The wooden structure sat on the water side of the boardwalk, though truthfully all of the buildings on both sides of the boardwalk sat on stilts sticking up from the tidal flats below, even the ones nestled up against the mountainside. Like most of the other buildings, the Pub & Grub looked like it had been there for a hundred years – the building wasn't nearly that old, but the dampness of the coastal climate made everything age faster.

There was no sign on the exterior of the building to indicate whether the establishment was open or closed. There were no windows on the boardwalk side of the building for Nora to peek in, either. Curious, she grabbed the door handle and pulled. She hadn't seen a single soul since she got off the ferry and lost sight of the four other passengers that had disembarked the ship at the same time. She was beginning to think this place was a ghost town, so she was actually surprised when the door easily opened and the soft sound of music drifted out from the building.

Inside, the Pub & Grub was rather dark, with dimly lit little lamps on each table. A bar ran almost the entire length of one wall and the rest of the building was filled with dining tables. The back wall was made up of tall windows, allowing an unobstructed view of the harbor and the inlet.

The place was empty except for a group of three burly looking men who sat at one of the tables, talking and laughing. All three of them stopped talking the instant Nora walked in and turned to stare at her.

She looked out of place. Her clothes were expensive, her jewelry ostentatious. She was striking and she knew it. Anywhere else, Nora would have relished having every head turn when she walked into a room. She usually enjoyed the attention, knowing all eyes were on her, that people admired her. But this was an altogether different feeling. It was actually unnerving, the way they looked at her, skeptically eying her up and down. The bearded men didn't look at her as most men did, with longing in their eyes, wanting her. They looked at her curiously, with distrust. Their nosy stares filled Nora with a sense of unease she'd never experienced before.

One nodded in her direction, said something to the others, and chuckled. *Are they... laughing at me?* she wondered.

Nora ignored their stares and turned her attention to the other side of the room, where the smell of burgers cooking on a grill reminded her just how hungry she was. At the far end of the bar, a pretty young blonde woman stood over a hot grill, preparing three plates. Nora walked in her direction, as the woman spread some butter onto hamburger buns then placed them on the grill.

The food smelled delicious. Nora hadn't eaten anything on the ferry ride from Juneau and she was getting quite hungry. She took a seat on one of the bar stools and grabbed a menu lying on the bar.

As soon as she sat down, the cook turned, saw her, and smiled invitingly. Nora guessed the woman was about the same age as her, in her mid-twenties. She was slender and tall. Very tall, Nora noticed, as she wiped her hands on a towel and walked toward her. *Is she really wearing shorts? In this weather?* Of course, Nora was wearing a skirt, but she was also freezing. This woman didn't seem the least bit fazed by the cold weather.

The cook grabbed a pot of coffee and a mug as she walked over, then set the mug down in front of Nora. Without asking, she poured a cup. Her long, curly blond locks had been hastily pulled up into a ponytail, and a few stray tendrils had sprung out during the course of her shift at the pub, where she apparently did everything. She was bartender, waitress, and cook.

"Cream or sugar?" she asked, looking Nora over and seeing the exhaustion on her face. "Or maybe a nip of whiskey?" she added with a wink.

"Black is fine," Nora said, smiling politely. "Thank you."

"You're welcome," she said. Conspiratorially, then, the woman leaned over the bar as if she were going to share a secret. Instead, she asked Nora a question. "So, why'd you bring a car all the way out here?" she asked quietly.

Nora's smile disappeared and was replaced by a look of both shock and embarrassment. She'd only been in town for a few minutes, she hadn't seen a single soul, and yet the bartender in the only restaurant in town had already heard about the stupid girl who brought a vehicle to a town with no roads.

Then the woman's face broke out into a smile.

"Don't worry about it," she said in an attempt to boost the newcomer's spirits. "You're not the first and you won't be the last. Why do you think they have that parking lot there, anyway?"

It was nice of her to say so, but it still didn't alleviate Nora's embarrassment.

The woman stuck her hand out, then. "I'm Lily, by the way. Lily Frontier. As in, Alaska, the last American frontier. Fitting, huh?" Then she stepped back away from the bar and dramatically bowed as if she were in a Shakespearean play. Nora laughed at that. The girl definitely had a flair for the dramatic. "And I'm guessing you're Nora, right?"

"Uh, yeah," she said. "How did you know?"

"Still a little too early in the season for tourists, so I figured you must be the one Mallow called me about. He sent some papers for you," Lily said, looking under the bar and not finding what she was looking for. "Now, if I can just remember where I put them," she said with a grimace on her face. "Hold on a sec. I'll be right back."

Lily walked over to the open kitchen area of the bar, pulled three hamburgers off the grill and stacked them onto plates already prepped with buns, lettuce, and tomato. Then she balanced one plate on an arm and picked the other two up in her hands and delivered them to the three men at the other end of the restaurant. Less than a minute later, Lily was back, but then she disappeared into a small office behind the bar. She reappeared a few seconds later with a large, thick envelope. "Here it is," she said, sliding the envelope across the bar to Nora.

Nora took the manila envelope and tore open the sealed end, eager to find out which house was hers. It looked like a bunch of paperwork, which she had expected. But she also figured there would be a set of house keys. Emptying out the envelope, she realized there were none.

"Not what you expected?" asked Lily curiously.

Nora shook her head and sighed. "No, I just thought there would be more…" She let her thought trail off, remembering Lily was a stranger. As nice as Lily seemed to be, Nora wasn't comfortable sharing the details of her life with someone she'd just met. "Um, can you tell me how to get to my uncle's house?"

"Who's your uncle?"

"Pete Cooley. The address just said Heron, Alaska." It hadn't made sense at the time that there was no street address. But now, knowing there were no roads, Nora understood.

As soon as Nora mentioned her uncle's name, Lily perked up. She knew him. She knew where his place was. "Yeah. I think you're going to like his place," she said. "The house needs some work, mind you, but the rest is absolutely beautiful." Lily smiled reassuringly.

Nora couldn't help but smile back. If she had felt even an ounce of apprehension about leaving everything behind and moving to a small town on a remote island in Alaska, it all dissipated in that moment. Leaving Conner and coming to Alaska might turn out to be the best decision Nora had ever made.

"Are you just visiting or are you planning to stick around?" Lily asked.

"I'm staying," Nora said confidently.

"Well, then, you are in for a real treat," Lily said enthusiastically. "Pete built that place up himself. I was just a kid back then, but from what I hear, he spent the first year out there sleeping under the stars. Don't know how he did it when winter rolled around. No shelter. No neighbors. Surprised he didn't freeze to death."

"Wait, what do you mean, no neighbors?" Nora looked at Lily, alarmed.

"Oh, Nora, that place is a good ten miles out," Lily explained. "Don't worry, though. It's right on the water. Real easy to get to."

Nora's breath caught in her throat. *I can't be hearing this right.* The house wasn't in town at all. It was out in the wilderness, with no neighbors and the only way to get there was by boat. But that couldn't be right at all. She'd spoken with Mallow over the phone. He had said the house was in Heron, not ten miles out. How was Nora ever going to survive on her own in the wilderness? She didn't know the first thing about survival or about being alone –

not that kind of alone, anyway.

"It might be real easy to get to if I had a boat," Nora spat out. Clearly, the whole idea of inheriting a house and property had been nothing but a cruel joke. For the first time, Nora began to question her decision to leave Los Angeles.

Lily watched Nora, her sudden anxiety evident. The property really was a gem as far as Lily was concerned, but she supposed it would take a certain type of person to live so far away from everything. Judging by the look on Nora's face, Nora was not that type of person. Lily thought about it for a minute and then decided to help her out. After all, if Nora planned to live out there, she would need all the help she could get.

"You know what? My brother Jake can take you out there." Lily reached across the bar and patted Nora's hand, trying to make her feel a little better about the situation. "You wait right here and I'll go call him," Lily said. Then, before she walked into the office behind the bar, she added. "You look hungry and I'll bet you didn't eat on the boat. Can I get you anything?"

Nora looked down at the menu in front of her for the first time. She'd grown accustomed to not even looking at menus, since Conner always ordered for her. She didn't even know where to begin.

"I think it's going to take me a while to decide," Nora said, unable to focus on the words on the menu. All she could think about was how foolish she'd been to get her hopes up.

Lily nodded and then disappeared into the office. Nora could hear her on the phone, telling her brother about the poor girl who needed a ride because she had brought a car to the island and not a boat. It all sounded so pathetic to Nora.

A couple minutes later, Lily hung up the phone. Nora's seat was empty, but since her purse was still draped over the backrest of the stool, Lily knew she hadn't gone far. Nora's cup of coffee was empty, so Lily refilled it. Then she went over to the kitchen area and tossed two more hamburger patties on the grill and readied some French fries for the deep fryer.

Feeling overwhelmed, Nora retreated to the ladies room and the tears came before she even closed the door. The ladies room wasn't much, but at least it was a private area to cry. It was a tiny room, smaller than most bedroom closets. In fact, there was barely enough room for her to stand up between the toilet and the sink. It was clean, though, Nora noticed as she lowered the lid on the toilet and sat down.

Maybe it hadn't been the smartest idea to leave everything to move to Alaska. But she couldn't go back. She wouldn't go back. Not to Conner and not to the elitist society she had become a part of... and grown to despise.

The sobs came silently and Nora was thankful for that. She didn't want anyone to hear her crying in the bathroom. That was the last thing she needed right now. She'd already made enough of a fool of herself just by showing up there. She didn't want to do anything else that might make her appear even more foolish in front of these rough-and-tumble people who would no-doubt be telling everyone about the fragile little thing that just got off the boat, literally.

Nora didn't know how long she'd been in the bathroom and she didn't care. She cried until the tears dried up, until she couldn't cry anymore. This was going to be her life now. At least she had a home and some property. She could adapt. That's what she told herself, deciding everything was going to work out fine. It had to.

When Nora emerged from the bathroom, Lily could tell she'd been crying. But Lily didn't say anything. Instead, she walked over to the grill and pulled a hamburger off the flames. Then she returned to Nora and set a large plate of fries and a big, juicy burger down in front of her.

"Hope you don't mind, but I took the liberty of choosing something for you. It's time for my break and I don't like eating alone," Lily said before Nora could say anything.

"Thank you."

"It's nothing," Lily reassured Nora. She reached into the cooler behind the bar and pulled out two cans of Coke. She placed one in front of Nora. The other one, she opened and took a long drink. Then Lily walked over to the grill and loaded up another plate and sat down next to Nora at the bar.

All she'd had for breakfast was an apple, so Nora was starving. She already had half of the burger eaten by the time Lily sat down and she was working her way through the fries before she took a break.

"Thanks," Nora said, beginning to feel a little better about her situation now that she had a full stomach. "You have no idea how much I needed that. What do I owe you?"

Lily simply nodded her head and shrugged it off. Swallowing a bite of her burger, she said, "On the house."

"That's very kind, but I..."

"Don't worry about it," Lily interrupted. "Out here, we look out for each other. We have to or else none of us would survive."

"Is it really that bad?" Nora asked, genuinely wondering what she was in for. She'd heard about harsh Alaskan winters with temperatures dipping down to 50 degrees below zero. "Are we going to have 10 feet of snow? And does it really stay dark all winter long?"

Lily laughed and shook her head.

"No. You'd have to be a lot further north," Lily said, grinning. "The days get short, mind you, but we still get six or seven hours of daylight in the winter. And the coldest it gets is usually in the low 20s. We have a coastal climate here, so you'll hardly ever see the temperature drop below zero. It's not too bad at all.

"No, it's not the weather here that gets to people. It's the isolation," Lily went on. "You'd think a town of more than a hundred and fifty people would be enough to keep each other company. And I suppose it is. We have plenty of people here and most of them get along fine. I think it's the realization you can't go anywhere that gets to some people. You already know what I mean. That ferry ride in from Juneau takes about seven hours and the ferry only comes twice a month in the summer, once a month in the winter. If you want to leave, say to go shopping in the city, it's a real ordeal to get out of here and then back again. Of course, if you can afford it, the float plane comes in almost daily if the weather's good, so there's that. But most folks have to wait for the ferry to come around and they can get a little stir crazy."

Lily didn't look up from her meal to notice Nora's face had grown paler at the portrait of Alaskan life she was describing. She kept on going, talking in between bites.

"It does rain a lot here, though," Lily explained. "And we do get a fair amount of snow, but that's not so bad either. The main thing you have to deal with in the winter here are the rough waters. High winds and choppy seas will make it difficult for you to get into town in the winter, so you'll want to make sure you have plenty of supplies to get you through. And then there's the fog, too. When winter rolls around, you could be stuck out there by yourself for weeks at a time, so you'll have to be prepared."

Lily looked up at Nora, then. The look on Nora's face had Lily wondering if she'd gone too far. Maybe she should let Nora see the property first and get settled in before she started telling horror stories about people who got stuck out in the wilderness.

"I'm not trying to scare you, now," Lily said reassuringly. "You're going to love it. That piece of property has the best view of the mountains across the inlet."

"If the property is so great, maybe I could sell it?" Nora asked hopefully.

Lily shook her head. "You could try, but I doubt you'd have much luck. It takes a certain kind of person to buy property that far out. The land is gorgeous, but there aren't too many people lining up to live that far away from everything. You know what I mean?"

Nora didn't say anything. She just nodded her head. She knew exactly what Lily meant because that's exactly how she felt. She didn't want to live ten miles out in the wilderness. She was a city girl. She had expected the house to be in town, around other people.

"I'm a little jealous, you know," Lily said, trying to reassure Nora. "I wouldn't mind getting out of town and away from all these yahoos." She cocked her head in the direction of the three older men across the room, one of whom was animatedly telling a story about a whale that had surfaced right next to his fishing boat the day before while he was out trolling. "These guys are mild right now, but they can get unbelievable rowdy. If I didn't have my dad to think about, I wouldn't mind disappearing into the wilderness for a bit. The peace and quiet would do me some good, not to mention what fun it would be. Fending for yourself. Surviving on nothing but your wits." Lily grinned. "Seems like it would be quite an adventure. And you came at just the right time... spring," she said. "Why, if I were you I'd plant a little garden or maybe build a small greenhouse. Then you could grow some fresh food and not have to buy that nearly rotten crap Nate sells at The General Store. Have you been to The General Store yet?" Lily didn't wait for Nora to answer. "It isn't much, but Nate carries almost anything you'll need. And if he doesn't have it, he'll order it for you. You should swing by there before Jake takes you out to the property. You're going to want to stock up on canned goods. I mean, it's not like you're going to be able to come into town every day for groceries, or anything."

Nora sat there, not sure what to say. She had some groceries in the car, but would they be enough? How long would her supplies last? Nora had no idea. Lily noticed her silence.

"I'm sorry," Lily said. "I'm rambling now, aren't I?"

Nora shook her head. "No, it's fine. You've given me a lot to think about."

"Well, don't think about it too much. You just need to get out there and see the place."

"But I've never been isolated from other people like that," Nora said. "What if I can't handle it? I could go crazy out there."

"Oh, well if that's the case, then don't risk it," said Lily jokingly. "The last thing we need is another crazy person out here. We have enough of those already. The ferry doesn't pull out for another 45 minutes, so there's still time to hop on it and go back home."

Nora shook her head. "No," was all she said.

"Good." Lily smiled. "You want my advice? Just go out there and see what it's like. I bet you're going to love it. Out there, you'll be just far enough away from all of these crazies," she said, raising her voice so the men eating their lunch across the restaurant could hear her. The scruffiest one of the bunch turned and flashed a bearded grin at her.

"Lily's the craziest of 'em all," he hollered back at them. "She keeps begging me to marry her. That's why I carry this umbrella around. Got to have something to beat her away with."

Lily turned back to Nora, laughing at the old man. "Anyway, you came here for a reason, right? Maybe it's not what you expected, but you're here now. You owe it to yourself to at least give it a try. You're the only one who knows if you're capable of surviving out there. And besides, if you need help you do have neighbors."

"Neighbors?" Nora perked up. "I thought you said there were no neighbors."

"Oh, well there weren't when Pete first moved out there. But like I said, that was a long time ago. Now there are three other cabins out that way, none of them terribly close to you but all of them a lot closer than town," she said. "Tom and Catty Baker live in a float house further down the inlet. Then there's Hilly Duncan. His cabin is about halfway up Long Mountain. And the closest one is Willie. I don't know his last name because he won't tell anybody. But he lives right on the water, about a mile from your place. If you need a hand, I'm sure any one of them would be willing to help you out."

Even though Lily had meant to offer some encouragement, Nora was even more skeptical. "So, my nearest neighbor is a mile away?"

"Yeah," Lily said enthusiastically. "There's even a trail you can take from your place to Willie's. No boat required."

Lily was smiling as if that should alleviate some of Nora's concerns. The thought of hiking through the woods for a mile to reach her nearest neighbor wasn't very encouraging, but in spite of everything, Nora couldn't help but laugh. "So, two of my closest neighbors are named Hilly and Willie."

"Yeah." Lily laughed too.

Trying to look on the bright side, Nora realized being so far removed from everything might be a good thing. Here, she could start a new life, a life completely different from anything she'd ever known.

"It does sound like it could be rather peaceful out there. That is, if the views are as beautiful as you say they are," Nora admitted. "Some solitude might not be so bad."

Lily perked up, then. "Now that's better," she said. "If you're looking for peace and quiet, then you've come to the right place.

It'll be worth it, you'll see."

The phone rang in the office behind the bar and Lily excused herself. The call was brief and a few seconds later Lily returned to the bar. "That was Jake, my big brother," Lily said as she picked up the empty plate in front of Nora and set it down in the sink under the bar. "He's ready to take you out to the property."

"Oh, okay," Nora said. While she was looking forward to getting settled in to the house and getting a decent night's sleep, she was still a little overwhelmed at the thought of being so far away from town. Truthfully, she was somewhat reluctant to leave the restaurant and the only person she knew.

"Don't worry," Lily said, sensing her hesitation. "Everything's going to turn out alright. You'll see."

Nora nodded her head, willing herself to believe Lily's words. "I know," she said, forcing a smile.

"Good. Jake is waiting for you down at the store dock." Lily told her where to go and assured Nora there was no way she could get lost in this town. After all, the boardwalk connected everything and everybody.

As an afterthought, Lily reached around and pulled a good Scotch off the top shelf behind the bar. She set it on the bar in front of Nora.

"Here," she said. "Take this. Consider it a welcoming gift."

"Oh, I don't really drink, not hard liquor, anyway," Nora said, hesitant to accept the gift.

"Doesn't matter. It'll come in handy when Willie stops by. You'll see," Lily said, placing the bottle in Nora's hands.

"Oh. Okay," Nora said. "Thank you… for everything."

Lily wished Nora good luck as she left the Pub & Grub, knowing Nora was going to need it, especially when she saw the "house" Pete had bequeathed to her. Poor girl didn't know what she had gotten herself into.

CHAPTER

2

When Nora emerged from the Pub & Grub, she turned left out onto the boardwalk, as Lily had directed her. Lily was right. There was absolutely no way she could get lost in this town. The boardwalk ran in a straight line along the coast, with only one other narrower walkway branching off and leading inland through a narrow valley. Nora saw a few houses down that way but, for the most part, the majority of the town sat right on the main boardwalk.

At the end of the boardwalk stood a large white building with absolutely nothing to indicate it was the town's only store. But Nora was certain this nondescript building was, in fact, Nate's store. None of the other buildings were possibly large enough to house any amount of merchandise.

A wide deck encircled the store, which hovered out over the water further than any of the other buildings in town. Instead of going inside, Nora walked around the building until the dock came into view, floating on the water at least a dozen feet below where she stood. Several small skiffs were tied off to one end of the dock and a much larger boat was pulled up in front of the dock. There was only one man on the dock and he was busy loading something onto the larger boat. Instead of steps leading down to the dock, there was a long, narrow plank with a railing on each side. The ramp was lined with one-inch wooden slats spaced about a foot apart, all the way down the plank. Nora stepped onto the ramp, and when her foot slipped, she realized the need for the wooden slats. Traction. Gripping the railings, Nora walked the rest of the way down the ramp much more cautiously now that she knew the wooden ramp was a little slick. The four-inch heels on her stylish, but impractical, boots didn't help.

The man was still loading boxes onto the boat when Nora approached him. She stopped right in front of him. Nora wasn't too sure about having a strange man take her into the wilderness, but she had no choice. There was no turning back now. Going back to California wasn't an option. She wasn't even going to entertain the thought. She'd rejected that life because she wanted something different. A fresh start somewhere new. Well, now she really could start over. Just not the way she had expected. The thought put her in a sour mood.

"Are you Jake?" she asked.

The man looked up, startled. He hadn't heard her coming. When Nora got a good look at him, she realized the man couldn't possibly be Jake. Lily had said Jake was her big brother, but this man, with a full, graying beard, had to be at least 50. When he smiled at her, Nora saw three of his front teeth were missing.

"He just went up to the store for a sec," the man said. Then, pointing at the ramp, "There he is now."

Nora turned to see a broad-chested man striding toward her. Like the dockworker, he also sported a beard, but he kept it well trimmed. In spite of what Nora considered chilly weather, he wore a short-sleeved shirt that tightly stretched across his chest and revealed an outline of well-defined muscles. A pair of blue jeans hugged his waist and disappeared below the knees into a pair of brown, rubber boots. He carried a cardboard box propped up on one shoulder and held out a hand in greeting when he approached her.

So this was the niece Pete had talked about, Jake thought. She didn't look at all like the adventurous kid Pete had described. No, this woman looked like the most adventure she'd ever experienced was a trip to the mall.

"You must be Nora," he said, his kind smile masking his curiosity.

Jake's smile revealed he still had all of his teeth, Nora noticed. Apparently, not every man in Heron was old, burly, and toothless. So that was a plus, she thought dryly.

Nora shook his hand and greeted him politely, coolly. The man looked trustworthy enough. Just like his sister, Jake was tall and lean. His hair was a sandy blond and looked like it had been freshly cut. His build was almost athletic looking, strong and capable.

"I appreciate this," Nora said, though the tone of her voice didn't convey much gratitude. "I assumed the house was in town. When I got out here and I realized I'd need a boat to get there, I didn't know what I was going to do."

Jake thought he heard a trace of agitation in her voice and he got the distinct feeling Nora was nothing more than a selfish, spoiled brat. She was beautiful, he had to admit, with her long amber-colored hair and those big blue eyes. He could tell her clothes were expensive. The kind that needed to be dry cleaned, not washed. And those black heeled boots had to be the most ridiculous thing he'd ever seen. She was definitely accustomed to a particular kind of life, so Jake had to wonder what would bring a woman like this to a small bush town in Alaska. She certainly didn't look too thrilled to be there.

"It's nothing," Jake said, forcing a smile. She'd barely spoken, but already he suspected the two of them wouldn't get along. Maybe he was making a snap judgment, but she seemed a little too self-absorbed for his tastes. But he'd promised Lily he would take her out to Pete's place, and that's what he was going to do. "If you're ready to go, we can run over to your car and get your things and then head out there. Come on, my skiff's over here."

He led her to a small aluminum boat, no more than 12 feet long. He stepped in easily and laid the box down on the bottom of the boat and then turned to Nora. He held a hand out and she took it. Steadily, he helped her into the boat and he didn't let go until she was safely seated at the bow.

The aluminum slat she sat on was hard, uncomfortable. Nora shifted in the seat and smoothed her skirt across her lap, unintentionally scowling at the thought of how miserable the ride was going to be in this thing that could barely be considered a boat.

When she looked up, Jake was staring at her. He looked at her the same way as those men in the restaurant. It made her feel uneasy.

"Have you spent much time on the water?"

"My ex had a yacht. We went out on it a few times. It really wasn't my thing," Nora said disdainfully. Then she realized why he was asking. He didn't want to know if she'd ever been a passenger on a boat. He wanted to know if she knew how to operate one. Because that's how she was going to have to get around from now on. "I have no idea how to drive a boat," she added.

"Well, don't worry about it. You'll get used to it," he said, trying to ignore the unpleasant tone in her voice. "Pete had a skiff pretty much like this one. It should still be out at the property. I'll show you how to use it and you'll be able to get around just fine, as long as you don't try to take it out into the open water."

Then Jake reached over and untied the boat from the dock. A few seconds later, the small outboard motor roared to life, making any further conversation nearly impossible without yelling. Smoothly, Jake maneuvered the skiff away from the dock. As soon as the skiff was clear of the other boats, he opened the throttle and turned in the direction of the ferry dock.

Even though the ferry dock was all the way on the other side of town, it only took a minute to get there. Jake turned the skiff in the direction of the shoreline, which had lengthened since Nora had arrived earlier on the ferry. The tide was going out and several feet of tidal flats were now exposed alongside the parking lot. Jake pulled the boat right up to the shore, then he jumped out into about a foot of water and dragged the boat further until the bow of the skiff rested on the pebbled flats. Taking Nora's hand again, he helped her out onto the beach.

Back on solid ground, Nora pointed toward the parking lot. "The Prius is mine," she said.

Jake chuckled, amused. "Yeah. I know," he said, leading the way up the embankment to the parking lot. Nora blushed with embarrassment, remembering no one brought their cars to Heron, so of course it would be obvious which vehicle was hers. When they reached the vehicle, Nora unlocked the doors and opened the trunk.

"How much of this stuff do you think we can take out there?" she asked.

Jake surveyed the overstuffed car. "For now, maybe a couple suitcases. Just the necessities."

"Just a couple suitcases? But I need all of this."

Jake shook his head, not feeling at all sorry for the woman. She needed to learn to go without a few of her so-called "necessities." It would probably do her some good.

"Like I said, Pete had a boat out there. You can always come back into town for the rest. By the looks of it, it's going to take three or four trips in a skiff."

"Three or four trips?" That wasn't acceptable. "What if we load the boat as full as we can? Do you think we could cut it down to two trips, maybe?"

Jake laughed at her. "Only if you want to sink the boat."

Defeated, Nora pulled two large suitcases out of the trunk and then reached into the back seat for a box that contained bedding and toiletries and a small grocery bag of food she had bought back in Juneau. "I guess this will do for now," she said reluctantly.

Jake picked up the suitcases and carried them to the skiff. Nora followed behind him with the box in one arm and the grocery bag in the other. While Jake loaded her things into the boat, she looked around one more time at the town, disappointed she would be so far away from it. It would have been nice to get up in the morning and take the boardwalk to the pub for a cup of coffee with new friends. She might have opened a shop of her own, something that catered to tourists and could generate a modest income. Then, in the evenings, she could have sat on her front porch and watched the sun set on the other side of the inlet. It was everything she had dreamed of on her journey north. A dream that wouldn't come true.

When Nora turned back to the boat, Jake already had the suitcases and other supplies loaded into the boat and was waiting expectantly for her to climb back in. With everything in the skiff, there was barely enough room for Nora to step over her things and sit down. When she was safely seated, Jake pushed the boat back out into the water and then jumped in and started the motor.

As Jake turned the boat away from the shore, Nora stood up abruptly. She'd forgotten something. The sudden movement rocked the boat, affecting her balance. Her legs wobbled unsteadily and the boat swayed from side to side.

"Whoa," Jake hollered. "Sit down."

"But I forgot to lock the car doors," Nora said as she carefully lowered herself back into the seat.

Jake laughed at the absurdity of her statement and shook his head. "You don't have to worry about that. No one's going to run off with anything."

Nora wasn't so sure. She may have only brought what she could fit in her car, but those few things she had were precious to her and she didn't want to lose anything.

"You're sure?" she asked.

"Yeah," Jake said reassuringly. "Your stuff is safe."

That was the last thing Jake said before he opened up the throttle and the roaring engine drowned out Nora's response.

The water was relatively calm and the skiff bounced along at a good pace as they headed south into the deep inlet. From where Nora sat, facing the rear, she had a good view of everything they were leaving behind. Her car full of books, movies, gadgets. Her computer. Her photographs and scrapbooks. All of her possessions. Everything she held dear. It all faded into the scenery as the town grew smaller. Before long, the town disappeared completely. Only the snow-capped peak of the mountain hovering over Heron remained in sight. Even that disappeared a few minutes later as the skiff rounded a bend and headed deeper into the inlet.

If Nora had thought it chilly outside before, she was wrong. Out on the water, it was absolutely frigid. The cold from the aluminum seat seeped right through Nora's skirt, freezing her bottom. She wrapped her arms tight and tried to distract herself from the chill.

"How long is it going to take?" Nora yelled over the sound of the motor.

"Another 25 minutes, or so," he hollered back.

Thirty minutes out of town. That wouldn't be so bad, Nora reassured herself. In Los Angeles she had lived thirty minutes from the beach and she had never thought much about driving that far. The only difference is she would be driving a boat instead of a car. *A boat... this is unreal.* She still couldn't believe there were no roads.

With the motor roaring, they really couldn't talk, so Nora fixed her attention on the shoreline. There were no beaches, only rocky ledges and a handful of little coves where the water stood nearly still. It was unchanging. More of the same for miles.

Nora's bottom was numb from the cold by the time she spotted the first hint that man had, in fact, stepped foot on this land at some point. Off in the distance, a tidal flat appeared and Nora faintly distinguished a tiny, little building sitting close to the shore. It was the first man-made structure she'd seen since they left town, so she kept her eye on it as they got closer, wondering if it belonged to one of the neighbors Lily had mentioned.

As the skiff rounded the point of rock where the building sat, the southerly side of the structure came into view. The weathered logs of the tiny log building showed its age. The south facing door was newer, as was the tiny window, but everything else had clearly been built many years ago.

It wasn't much larger than a shed. Perhaps it was used as storage by one of her neighbors or maybe it was a small cabin that had been abandoned long ago. Nora wondered about it right up until the moment Jake turned the skiff toward the shore and cut the throttle. That's when Nora realized the cabin on the shore was their destination.

"Please tell me this isn't the place," Nora pleaded, a touch of dread in her voice. She looked at Jake for reassurance, but he just looked back at her apologetically. "No," she said emphatically. "This can't be the place. The lawyer said there was a house and a couple of outbuildings. This is a shack." She sounded almost hysterical.

Jake wasn't surprised by her reaction. It was exactly what he'd expected. Not everybody was cut out for living in the Alaskan wilderness, certainly not a woman who was obviously accustomed to a more luxurious lifestyle.

"I can take you back into town, if you want," he offered.

"And what good would that do?" she shot back, not expecting Jake to have the answer. "I don't have anywhere else to go. In case you didn't realize it, the ferry only comes to town twice a month."

There really was nothing Jake could say. It was true. Unless she was willing to charter a flight out on a float plane, she was stuck in Heron for at least the next two weeks. But she didn't have to spend those two weeks alone in the wilderness.

"There are a few small lodges in town. A woman like you shouldn't be out here, all alone."

That caught her attention. Nora looked up at him sharply.

"What do you mean, a woman like me?"

"You know what I mean."

Nora shook her head. She was irritated with herself for getting her hopes up in the first place. But even more than that, she was irritated with Jake for thinking she would high-tail it back to town the first chance she got. He didn't even know her, and already he figured she was going to throw in the towel, call it quits. "No," she said, determined to prove him wrong. "I'll just have to manage."

"You'll be better off in town," he said firmly.

"No." Her stubbornness was getting the best of her.

"Fine," Jake said, pulling the skiff to shore. He quickly unloaded all of her belongings and helped her out of the boat. Picking up her suitcases, Jake led Nora up the slight incline toward the cabin. He set the suitcases down beside the door and glanced at Nora. For the first time since meeting Nora, he felt sorry for her. He really did.

Jake turned and opened the cabin door and walked into the darkness. Memory led him to the round wooden table at the far end of the room and then he groped around until his hands found the oil lantern he knew would be sitting in the center of the table. Jake reached into his pocket and withdrew a book of matches and expertly lit the lantern. Then he turned the knob on the side to lengthen the wick. The soft light grew a little brighter and illuminated the entire cabin.

He turned around, then, and saw Nora was still standing outside the cabin, a blank expression on her face. She was doing everything she could to hide her disappointment. It wasn't working.

"No electricity," she said dryly. "And no running water. That just figures."

"What did you expect?"

Apparently too much. She'd anticipated a nice little house in town. When that hadn't panned out, she'd at least expected to find a livable home on the water's edge. Instead, all she had was a shack of a cabin with absolutely no utilities.

"I don't know. Something, at least. Plenty of people live off the grid with solar power."

"Well, out here most people use generators if they need power. Look on the bright side. No electric bills. No heating bills. Some people actually prefer living in a dry home like this. You'll be free to come and go as you please and never have to worry about the water pipes freezing."

Nora looked at him skeptically.

"Come on," he said. "Check out the place." He held out a hand to her, but she didn't take it. Jake dropped his hand to his side as Nora walked past him into the cabin.

The place was small, but not as bad as she had expected it to be from the outside. A lumpy, worn-looking couch sat along one wall, with a wood-burning cook stove sitting opposite it. A wooden ladder led up to a loft above and when Nora stood on her tiptoes she saw a bed perched up there, filling most of the loft space.

Along the rear of the cabin, the wall was lined with shelves cluttered with books, plates and cups, and probably everything Pete had used to survive out there. On one shelf, Nora spotted a lone framed photograph. It was a family portrait taken when she was probably 4 years old. She sat in her mother's lap and her father stood behind them. They were all smiling. That would have been before her parents divorced, a rare occasion when her parents weren't fighting.

"Pete talked about you from time to time, you know," Jake said when Nora's gaze lingered on the photograph. He had mistaken the look in her eyes, thought he saw sadness for her uncle's death.

That surprised her. "Really?" she said. "That seems so weird to me."

"Why?" he asked.

"Well, I never met him," she said simply.

Jake looked at her, puzzled. "The way he talked about you, I always assumed the two of you were close."

"He talked about me? What did he say?"

"Mostly about you as a kid. He said you had an adventurous spirit. He liked to think you got that from him." Looking at her now, Jake had to wonder how Pete had been so wrong about his niece. As far as Jake could tell, Nora wasn't the kind of woman who sought out adventure. Maybe at one time, she might have been different. But now, she looked fragile and delicate, more like the kind of woman that needed to be taken care of. "You really didn't know him?"

"All I ever knew of him was that he was my dad's older brother. He never came to visit us and we never went to visit him."

"That's not true. Pete showed me a picture once. It was of you and him. You were pretty young, though, so I suppose you might not remember it."

Nora shook her head. "I don't. I don't even know what he looked like."

"And yet, he left everything he owned to you," Jake said.

"I suppose he didn't have anyone else to leave it to," Nora replied. She said it casually, as if it didn't mean anything to her. But deep down she was thankful he'd thought of her. He had been her lifeline. He had given her the means to walk away from a difficult situation, a bad relationship. Even if he'd only left her a dilapidated cabin in the middle of nowhere, it was still a chance to start over. It was a better alternative than what she might have become if she'd stayed with Conner. She would have tried to be the perfect wife, but she never would have measured up to his impossible standards. And it would have driven her crazy.

"Maybe you're right," Jake said. Then he turned toward the door. "I'll be right back."

Nora watched him trot back to the boat and bring the rest of her things up to the cabin. He brought the grocery bag in and set it on the table and then hauled in the suitcases.

When he finished, Jake turned to Nora, who stood there watching him. She honestly didn't know what to do with herself.

"Well, would you like me to show you around the place?" Jake asked, sensing Nora's uncertainty.

"I think I've seen it all," Nora said unenthusiastically, "I could probably touch both walls if I stretched my arms out." To prove her point, Nora raised her arms to her sides. The cabin wasn't actually small enough for her to touch both walls, but it was close enough as far as she was concerned.

Jake's lips turned up slightly at the edges. "No, I meant the rest of the property," he said. "You have five acres here and, like the lawyer said, there are a couple of outbuildings."

Nora was worn out from the long trip and exhausted at the thought of how hard life would be in a rustic cabin. She didn't really feel like walking the grounds, but she followed him outside anyway.

Jake led her toward a smaller building immediately behind the cabin. It looked to be in about the same condition as the cabin, and it held a variety of fishing poles, nets, fishing tackle, some large metal traps, a couple pairs of snowshoes, and a couple axes and metal wedges for splitting wood, as well as a collection of old burlap sacks. Alongside the shed, an aluminum skiff sat upside down.

"Well, this isn't going to work," Jake said as he looked over the boat. A hole about three inches wide had been torn through the underside. He looked up at Nora and saw the look of disappointment on her face. "Don't worry," he said. "We'll get you another boat. You're not going to be stuck out here."

"Come on," Jake said, leading her away from the supply shed and the useless boat. He pointed out a stream flowing through the rear of the property, as well as the outhouse that stood well away from the cabin. Then he walked Nora over to the woodpile. Thankfully, there was a good supply of wood already split and stacked.

"It looks like the axe and maul are still in good shape. If you start now, you'll be able to store up enough for the winter."

"Start now?" Nora had no idea what he meant.

"Chopping wood," Jake explained.

Nora's eyebrows shot up in surprise as she began to understand the reality she was faced with. She was going to have to chop wood. She'd never done anything like that before. As a child, she'd gone camping a few times with her parents, but the wood they'd used for campfires had been bought at the store, already neatly chopped and bundled.

Jake chuckled at her expression.

"Don't worry," he said. "It's not that hard, once you get the hang of it. Just swing the axe hard and straight. And if you need help, there's always someone willing to lend a hand."

Help. Just looking at the place, Nora knew she was going to need help. No running water, only a wood stove for heat. She was going to need a lot of help, if she could bring herself to ask for it. There was only one problem. Nora didn't want to ask for help. For the first time in her life, she had a chance to do something on her own, without anyone else stepping in and taking charge. She desperately wanted to prove she could do it, not only to everyone who had ever doubted her, but to herself.

"I'm sure I'll be fine," Nora said stubbornly, not willing to admit that she was in over her head.

"If you say so," Jake said, unconvinced.

Grabbing an armload of wood, Jake led Nora back to the cabin and stacked the wood beside the stove.

"You know how to build a fire, right?" Jake asked her.

Nora lied and said she did. She felt inadequate enough as it was and she didn't want to admit she couldn't do something as simple as build a fire. Everywhere Nora had ever lived, all she'd had to do was turn a little knob on the wall to adjust the temperature. And on those camping trips with her parents, her dad had always been the one to build the fire. All of her life, Nora had stood by while someone else took care of the details. But not anymore.

"Anyone can build a fire," she said, cocking her chin up in defiance.

In spite of Nora's insistence that she'd built fires plenty of times before, Jake still showed her how to load the wood into the stove on top of the kindling and how to light it so it would stay lit. "Even though it gets up into the 40s and 50s during the day, it still gets chilly at night, so you'll have to add more wood later on to keep it going," Nora vaguely heard Jake say. All she could think about was how different their definitions of "chilly" were. All day long Nora had been cold. She was expecting it to be downright freezing at night, not just a little chilly.

With Nora delivered safely to the cabin and a fire roaring in the stove, Jake figured he'd done his job. But he was still a little reluctant to leave her there.

"Well, I guess that's everything," Jake said. "Is there anything else you need help with before I go?"

Nora put on her bravest smile. "No. I'll be fine," she said, trying to convince herself as much as him.

"Are you sure you don't want me to take you back into town? We have a spare room…"

"No," Nora cut him off. "I'll stay." She was determined to make a go of it. Like it or not, this was her home now.

"Ok," Jake said grudgingly.

Nora walked him out to the skiff. The tide was at its lowest and the boat now sat far up on the tidal flats, a good distance from the water.

"Thanks for bringing me out here," she said.

"No problem." Then Jake picked something up out of the skiff. "Oh, I almost forgot. Lily said you probably didn't have too many supplies, so I picked up a few canned goods and some other things I thought you might need." He handed her the cardboard box full of food. Then he quickly pulled the skiff out into the water, jumped in, and started up the motor. He waved one last time before he turned the boat toward town and sped away.

Nora, shocked at receiving yet another welcome gift, stood there holding the box and watching until his boat disappeared from sight. Alone, she walked back up to the cabin. She set the box down on the table alongside the grocery bag and then looked around. It all looked so depressing.

The fire Jake had built was roaring in the fireplace and the cabin had grown rather toasty in a matter of minutes. Nora still couldn't believe she was going to have to chop wood in order to keep warm. She'd only ever seen people chop wood in movies, the ones about early settlers in the west. Is that who she was now? A pioneer?

At least she had a roof over her head, Nora reminded herself. In a way, it was like those camping trips she'd taken with her parents. It wouldn't be so bad to "rough it" for a while in the cabin. That's what she tried to tell herself, anyway.

Not knowing what to do with herself, she curled up on the small couch and laid there. Everything felt so foreign. She didn't want to unpack her things, not yet anyway. It didn't feel right, like she was taking over her uncle's home, edging him out before she even got to know him. No, for now Nora would leave things as they were.

She lay there for a long time. Night eventually set in. The shadows from the lantern flickered against the walls, giving the cabin a spooky feel and Nora had second thoughts about staying there. But with no boat, no roads, and no trails, there was no way out. The cabin was her only refuge.

CHAPTER

3

Nora was still lying on the couch when she heard a knock on the door. She must have dozed off again, she decided in a half-awake state. She'd been dreaming about being back in the 5,000 square foot home she'd shared with Conner. It was Thanksgiving Day and Nora was trying to make a nice dinner for herself. Conner was too busy at work and had chosen not to take the holiday off. But Nora was okay with that. She told herself it would be good for her to be alone on the holiday, and instead of choosing to wallow in self-pity, she had rolled up her sleeves and started making a Thanksgiving dinner for one. The pie was cooling in the window, the turkey was almost finished, the potatoes were mashed, and everything was coming together nicely when a stream of people she didn't know started showing up at her door. They barged in without being invited and quickly filled the living room. Nora didn't know what to do. She didn't have enough food for everyone, but the strangers were intent on having dinner with her. They were all dressed like they were ready for a red carpet event, making Nora feel inadequate in the everyday clothes she was wearing. To make matters worse, every time she went back to the kitchen to finish the meal preparation, more people showed up at her doorstep. Things kept getting more hectic and more out of hand. Nora was about to boot them all out of the house, when she heard another knock on the door. The last knock awoke her from the dream, thankfully.

She had been lying there on the couch for hours, dozing off and on despite the fact that the sun was up and she knew she should get up. Instead she lay curled up under a throw blanket Pete had left slung over the back of the couch. The blanket smelled of smoke and something else Nora couldn't identify. Frankly, the stench of the blanket was nearly unbearable. Nora could have gone through her things and pulled out the blanket she'd brought with her to Alaska, but she didn't feel like moving. In spite of the smell and her discomfort, she was too tired to move. That's the way she'd been all night long. She felt a growing ache in her back, no doubt from lying on the lumpy old couch for too long, and shifted slightly to relieve the pain.

Her first night in the cabin had not gone well. Nora wasn't usually the type of person to be afraid of the dark, but for the first time in her life she had felt frightened of the unknown. There were so many unfamiliar things lurking outside the walls of the cabin, so many unusual noises in the night. And then there was the blasted lantern that kept casting spooky shadows on the walls. No, Nora had not slept much the entire night. And so, when daylight came, she didn't bother getting up. She was exhausted and all she wanted to do was sleep. Unfortunately, sleep was the one thing she seemed to be incapable of doing. All she managed to do was drift off for a few minutes at a time, so she wasn't getting the rest she so badly craved.

The fire had gone out hours ago. Even though Jake told her she would need to add more wood every few hours, Nora hadn't bothered. Initially, the cabin had been roasting. The fire had rapidly warmed the small space up to an unbelievably hot temperature and Nora had laid there sweating. When the fire finally died down a little, Nora was thankful for the relief. Hours later, the warmth completely dissipated and Nora pulled the throw blanket over her in an attempt to stay warm. Now, she pulled the blanket over her head to block out the sun peeking through the window. She was determined to get some sleep.

But sleep wasn't in the cards. A knock at the door brought her the rest of the way out of the half-awake state she'd been in all morning. Maybe she hadn't been dreaming when she'd heard the knocking before, Nora thought as she threw back the blanket and sat up. The last thing she'd expected on her first day at the cabin was a visitor. *Who in the heck would be all the way out here, anyway?* Lily had told her there were only three neighbors, and none of them lived close by.

"Nora?" she heard from the other side of the door. She recognized the voice. It was Jake. He knocked again and Nora jumped up from the couch.

"Um, just a second," she hollered. Nora looked around frantically. *Was there seriously no mirror in this place? Of course, there wouldn't be a mirror. A backwoodsman like Pete would have had no use for such things*, Nora thought, running her fingers through her hair in an attempt to fix her appearance. She'd slept in the same clothes she'd worn the day before. They were wrinkled and probably smelled, but she didn't have time to change. Grabbing her jacket off the peg on the wall, Nora slid it on to hide her wrinkled clothing. She knew she must look horrid, but she did her best to tidy herself up before opening the door.

When Nora opened the door a few seconds later, she found Jake leaning casually against the door frame, gazing in the direction of the water... and looking extremely attractive. The sight of him made Nora even more self-conscious about her disheveled appearance. *Did he look this good yesterday when I first met him?* Sure, Nora had noticed his firm build, but she hadn't noticed the way his hair glinted in the sunlight. Maybe he only looked so good because she'd spent the night alone and scared, and now she practically had a knight in shining armor standing at her door. Or maybe she'd been a bit self-absorbed the day before, to the point where she didn't even think twice about the hunky guy taking her out to the property. But who could blame her – after such a long trip and the disappointment of finding out she'd inherited a shack instead of a house – for being a little preoccupied?

If she hadn't noticed what was right in front of her the day before, she certainly did now. The way his arms were crossed over his chest, his biceps bulged out through the cotton t-shirt tucked neatly into his faded blue jeans. He wasn't wearing a coat and he looked perfectly comfortable without one.

"Aren't you cold?" As soon as the words were out of her mouth, Nora winced inwardly at her blunt question. She hadn't bothered to say hello or how are you.

Jake chuckled and glanced up at the sky. The sun was shining. "No. Not at all." When he turned back toward Nora, he realized he'd obviously woken her.

"Is this a bad time?" Jake asked, only mildly concerned he had come too early. In spite of the bad impression Nora gave him the day before, Jake wasn't the kind of man to leave a woman stranded. Nora might had come across as spoiled and selfish, but she did need his help.

Seeing her now, he wasn't at all sorry he'd caught her in such a state. Her hair was untidy. It draped softly down her back and seductively over her shoulders reaching down to her breasts. He wouldn't mind running his own hands through her hair, twisting it around at the nape of her neck, and pulling her in close. Maybe he could kiss the spoiled brat out of her.

A lock of hair slipped out from behind her ear and Jake had to suppress the urge to reach out and tuck it back into place. If this was how Nora looked every morning, it would be a pure pleasure to wake up next to this woman, in spite of the fact she was a general pain in the ass to be around.

Nora shook her head. "No, of course not," she said reassuringly. "I just wasn't expecting any visitors." The previous day had been a little awkward, traveling to her new home with a complete stranger. Even though it was only a day later and Nora still didn't really know Jake, she was eager to see a familiar face. Any face would do, in fact, after the sleepless night she'd had in that spooky cabin. "I'm glad you came. I honestly wasn't expecting to see another person until the next time I go into town. And since I don't have a boat, I figured that would be a very long time."

"Well, that's kind of why I'm here," Jake said. He stepped aside and pointed toward the water. "I brought you a skiff."

Looking past him, Nora saw he had towed a small boat behind his own. Both were pulled up onto the shore.

The sight of the boat brought a smile to Nora's face. A little aluminum skiff had never looked so good. It was a beacon of hope, a lifeline to civilization. She lit up at the mere thought of being able to make runs into town to get the rest of her things from her car.

Then she realized she really shouldn't accept it. Things had begun the same way with Conner. A handsome man. Gifts. Before long, she'd lost herself. She wasn't going to let that happen again.

"Jake...," she began. She was thankful for the kind gesture and didn't want to offend him by turning down his offer of a boat, but for the first time in a long time she had an opportunity to forge a life of her own, without anyone's help, most especially without the help of a man. "It was very nice of you to bring it out here, but I think I'd rather repair the one I have," she said.

"It's not that big of a deal," he responded casually. "It's just on loan.

Jake could tell she was still hesitant to accept the boat, but he wasn't about to take no for an answer. He hadn't felt right about leaving Nora alone at the cabin the day before. Pete had been a friend and Jake knew how much Nora had meant to him, even if Nora didn't realize it. Jake owed it to Pete to make sure Nora was taken care of. She was too delicate for this kind of life, too ill-prepared. The boat wasn't much, but it was a necessity for anyone living so far from town and it was the least Jake could do.

"Look. I brought you out here with next to nothing. I couldn't leave you alone in the wilderness with no way to survive. It wouldn't be right. If anything happened to you, it would be my fault for leaving you here unprepared and unequipped," he tried to explain. "At the very least, you need a way to get back into town," he added.

Nora had to admit she needed the boat. The only way to repair the boat she had was to run into town and buy supplies, and she couldn't get to town without a boat. She just wasn't sure how much help she should accept from Jake… or if he would expect anything in return.

When Nora didn't object further, Jake took her silence as acceptance. "Come on," he said, turning and walking toward the boats. Nora slipped on her shoes and followed him out the door. The boat was almost exactly the same as the one Pete had left behind, a simple aluminum boat with three wooden seats, except it didn't have a huge gaping hole in it like Pete's did. As they got closer, Nora saw the skiff was loaded up with cage-like wire contraptions, along with a box of supplies and a casserole dish. She looked over at Jake questioningly.

"Okay, so I also brought a couple other things I thought might come in handy," he said, explaining the supplies. "Lily sent a few things she thought you'd need. There's a chicken casserole. And I also brought a couple crab traps."

"Crab traps?" Nora said incredulously, wrinkling her nose at the thought of trying to catch crab. "I assume I'd need to go out on the water to catch crab, and you already know I don't know how to drive a boat."

Jake grinned, a gleam in his eye. There was a dimple in his left cheek when he smiled. She hadn't noticed that before, either. "In case you don't remember, I told you yesterday I would show you how to use the boat. I tend to keep my promises." Jake saw the uncertainty on her face. "Don't worry," he reassured her. "A little skiff like this is pretty easy to handle."

"Okay," Nora said, giving in to the boating lesson. "But catching crab? I'm not sure I'm up to that. Don't they have pincers?"

Jake laughed at her, glad to see some of her arrogance from the day before had disappeared. She seemed more relaxed now, certainly less irritating. "Just stay away from the pincers. And if one happens to catch a hold of you, think about how good that little bugger is going to taste with melted butter. I think it's worth the risk."

The thought of fresh crab for dinner brought a smile to Nora's face, even if the idea of catching them herself made her a little uneasy.

"Alright," Nora said, agreeing to go crabbing. "When do you want to go, then?"

"Just let me unload this stuff and then we can get started," he said, picking up the box and the casserole dish from inside the skiff and carrying it to the cabin. Nora rushed to get ahead of him so she could hold open the door, since his hands were full.

Inside, the cabin looked exactly as it had when they'd arrived the day before. Jake looked at her curiously.

"You haven't unpacked anything?"

Nora didn't know what to say. "I was just so tired," she said lamely.

"That's understandable. It's a long trip getting out here," he said, sitting the box and the casserole on the table. "Why don't you sit down and I'll get this place aired out?"

"No, don't," Nora said. "Really, I'd rather you didn't..."

"Sit," Jake commanded, placing his hands on her shoulders and moving her in the direction of the couch. "I insist."

The tone of control in his voice reminded her of Conner and, out of habit, Nora did as she was told. She sat there while Jake opened the window, letting a cool breeze waft through the room. Almost instantly, the stuffy smell of the wood stove dissipated and was replaced by the scent of salt water. Looking around at what else needed to be done, Jake picked up Nora's suitcases and hauled them up the ladder and into the loft. He set them next to the dresser alongside the bed. Then he quickly removed all the bedding from the bed and tossed it down on the floor below and dusted out the cobwebs in the loft. Coming down from the loft, Jake scooped up the old bedding, took it outside, and hung it on a clothesline to air out.

"That's better," he said when he entered the cabin a few minutes later. "Oh. One more thing." He reached behind Nora and grabbed the old throw blanket from the back of the couch. He trotted outside and tossed the blanket over the clothesline, as well, and then came back in. "Now there's no more Pete stench in here," he said, satisfied.

"I could have done that myself."

"A simple thank you would suffice."

"Thanks," she said grudgingly. Nora had to admit the cabin looked and felt a lot better. It still needed a good cleaning and Nora still needed to sift through her late uncle's possessions to see what she could use and what she should give away. But at least some of the "Pete stench" was gone, as Jake had said.

"You're welcome," Jake said, pleased. "You ready for that boating lesson?"

Nora nodded her head and stood up. She wasn't feeling particularly confident about it, but she forced a smile anyway. "Now's as good a time as any. Just give me a few minutes to change my clothes. I'll meet you out there."

After Jake walked out of the cabin, Nora climbed up into the loft and opened one of the suitcases. Most of the clothes were completely impractical, but she managed to find a pair of skinny designer jeans, a plain white blouse, and a pair of barely worn sneakers. She also found a hair brush and quickly pulled her hair back into a ponytail. Feeling at least a little better about her appearance, Nora climbed back down from the loft and trotted down to the shore.

It took three pulls before Nora managed to start the outboard motor. The final pull, she tugged so hard she almost lost her balance. For a split second, Nora thought for sure she was going overboard. Even if the water was only a couple feet deep, she didn't like the thought of falling into the icy water. Thankfully, Jake reacted quickly. He caught her by the arm and helped her into the seat. Then he sat back down in the middle seat, directly in front of Nora.

"Okay," Jake instructed, "Now gradually turn the lever, just a little bit at first."

Nora turned the throttle too quickly and the boat lurched forward. Shocked at how fast the boat had moved, she released the throttle and the boat slowed instantly.

"That's alright," Jake reassured her. "You'll get used to it. Now try again."

This time, she did a little better. The boat took off slowly with Nora steering it away from the shore. Gradually, she opened up the throttle a little more and the boat began to pick up some speed. Nora was careful not to open the throttle all the way, though, unsure if she would be able to handle the boat at its top speed.

Jake expertly guided her through turns and directed her where to go. He pointed out areas of the inlet Nora should avoid, especially the few spots where rocks jutted up almost to the surface and could catch unknowing boaters unawares.

Nora still didn't feel very confident, but she was starting to get the hang of it by the time they reached a small cove on the opposite side of the inlet. Just as Jake instructed her, Nora let up on the throttle and the boat slowed.

The rise and fall of the boat on the waves was calming and, now that Nora wasn't so focused on her disappointment in the cabin, she began to really appreciate the beauty of her surroundings. It was like she was seeing it for the first time. *Lily wasn't kidding... it really is beautiful out here*, Nora thought as the sun's rays lit up the mountainside, bringing out the colors of the trees and the rocks and the snowcapped peaks. Everything looked so much more beautiful and inviting than it had the day before when it had been shrouded in cloud cover. Maybe it was the sunshine or maybe it was the scenery, but Nora was beginning to feel more optimistic than she had when she'd first arrived.

"Can we just sit here for a while?" Nora asked.

"Sure," Jake said, "Just let the motor idle." Even as he said the words, he could tell Nora wasn't paying attention to him. She was focused on the sound of the water lapping against the slate shoreline, the beauty of the towering mountains and the sight of a pair of bald eagles circling overhead.

"Look," he said, pointing toward a disturbance in the water about 50 feet away. "Sea lions."

Nora's eyes turned in the direction Jake pointed, toward the edge of the cove. Sure enough, there were five little bodies floating on the surface. One dipped under the water and two more surfaced. Then Nora noticed, if she looked really hard, she could see others swimming below the surface.

Living out here might not be so bad, Nora thought, relaxing a bit. At least she would have sea lions, and who knows what else, to keep her company. It was breathtaking, watching them float on the surface, lounging on a bed of seawater. Nora counted nine more sea lions before the weird-looking creatures dipped back underwater and disappeared from sight.

When Nora turned back toward Jake, she was smiling. "That was amazing," Nora said, grinning from ear to ear. Her excitement was infectious.

"You'll see a lot more of those," Jake promised her, forgetting he'd ever thought she was a spoiled brat. She was the most beautiful woman he'd ever seen. And the way she delighted in something as simple as sea lions, well that had him second-guessing his first impression of her. "Along with the occasional whale and porpoises."

Almost on cue, Jake spotted movement in the water ahead. He pointed in the direction of the wake left by two dolphin-like creatures as they moved closer to the skiff. "Speak of the devil," Jake said, surprised by their sudden appearance.

"What are they?" Nora asked excitedly, glimpsing only a bit of their dark-colored flesh as they skimmed the surface and descended back under water.

"Porpoises."

Nora leaned over the edge to get a better look.

"I've never seen porpoises before," Nora said, delighted at the sight. "Not in real life, anyway."

"Really?" He found that hard to believe.

"Like I said, I've only been on a boat a couple times. I'd rather lie on a beach somewhere than go out on the water."

"Well you'll have to get used to it, being out on the water. It's the only way to get around out here. And you'll see a lot more of these things."

One of the porpoises surfaced a few feet away from Nora, leaping out of the water and splashing her with the frigid waters of the inlet. Nora let out a squeal and she couldn't help but laugh. "I wasn't expecting that," she said, giggling. Jake was laughing, too. He had narrowly escaped the porpoise's splash.

"They don't usually come up quite so close," Jake explained.

Nora watched as they swam away, thinking about how awesome it would be to experience this every day. "It's beautiful here," Nora said, all of her apprehension about living in the cabin slipping away, at least for the time being. She closed her eyes and breathed in the cool ocean air, the feeling of serenity enveloping her.

"Gorgeous," Jake agreed, but he wasn't referring to the outdoor scenery.

She opened her eyes and saw Jake was watching her closely.

"Anyone would be lucky to live here," Nora said, ignoring the look in Jake's eyes and turning her attention back to the water. The day before, Lily had said it would be nearly impossible to sell the property, but looking around, Nora decided to give it a try. A place this beautiful couldn't be too hard to sell. It might be tucked away from the world, but that could be a selling point, Nora thought. There was an indescribable amount of natural beauty there. It was virtually a playground for the outdoor lover. Taking in the beauty of the inlet, Nora was almost sorry she'd never been much of an outdoorsy person. But for the right person, this could be a paradise. "Paradise," she whispered, thinking of how to word the listing.

Jake smiled at her. It was paradise. And he was glad she could see it that way. He hadn't thought Nora was cut out for living in the wilderness, but she seemed content out there on the water, bobbing up and down on the waves as the boat drifted, lost in thought.

Nora reached into the pocket of her jeans and pulled out her cell phone. Out of habit, she still carried it around with her, even though she hadn't gotten a cell phone signal since she'd left Juneau.

"Planning to make a phone call?" Jake chuckled.

She smirked back at him mockingly. "Maybe."

Nora knew there were no cell phone towers. There was no signal. But she turned the phone on anyway and used the built-in camera to snap some photos, one of the mountains with their snowcapped peaks glistening in the sun and one of the cove. Then Nora pointed the phone toward the eastern shore. Across the inlet, the old cabin stood tucked under the shadow of the tall trees. From this distance, it looked rather quaint. It was a picturesque scene, Nora realized as she took several photos of the cabin in the distance.

The photos would be perfect for an advertisement. Maybe she'd get lucky and someone would see the advertisement and buy the property. The beauty of the inlet alone would be enough to catch the attention of potential buyers. It was at least worth a try. And she felt certain now, she would be able to sell it. No matter how long it took, Nora would find a buyer. In the meantime, she had no choice but to live in the cabin. But with surroundings like this, it might not be too much of a hardship.

Nora decided that when she got back to the cabin she would

take some more pictures of the property, perhaps a few snapshots of the cabin from the right angle to make it look bigger than it was. If she could just show people how beautiful it was out there, maybe it wouldn't be so hard to sell the property after all.

Spontaneously, then, she turned the camera toward Jake. She snapped a shot of him sitting at the bow of the skiff, leaning over the edge and running his fingers through the water. His eyes were focused on the shore and the edges of his lips were turned up in a faint smile. When she snapped the photo, Jake looked up at her and grinned. He looked comfortable there, like it was absolutely where he belonged.

"No fair," Jake said, playfully reaching for the phone. "You have to be in at least one of the pictures." He held the phone up and clicked the shutter button, capturing the image of Nora smiling with her cabin far off in the background. Then he turned and leaned over next to Nora, holding the phone out as far as he could. He smelled good, Nora noticed. Maybe too good. She felt the rhythm of her heart pick up the pace as he leaned in closer and snapped a photo of the two of them. The close contact only lasted a second before Jake moved back to his own seat, and Nora was grateful for that. She didn't want to be attracted to Jake, whose actions had more than once reminded her of Conner's controlling ways. She wasn't going to let herself end up in another relationship like that, no matter how good Jake smelled or how he looked at her... or the way his eyes seemed to smile at her.

When Jake handed the phone back to her, Nora quietly put it away. "What now?" she asked, unsure of what else to say.

"If you're ready, we could start crabbing."

Nora wrinkled her nose at the thought of the crabs with their pincers, but then decided steamed crab would be worth the effort, especially if she could convince Jake to do most of the work.

"Yeah, let's do it," she said with as much enthusiasm as she could muster. "Where should we go?"

"Let's go back to the edge of the cove," Jake pointed.

Nora reached for the throttle of the motor, still idling softly. When she turned the throttle, though, the motor stalled.

"That's alright. That happens sometimes. You remember how to start it, right?"

Nora nodded her head and turned to restart it.

"You're going to flood it," Jake told her after her fourth unsuccessful pull on the cord. Nora didn't understand what he meant, so she tried it one more time. When the motor still didn't start, she gave up and turned around. Jake was sitting there, patiently watching her, with an amused grin on his face. "Told you so."

They rocked gently on the waves and drifted with the current as Jake explained what she'd done wrong.

"We'll have to wait a few minutes before we try it again, unless you want to get your phone out and call for help."

It took a second for Nora to realize he was teasing. She actually almost reached into her pocket for her cell phone.

"Very funny."

But it did get her thinking. She was completely isolated out there. There were no cell phone towers, so there was no way to call for help if she needed it. Aside from the boat, there was no way out. No roads. No nothing.

Nora glanced up at the towering mountains. Just a few minutes earlier, they had seemed beautiful, but now Nora saw them for what they really were. An obstacle. A resolute force keeping her isolated from everything. The enormity of it all was almost overwhelming. Nora felt like she was in an enormous bowl. She was trapped and the only way to get out was to climb those impenetrable-looking peaks. The beauty of the inlet was intimidating, its remoteness intensely unnerving.

She wondered what might lie beyond those peaks. Did they go on for miles and miles? Were there other communities tucked away back there, accessible only by air? Nora thought of the trail she'd seen leading away from town and into the back country.

"Yesterday I saw a trail leading away from the parking lot at the ferry terminal. Where does it go?" Nora asked.

Her question surprised Jake.

"Oh, it cuts through between the mountains and leads back about 10 miles. People use it for hauling firewood and hunting, but other than that, there's nothing back there," Jake explained.

Then he looked at Nora and saw the curiosity in her eyes. That look sent a surge of unease up his spine. Maybe there was some adventurous spirit in the woman after all. "If you get a bug up your butt and decide to do some exploring, don't even think about it," he said firmly. "You'd need a four-wheel-drive truck, and even then, the trail is pretty dangerous. Your car wouldn't make it past the first bend."

Nora flinched at the commanding tone of his voice. She didn't like the idea of having a man tell her what she could and couldn't do. Wasn't that why she'd left Conner? She hadn't come all this way to be bossed around by another man.

Truthfully, the idea of exploring some back country appealed to her. She'd never been confined to such a small space. Strange, to think Alaska was confining. It was the largest state in the U.S., but also the least accessible. Nora couldn't venture inland. There were no roads and she didn't know the first thing about surviving in the wilderness. With absolutely no boating experience, she couldn't really explore the waters, either. She'd be stuck on the edge of a massive island, with nowhere to go. The idea of the trail, and the knowledge that it led somewhere, intrigued her.

"I mean it," Jake said, sensing Nora's interest in the trail. The tone of his voice had grown more resolute. "It's not safe for someone like you."

Nora bristled at the comment. Instantly, she forgot about finding out where the road led.

"What do you mean, someone like me?" She had no right to be offended, but she was. Sure, she didn't know the first thing about the Alaskan wilderness, but that didn't mean she couldn't drive down a road. It was a road, for God's sake.

"I just meant someone who's not familiar with the back country. That's all," Jake said apologetically. "I didn't mean to offend you. Really. It's just... we get these people who come in for a few days and think they're going to hike the mountain or do some back country hiking and it seems like half the time we have to go in and rescue them. If you really want to explore the trail, I'll take you back there sometime. But, please, don't try it by yourself."

Nora didn't notice the sincerity in his voice. All she heard were the words of an overbearing, domineering man telling her what to do. His comments annoyed her. "Okay," she said, not bothering to hide the irritation in her voice. "You've made your point. I understand. I have no business being here. I might as well pack up my stuff and head back south."

"That's not what I meant," Jake said, thinking he ought to change the subject. Then he added cautiously, "Do you still want to learn how to catch crab?"

"I think I've had enough bossing around for one day, don't you?" she said, a little more crossly than she'd intended. Nora turned in her seat and yanked hard on the pull cord. That time, the motor roared to life.

* * *

Jake didn't stick around long after they got back to the cabin. He offered to help her retrieve the rest of her things from her car, but she turned him down flat before not-so-kindly asking him to leave, her tone making it clear she didn't want any more help from him. Not then, not ever.

He'd obviously upset Nora out on the water more than he'd realized, even though it hadn't been his intention. He had only wanted to impress upon her the necessity of playing it safe. The rules were different out there and the road was no exception. It was a dangerous trail even Jake didn't like to use if he didn't have to. He could only imagine Nora deciding to take a pleasure drive into the backwoods all alone. If she got into trouble, she couldn't call AAA. He thought he'd gotten his point across, but he wanted to avoid angering her any further. So as soon as Jake showed her how to moor the boat and ensured she was safely back in her cabin, he left.

At first, Nora was glad to see him go. But as the realization that she was all alone set back in, Nora's irritation with Jake quickly dissipated and she wished she hadn't ended their boating lesson early. Sure, Jake had been acting like a typical dominant male, telling her what she could and couldn't do, but then again, maybe she had overreacted a tad. She had to remind herself, he wasn't Conner. He was only trying to help, but Nora needed to learn how to do things on her own.

She walked over to the table and sampled the casserole. It tasted good. Really good. Eating right out of the casserole dish, she took another bite and opened the box of supplies Lily had sent. There was a note on top.

Heron doesn't have an official welcome wagon, but I figured you could use some things to make the place feel a little more like home.   *- Lily*

Nora smiled when she saw the contents of the box. There were several scented candles, a jar of homemade jam, a well-worn paperback romance novel, and, of all things, a hand mirror. Nora picked up the mirror and looked at her reflection. "Ugh," she groaned, wishing she'd had the mirror earlier. She looked a mess. Even with her hair pulled back in a ponytail, the damp ocean air had frizzed and curled a few tendrils that had gotten loose.

She set the mirror down on the table, picked up the casserole dish, and carried it over to the couch. As she picked at the casserole, Nora looked around the cabin, wondering if anyone would actually be interested in the place. She hoped someone would. In the meantime, she had no choice but to live there until a buyer came along, no matter how long it might take.

She ate a few more bites and then lay down and closed her eyes. It was only mid-afternoon, but the exhaustion from the long trip caught up with her. She'd spent more than two full days on the ferry from Washington to Juneau, and then a good part of another day on the ferry to Heron, followed by a long trip out to the cabin and a sleepless night in her new surroundings. By the time the boating lesson had finished, she was exhausted, both physically and mentally.

CHAPTER

4

Jake didn't like leaving Nora behind in Pete's old cabin. He'd done it twice now, and each time he felt like he was leaving her to die out there in the wild.

In his experience, people generally fell into one of two categories: those who could and those who couldn't. One thing was certain, Nora *couldn't* make it out there on her own. From the looks of her, she'd never had to chop and stack wood in her life. She probably didn't know the first thing about hunting or fishing. Heck, she barely knew how to operate a boat.

As far as Jake could tell, Nora was the kind of woman who needed to be taken care of. She needed a man to do the heavy lifting and to protect her on those cold, dark nights. With summer coming on, the days were getting longer. But winter would roll back around soon enough and the nights would turn long and dark. Darker than Nora could understand, at least until she experienced it for herself. And when those dark nights enveloped the cabin and shrouded everything in blackness, who would be there to wrap his arms around Nora and keep her safe?

On the other hand, maybe she'd be gone by then. A woman like Nora had no business in the wilds of Alaska, and he expected she'd realize it quickly enough. As soon as she got a taste of life in the last frontier, he was betting she'd come to her senses. Already, she was realizing she didn't belong out there. Hadn't she said as much on the boat? She'd end up high tailing it out of there the first chance she got, which would be in another two weeks when the ferry was scheduled to come back to town. Yeah, if she had any common sense, she'd leave. And therein was Jake's dilemma, because the last thing he wanted to see was her boarding a ship and leaving Heron for good. For the life of him, he couldn't figure out why, but he hoped she would stay.

For now, all he could do was make sure she survived out there all by herself. At least he left her with enough supplies to keep her alive and a little knowledge to help her navigate her new surroundings, Jake thought as he turned his skiff toward town. But he still didn't feel right about leaving her alone in the drafty old cabin to fend for herself.

Jake was only a mile from Nora's cabin, still another nine miles from town, when he turned the boat toward the shore. He needed some peace of mind. Short of setting up camp next to Nora's cabin, there was only one other way to make sure she would be safe in that ramshackle cabin.

There were no tidal flats there, so Jake pulled up as close as he could to the rocky shore and carefully climbed out of the boat, tying it off on the rocks. With sure steps, he followed a narrow footpath through the lush forest leading to Willie's doorstep.

The house sat out of view of the inlet, exactly the way Willie wanted it. All of his life, he'd dreamed of living in the Alaskan wilderness, far enough from everybody so no one would come knocking on his door. When he retired from his job at the factory at the age of 50, he packed up his belongings, left Ohio, and headed north. He didn't have a plan, just an idea of where he wanted to be. He wandered around for a while and somehow ended up on a fishing boat based out of Sitka. It was hard work, especially for a man of his age, but he stuck with it for as long as he could. When he heard about a piece of land for sale near Heron, he bought it without even seeing it and left the rest of the world behind for good. It took Willie less than a month to build a small cabin to live in, tucked away from the inlet and the curious eyes of passersby. Only those who knew where to look could find the path he'd made from the shore of the inlet, through the thick forest, to his house.

Jake had walked the path many times. He knew every twist and turn of the trail, every blasted root jutting up out of the ground attempting to trip him. He could probably walk it blindfolded.

At the end of the trail there was a large clearing and right in the middle sat a beautifully crafted log home. After he'd built a small cabin to live in, Willie had spent years designing and building the house he'd always dreamed of. Everything had been done with his own two hands and a very well-worn set of tools. Even though he had a generator right from the start, he'd chosen not to use any power tools. He had wanted to feel the wood in his hands as he cut and shaped the logs. It had been a labor of love, and it was the only thing in Willie's life of which he was truly proud.

An old, rusty saw blade hung on the door of the home, the serrated edge sticking out to catch the paws of any animal large enough and hungry enough to try and break in. As long as Willie had lived there, no bear had tried to push down his door, but he believed in taking precautions, and he had come up with various methods of questionable effectiveness in an attempt to keep the bears away.

Jake raised his hand to knock on the door, but before his

knuckles rapped on the wood, he heard the old man call to him from somewhere in the woods. Jake couldn't see him, but obviously Willie had spotted Jake. Somehow, Willie always knew when someone came to call on him. A second later, Willie stepped out from behind his workshop, a small shack that housed Willie's not-so-secret distillery.

Willie zipped up his pants as he trotted toward Jake. "I was just markin' the perimeter with my scent," said Willie when he got closer. He was short and stocky, firm with the muscle that only comes from years of working outdoors. "Thought I heard somethin' scratchin' around out here last night and I want to make sure it doesn't come back."

"You know that doesn't work."

Willie shrugged and walked past Jake, into the house. "Worth a try," he said.

Inside, Willie went straight into the kitchen and pulled a hot meatloaf out of the oven. Over the past 15 years since Willie spent his first winter in the tiny cabin, the home had grown considerably. The original cabin, a space barely larger than 10-foot square, now served as the entryway to a comfortable, two-story home. The house was a bit larger than Willie needed, but once he'd started building, he couldn't seem to stop. It had taken a great deal of restraint for him to call it quits when he'd reached 1,200 square feet and to focus his efforts instead on the finishing touches.

Even though it was off the grid, Willie didn't go without at least the basic modern luxuries. He had running water and electricity, both installed entirely on his own. An outbuilding served as the powerhouse and held battery units for a combination of solar and hydro power, and he always had the gas-powered generator as back-up. Willie hadn't gone as far as installing a satellite and wasn't sure if he ever would. He didn't want to be connected to the world, but he still enjoyed the comforts of modern life. Just that past summer, he had installed new floors with built-in radiant heat, a luxury he really enjoyed because it meant he no longer had to spend hours of back-breaking work, chopping and hauling wood to burn. Other than a slight limp, Willie was in good shape for a 67-year-old man, but after a life of hard labor, he was looking forward to settling in and enjoying his golden years.

"You're just in time for supper," Willie said, grabbing a gallon of goat's milk out of the fridge and pouring two glasses. To his own glass, he added a bit of coffee and a shot of Irish Cream liqueur. "You want a nip?"

"No, thanks."

In spite of all the measures he took to ensure people couldn't find him, Willie was actually a rather friendly man. He welcomed his friends and helped his neighbors whenever they were in need. For a hermit, he was remarkably genial. Without even asking, Willie already had two plates out and was cutting into the meatloaf. He slapped a slice of meatloaf onto a plate and slid it across the table to Jake.

"This is from the bear I shot last season. The one that broke into the goat house."

Jake sat down at the table. He wasn't hungry, but he also wasn't going to insult Willie by not eating. He picked up his fork, ate a bite, and then grinned up at Willie.

"You know, for an old coot, you're cooking isn't half bad," Jake joked.

Willie smiled, ready to get down to business.

"So what brings you here? It ain't that new girl down at Pete's, is it?"

"How do you know about her already?"

Willie shrugged. "I may live in the middle of nowhere, but I still have eyes. Saw you and her headin' down that way yesterday."

"I suppose you've already been down there checking things out."

"Can't say I didn't take a little walk last night."

Jake smiled and took another bite of the meatloaf. "Then you must know everything about her, right?"

Willie chuckled. "I know enough. I can tell by the looks of her she ain't used to this kind of livin'. I also figure she didn't find what she was expectin'."

"What do you mean?"

"A woman like that wouldn't have come all this way if she knew Pete's place was just a shack. I figure she was expectin' somethin' a little more..." He hesitated, trying to think up the best word to describe it. "...up-to-date, I suppose you could say."

"You may be right," said Jake. "That's actually why I'm here."

Willie chuckled again. "I think I know exactly why you're here. You want me to check in on her every once in a while, am I right? You want me to make sure she's okay out here all by herself."

"Maybe," said Jake, shoving a forkful of meatloaf into his mouth. He had the distinct feeling Willie understood all too well Jake's interest in Nora and it made him feel a little uncomfortable.

Willie grinned and leaned back in his chair, enjoying the sight of Jake's sudden nervousness. "Yep, she's a pretty one. You don't see too many lookers like her around these parts. I suppose if I was young like you I'd be fallin' all over her, too."

"That's not it at all," Jake said defensively. "I just think she came out here unprepared. She doesn't know what she's gotten herself into."

"So, you're sayin' you haven't noticed her good looks?" asked Willie teasingly.

Jake smiled. "Oh, I noticed, all right. She's hard to miss." He sighed then. "I just can't figure out what the heck she's doing out here. She doesn't belong all alone in a cabin in the middle of nowhere."

"So where does she belong?" Willie asked.

Jake shook his head. "I don't know."

"Well, I wouldn't worry too much 'bout her," said Willie. "She likely just showed up here on a whim. Maybe she got word she inherited some property and thought she'd come out and check it out to see if she could sell it. Maybe when the ferry comes back through, she'll get on and go back home and tell all her friends 'bout her Alaskan adventure and the quirky people she met out in the bush."

Willie's words echoed Jake's own thoughts. "Could be. I mean, she doesn't strike me as the type that can hack it out here... or even the kind that would give it a try. But I guess she doesn't have much choice in the matter, at least not for the next two weeks when the ferry comes back to town."

"Two weeks ain't very long," Willie said. "I'm sure she'll be fine."

"For someone like her, two weeks alone in a rustic cabin could seem like a lifetime."

Willie nodded his head, thinking about Jake's words. If the new girl was going to stay out there in Pete's cabin, then he supposed she was going to need some help.

"Okay," said Willie. "There's one more thing I've been wonderin' 'bout. What I want to know is why you don't do it? Why don't you come out and check in on her every so often, if you're so concerned 'bout her well-bein'?"

"I don't want to get involved. Like you said, she probably won't stick around too long. No sense getting entangled with a woman who may only be here for a couple weeks."

Willie was satisfied with Jake's answer. At least he was being honest. Jake was playing it safe. Getting involved with someone like Nora, someone who would likely up and leave, can be rough on the heart. But Willie wasn't sure how smart it was for Jake to stay on the sidelines.

"You know, there are a few dozen other men in town, probably linin' up for a chance to take care of that girl. You might miss your chance," Willie said with a wink as Jake took another bite of the meatloaf. Jake swallowed and looked up with a scowl on his face that only made Willie chuckle. "All right," Willie finally agreed. "I'll check in on her every so often."

"Thanks," said Jake, standing up and taking his empty plate to the sink. He downed the glass of milk Willie had given him. "Good eats."

"Did you expect anythin' less?" asked Willie with a grin.

Jake smiled back. "You're the second-best cook in town, but don't tell anyone I said that. Lily might be offended."

"Why would she be offended?"

"Because it puts her in third."

Willie laughed at that." Some might argue with you 'bout that."

"Yeah, they might," Jake conceded. "Just keep an eye on her, okay, but don't make it obvious," Jake reminded Willie one more time as he walked to the door.

"You know I will. I'd have kept an eye on her even if you hadn't asked me to."

Jake nodded. He knew he could count on Willie to watch out for Nora. Willie was just about the only man in town Jake trusted to keep her safe… and single.

CHAPTER

5

Jake leaned against the railing of the boardwalk, looking out over the harbor and thinking about her. Why couldn't he get that woman off his mind? No matter how hard he tried to focus on something else, she always crept back into his thoughts. He found himself wondering whether his first impression of Nora might have been all wrong. Judging by the looks of her the first time he'd seen her, he'd thought she would take one glance at the old cabin and head right back to town. But she hadn't. She'd surprised him with her stubborn determination to stay out there.

Off in the distance, Nora's skiff appeared. Even from far away, Jake recognized the pale green color of the skiff he'd loaned to Nora the day before and the familiar hum of the motor he'd rebuilt himself. Jake watched intently as the boat came in from the south. She was slow and awkward, but she was doing alright for someone who had just learned how to operate a boat. He felt a small tinge of pride as Nora clumsily maneuvered the boat toward the shore. He'd taught her how to do that.

"What are you grinning about?"

Jake hadn't heard his sister approach. He'd been so focused on watching Nora, he hadn't noticed anything else the entire time. He hadn't even realized the sight of Nora brought an instant smile to his face.

"Nothing," he said, quickly looking away. But it wasn't quick enough. Lily followed the direction of his gaze. When she saw Nora's skiff rocking on the waves, she smiled, too.

"Ah," she said, understanding instantly why Jake had been grinning like a school boy. "You like her, don't you?"

"I'm concerned for her," he shot back gruffly.

"That grin didn't look like concern to me," Lily teased, jabbing him in the ribs.

Jake shrugged and glanced back across the harbor at Nora's skiff. He wasn't lying. He was concerned for her. But there was something more to it, too. Jake couldn't deny he felt something deep inside of him whenever he saw Nora. He liked her, in spite of the poor first impression she'd made. But she had been clear the day before. She didn't want anything to do with him. That's probably a good thing, Jake reminded himself, since she was most likely not going to stay in Heron, anyway.

"Jake?" said Lily, trying to get his attention. He had drifted off in thought and by the time he snapped out of it, Lily was looking at him grinning. "I was right. You really do like her."

"Maybe," Jake reluctantly admitted. "But it doesn't matter."

"What do you mean?"

Jake shook his head, not wanting to explain it, but somehow needing to say it out loud. "She reminds me too much of Mom, and you know how well Mom liked living here. Every minute of every day was a struggle for her. She always wanted more than what this place has to offer. I have a feeling Nora will feel the same way after she's been here for a while."

"You can't assume to know her that well, Jake. She's only been in town for two days."

"Yeah, and she'll probably be leaving on the next ferry out of here."

"And if she's not?"

"Then it'll be the next one after that," he said stubbornly.

* * *

Awkwardly, Nora maneuvered the skiff up to the shore as close as she could get to the parking lot. Concerned about ramming into the rocky shoreline, she cut the throttle too soon and found herself sitting more than 20 feet from the shore. Gripping the handle, Nora turned the throttle and gave it too much fuel this time, sending the boat forward faster than she had expected. She quickly pulled the lever to the right and the boat turned, but it still collided against the rock. That's exactly what Nora was trying to avoid.

Everything had been much easier when she and Jake had made this approach two days earlier. But the tide had been low then and he had easily coasted the boat right up onto the tidal flats. Now, the tide was at its peak and there was no sandy landing. Not to mention, a novice was at the throttle this time around, too.

Grabbing hold of the rock, Nora clumsily tied the boat off by looping a rope around one of the smaller boulders and tying an awful-looking knot. Then she carefully stepped out of the boat and onto one of the flat topped boulders. At least that had worked out better than she'd expected.

It was Nora's third day in Alaska, but only her first real day alone, and she was determined to figure out how to make it on her own. The day before, Jake had offered to help her retrieve the rest of her belongings, but Nora had politely declined. Well, she may not have been very polite about it, but considering her mood at the time, she hadn't really cared. Besides, Jake had already done enough and she wanted to know she could do things for herself. Her first boat ride by herself had been a little nerve wracking, but Nora had made it in to town, even if her first attempt at docking the boat had been a little rough.

The car sat undisturbed, just as Jake promised. Even though it was unlocked, everything was still there, Nora realized, as she took her time sorting through her things and prioritizing what she'd need. The television and computer, she decided, could stay in the car. She had no use for them at the cabin and didn't see the point in wasting the time and energy of hauling them out there for nothing. For now, they would be safe in the car until she needed them again, when the cabin sold and she moved back to the real world. The things she absolutely couldn't live without, which was really only a few boxes and a large duffel bag, Nora carried back to the skiff.

With her most important belongings safely stowed in the skiff, Nora left the boat tied to the boulder and turned toward the boardwalk. She needed to find a computer with internet. With all of the satellites on top of the houses in town, someone was bound to have internet she could use, and Lily could point her in the right direction. Her first stop was the Pub because she figured she'd find Lily there. She was right.

"What do you need the internet for?" Lily didn't even try to hide her curiosity when Nora asked about internet service. She liked to know what people were up to, that was no secret. The best way to find out, she'd learned, was to ask.

"Oh, you know…," Nora stalled, not ready to let anyone know she was trying to sell the property. It was a long shot, after all, that anyone in their right mind would buy it. "I just need to update my Facebook status to let everyone know I've dropped off the face of the earth and I'll never be heard from again."

Lily looked at Nora, confused. "Facebook? What's that?" She could only hold the feigned look of bewilderment for a moment, but it was long enough to fool Nora.

"Very funny," Nora replied when Lily burst out laughing. "Seriously, though. I'm debating what to post as my new status. Probably something along the lines of 'I'm about to become bear food' or 'a very handsome yeti has proposed and we're going to make our home in the wilderness.' That sort of thing."

Lily giggled. "And they say I'm a drama queen."

"When one of them comes true, you'll see I'm not being overly dramatic," Nora shot back, but she was laughing too, now. "The yeti thing might actually happen. Have you noticed some of the men around here? I saw one hairier than Bigfoot on the way here."

Lily laughed harder. "Was he walking like this?" She turned and struck a Bigfoot pose. Nora nodded, trying not to laugh and failing miserably. Spurred on by her audience, Lily dramatically stomped back and forth behind the bar, Bigfoot style, occasionally stopping mid-step and looking sideways to mimic the infamous photo of Bigfoot.

Nora laughed so hard her stomach ached and she could hardly breathe. She clutched her belly with her arms, trying to catch her breath. "Stop, stop." She begged.

"Okay. Since you ask so nicely," said Lily, bounding back to her seat behind the bar. "You can use the computer in the office to place your ad."

Nora's face drained its color. *How did Lily know she was going to place an ad for the property?* "What do you mean?" Nora asked cautiously.

Lily grinned. "You know, a personal ad. Attractive woman seeks very hairy, reclusive yeti for long term commitment."

Nora chuckled, relieved. "Yeah. That's just what I need."

"Come on," Lily said, gesturing for Nora to follow her into the office. "I'll get the internet up. It's a little slow, but that's a good thing. It teaches you patience."

A few minutes later, Nora was seated at the desk, with a Yahoo homepage staring back at her. Lily had left her alone in the office and had gone back to work in the restaurant. She hadn't been kidding about the internet connection being slow. It was like having dial-up.

It took a few minutes to find the website Nora was looking for, a publication in Los Angeles that specialized in real estate. Then it took another minute or so for the page to load. The office door was closed to prying eyes, but Nora still felt a little uneasy about using Lily's computer to place an ad for the property. It almost felt like she was betraying her new friend, letting Lily believe she was staying in Heron when she was really doing everything she could to find a way out of there. Typing as quickly as she could, Nora tried to make the property and its rustic cabin sound as appealing as possible.

Then she pulled out her phone and connected its USB cable to the computer to upload the photos of the property to the website. Slowly, ever so slowly, the photos uploaded one by one. The place really did look good in the pictures. The water was so clear, the sky so blue. The mountain backdrop made even the ramshackle cabin look inviting. And then there was the photo of Jake in the boat. What had possessed her to take his photo?

For some reason, the image of them living out there together popped into her head. She could see him cutting and stacking wood alongside the cabin, while she brought him a glass of ice cold lemonade. In her imagination, he stopped working long enough to wipe the sweat from his forehead and to pull her into his arms, forgetting about the lemonade, losing themselves in a kiss.

Wait! What am I thinking? She had no romantic interest in Jake. He was such a typical dominant male, and that was the last thing she was looking for.

Nora took a deep breath and tried to push all thoughts of Jake out of her mind. She needed to focus on the advertisement, which was actually looking pretty good with all those photos. Being realistic, Nora knew it would take a while for the property to sell. She hoped to find a buyer before the next winter, before the choppy waters and thick fog Lily had warned her about would have a chance to hold her hostage in a cabin in the middle of nowhere. Then again, maybe it wouldn't be so bad, being trapped in a cabin with Jake, nothing to do but spend all their time making love.

"Stop it," Nora whispered to herself. She didn't even like Jake, did she? He was controlling and stubborn... and built like no man she'd ever known before. Strong and handsome. "No," she said, trying to convince herself. "I am not interested in Jake."

Refocusing her efforts on the ad, Nora read through the advertisement one more time. It was perfect. With a single click, the listing would become active on the site. Nora's finger hovered over the mouse, hesitating. For some reason she was suddenly reluctant to list the property. Was she being hasty, trying to sell the place before she'd even given it a chance? Or was it the thought of living there with Jake that made her hesitate? Nora wasn't sure.

It's never going to sell, anyway, she thought. *Just place the ad.* It was a long shot that anyone would buy the property, so there was no harm in listing it while she was still undecided. She would stay in the cabin for now. Being alone in the wilderness would test her limits, but it would also give her plenty of time to decide whether she really wanted to sell the property. She clicked the icon to submit the ad for publication. *There, it's done.*

* * *

Nora held tightly to the boulder the boat was tied to, carefully stretched one leg out and stepped onto the middle seat of the skiff. The boat leaned dramatically to the side and Nora moved her foot over more to the center before quickly jumping in the rest of the way. She smiled to herself. She was actually getting the hang of this.

A few minutes later, Nora steered the skiff south and was on her way back to her new home. The cool air in her face and the beautiful surroundings put Nora at peace with her situation. She didn't even care about the things she'd left behind in the car. Everything seemed so much simpler now. Even though her time in Alaska might be temporary, she felt lighter than she had in years, Nora realized as she turned the skiff toward the narrow strip of beach in front of her cabin.

She pulled the boat up as far as she could on the shore, but she still had to jump out into about nine inches of water.

"I need to get some of those rubber boots like the ones Jake wears," Nora said aloud. That was weird. For the first time ever in her life, there wasn't anyone within earshot. "Okay, quit talking to yourself, Nora," she said as she grabbed the bow of the skiff with both hands and dragged it up onto dry land as far as she could. She wasn't about to become some crazy person who carried on entire conversations with herself.

Leaving the boat on dry ground, Nora grabbed two of the boxes and carried them up to the cabin, her feet squishing into the water-logged soles of her sneakers with each step. Then she went back to the boat and grabbed the other box and the duffel bag. As soon as she finished hauling everything to the cabin, she kicked off the wet shoes and peeled off her socks. The soaking wet pant legs of her jeans clung to her calves, so Nora took those off, too.

She stood on the front stoop of her cabin in only a heavy wool sweater – something Pete had left behind – and her underwear, not caring that she was outside. There was no one around to see her, anyway. Bending down, Nora unzipped the duffel bag and rummaged through it for a few seconds until she found a pair of flip flops. She put them on and then carried her wet clothes and shoes over to the piece of clothesline strung up between two trees. She tossed the jeans and socks over the line. Then she tied the shoe laces of her sneakers together and tossed them over the line, as well.

"Hi, there."

Nora almost jumped out of her skin at the sound of a man's voice. She turned around to find a brawny-looking man emerge from the woods about 20 yards away. He stopped abruptly when he got a clear view of Nora, and then awkwardly turned his back to her. Nora didn't immediately realize why. Then she remembered she was standing there in her underwear. Grabbing the blue jeans off the line, Nora hurriedly pulled them back on, cringing a little at the wet pant legs but more so because she'd been caught with no pants on.

"Sorry about that," the man said, still turned away from Nora. Even at that distance, she could see his neck and ears were slightly reddened. He was blushing. At least she wasn't the only one who was embarrassed.

"Not your fault," Nora said, trying to hide the irritation in her voice. "I'm decent now."

He slowly turned around, and Nora got the distinct impression he didn't quite believe her. When he saw she was, in fact, fully clothed, his face relaxed and the pink hue gradually faded from his cheeks.

"I… I didn't mean to sneak up on you," he said. "It's just that Jake mentioned you were here and he asked me to stop by and check in on you." Willie regretted the last sentence the second it came out of his mouth. He wasn't supposed to mention that fact, but he was a little flustered after seeing Nora half naked, he hadn't known what else to say. So much for discretion.

So, Jake thinks I need to be looked after, Nora thought, slightly annoyed. Here she was, trying to be an independent woman, but Jake went and asked her neighbor to check up on her. Were all men control freaks? Did they all think women needed to be taken care of, looked after, and told what to do? Jake clearly thought Nora needed help and, as a result, a strange man had found her half naked. Nora didn't feel comfortable about that at all. She had no idea who this guy was or what he was capable of. But she did know she had no way to defend herself if he turned out to be a lunatic and no way to call for help, either.

The man still stood a good distance away from Nora. Other than turning around to face her, he hadn't made a single move.

"I brought you some homemade jerky. Thought you might like it," he said uncertainly, trying to fill in the silence. He held up two clear plastic bags. "This bag's black-tailed deer and this one's brown bear. Oh, I'm Willie, by the way."

Willie. Lily had mentioned her closest neighbor was named Willie and there was a walking path connecting her property to his. Nora nervously smiled at him. If he was her neighbor, she would need to get over her fears. As she'd been told more than once now, neighbors were an important part of surviving out there. She'd have to be friendly with her neighbors, even if they did look a little scary.

"Willie," she said as welcoming as she could given the circumstances. "It's nice to meet you. I understand we're neighbors?"

He smiled back then, and began walking toward her. Nora saw he walked with a noticeable limp, but it didn't seem to slow him down much.

"I really am sorry 'bout sneakin' up on you like that," Willie said when he reached the clothesline. He stood a few feet away from her and smiled at her through his unkempt beard. He stood no taller than Nora's five and a half foot frame. His gray eyes emitted a sense of serenity and Nora wondered how she could have ever doubted this man's intentions.

Willie held the two bags of jerky out to Nora with friendly smile.

"Thank you," she said graciously, taking the bags of jerky and wondering what to do next. The proper thing, Nora decided, would be to invite him in. She remembered the gift of Scotch that Lily had given her, along with Lily's comment that it would come in handy when Willie came calling. "Would you like to come inside?"

"No, no," Willie said shaking his head. "I have work to do. Just wanted to make sure you was okay out here."

"Are you sure?" Nora asked, strangely reluctant to see him go. Just a moment before she had questioned his motives, and now she was hesitant to be left alone. "I have a nice bottle of Scotch…"

"Maybe next time," he said, turning to leave.

"Next time," Nora repeated, wondering when that might be.

Nora watched him make his way down the trail until he disappeared, then she turned and walked up to the cabin, wishing Willie would have accepted her offer to come inside. This whole being alone thing sucked.

Inside, Nora's loneliness was even more difficult to deal with. She tried to ignore the feeling of isolation by keeping herself busy. This wasn't her home, and yet it was, at least for the time being. But it still felt like someone else's cabin. If she was going to stay there for any length of time, she needed to make it feel like her own. The old, worn out couch was depressing to look at and the soot-covered wall behind the wood stove filled the whole place with a stagnant, thick odor. What she really needed was to make the place more livable. She remembered how Jake had swept through the cabin the day before, tossing out Pete's old smelly blankets. "Pete stench," she said aloud, recalling Jake's words. He had looked so pleased with himself as he'd thrown the nasty old blanket over the clothesline and dusted his hands off on his blue jeans. Even though she hadn't wanted him to take charge the way he had, it was actually kind of cute. Why was she thinking about him again? The last thing Nora needed was a man, especially one like Jake. Nora had gotten the distinct impression Jake liked to take charge, to be in control, to step in and save the day. Well, she didn't need a knight in shining armor. She could get by on her own just fine. She definitely hadn't liked how domineering he'd been out on the water, telling her she wasn't fit to drive down a road. But, she had to admit he was great to look at. The image of him in the boat, with his hand over the edge snaking his fingers over the surface of the water, popped into her head. He had looked so perfectly content out there on the water, so incredibly gorgeous. Ugh, she needed to get Jake off her mind.

Work always helped Nora clear her mind, and she definitely had plenty of work to do. She picked up one of the boxes and tore the packing tape off the top. In the first box, Nora had packed more practical things like her favorite coffee mug, a French press to make her precious coffee, and a small electric hand-held coffee bean grinder. Nora took everything out of the box and set the things on the table. The coffee grinder, she stuck her tongue out at and tossed it carelessly aside. She would have to settle for pre-ground coffee from now on. She picked up the second box and began unpacking those things next. That box held more clothes, along with her iPod and a handful of DVDs. There was also a scrapbook, a few framed photographs, and a pair of decorative

76

candles she had never lit because they were merely for looks. Now, they would get some use, Nora thought as she set them out on the table. The final box held mostly shoes. All kinds of them. Absolutely none of them were very practical.

The duffel bag, Nora dragged up the ladder and into the loft. Her suitcases still sat at the foot of the bed where Jake had left them. Nora eyed up the dresser next to the bed. It was small. Only three drawers. She pulled open the top drawer. It held Pete's socks and underwear. Nora didn't have to look hard to see the holes in the old garments. They looked like they should have been tossed out about 100 wears ago. Nora pulled the drawer out all the way, carried it to the edge of the loft, and dumped it out onto the floor below. She replaced the top drawer in the dresser and opened the next. More clothes. Shirts mostly. She pulled them out and tossed them over the loft railing, too.

The bottom drawer held a few pairs of pants. When Nora reached in to grab the pants, she found something else in there, too. Hidden under the pants was a long, flat wooden box. Nora pulled it out and sat down on the bed. The clasp was rusty, but it opened easily enough. She reached into the box and pulled out Pete's journal. Flipping through the pages, it looked pretty mundane. More like a record of how many fish he'd caught and how much wood he'd chopped, keeping track of how much he'd need for the following winter. Nora made a mental note to read through it later. The long lists of supplies, along with Pete's notes on when they ran out, would be helpful. She put the journal back in the box and resumed her work.

With the dresser cleaned out, Nora took her time unpacking her clothes and neatly placing them in the dresser, organizing them almost the same way Pete had kept his clothes, though her clothes weren't nearly as practical as Pete's had been. Tight skirts and low-cut blouses were useless here, unless Nora wanted to attract a lumberjack or a lonely backwoodsman... or the yeti she had joked about with Lily. She had a feeling she wouldn't need the fancy clothes and make-up to do that, though. All she had to do was be female. *Oh, well,* Nora thought. *These clothes will have to do for now.* But the next time she went into town, she would have to stop by The General Store and hope they carried women's clothing.

Her work in the loft was done. Nora's clothes were unpacked. The bed was made. Her quilt was spread out over the twin mattress. It looked as homey as it was going to look in her new bedroom.

Picking up the wooden box and the three pairs of jeans Pete had left in the bottom drawer, Nora carefully climbed back down the ladder. She tossed the jeans on the pile of clothes littering the floor and set the wooden box down on the table. She still had a lot of work to do, so she sat down on the floor and sorted through the clothes, tossing the unusable items into a throw-away pile to burn. The jeans she folded and packed into one of her now empty boxes. She did the same with the shirts, determined to save them and use them for something. At the very least, the shirts could be used for rags.

After Nora sorted through Pete's old clothes, she pulled everything Pete had left in the cabin off the shelves. She arranged the canned goods according to the type of food and expiration date, but also found quite a few cans with the paper torn off and absolutely no indication of what the cans held. Those, she stacked off to the side, thinking someday she might feel adventurous and open up the cans to see what was inside.

On the bottom shelf, she found two large jugs of distilled vinegar next to a metal bucket. Nora went outside to the hand pump and filled the bucket part way with water. She came back inside and added some vinegar, making a cleaning solution to get rid of the musty smell in the cabin. Then she set to work scrubbing down the walls, ceiling and floor of the cabin. Every surface and every fixture got a good scrubbing.

By the time the sun disappeared behind the mountains, Nora had everything unpacked and in its place. The work didn't quell her loneliness, but at least the cabin felt more livable.

That evening, instead of sleeping on the couch as she had done the first two nights, Nora slept in the small bed up in the loft. As it turned out, the bed was actually rather comfortable, but in the morning, the sun awoke her much earlier than she would have liked. That's when she noticed the cold. Even through the covers, Nora felt the chill of the early morning and she knew the fire had gone out.

Wrapping the blanket around her, Nora hopped out of bed and climbed down the ladder. The wood stove still held a few hot coals, so Nora shoved a couple small pieces of wood in and hoped they would catch fire quickly. When that happened, it took no time at all for the entire cabin to warm up and Nora shed the blanket, as well as the sweater she'd worn to bed over her pajamas. She still couldn't get used to how fast the cabin could go from freezing temperatures to a sauna. It was so warm she had to open the window a crack and let some cool air in to balance the temperature.

Still in her pajamas, Nora slipped on her shoes and ran out into the cold to pump some water into a pitcher and then ran back inside. She put a pot of water on the wood stove to make coffee, along with a big kettle of water she would use to wash up with once it got warm. It was a good thing Lily sent some ground coffee with all those other supplies, or else Nora would have been trying to grind up her whole coffee beans on the rocks outside.

When the coffee was ready, Nora sat down at the table with a large mug, looking out the window at the water. Once, she saw a ripple on the surface of the water that caught her attention. She couldn't really tell what it was, but she imagined it was a whale. She hadn't seen one of those yet and she liked the idea that there might be a giant whale swimming in the inlet a few dozen yards from her home, that just under the surface there was something beautiful waiting to be discovered. If only it would break through and reveal itself to the world.

That's kind of how Nora felt, like she'd been hiding her true self from everyone. That's what she'd done with Conner. While he paraded her around like a prize, she played the part of the ideal girlfriend. She willingly let him control every aspect of her life, hid pieces of herself to make him happy. But not anymore. Now, she was on her own and she was so close to breaking through the barrier, to becoming her own person, to letting people see her for who she really was.

There's too much time to think out here.

Never in her life had Nora been so introspective. No matter how much she tried to enjoy the peace and quiet, she couldn't get past the overwhelming sense of loneliness she felt, and it wasn't only because she didn't have any close neighbors. She'd never gone an entire day without seeing another human being before. But this feeling of isolation had begun before Nora ever reached Alaska. Honestly, it may have been inside of her all along, even when she was with Conner, even when she'd been happy with him. She'd tried to cover it up with pretty clothes and to distract herself with a full social schedule, but inside she had always felt like she didn't belong, like no one really understood her, like she was alone in the world. And now, she truly was alone.

She needed something to distract herself from her thoughts. The paperback romance novel Lily had given her still sat on the table. There wasn't much else for Nora to do, so she curled up on the couch and settled in for a long reading session.

Around noon, Nora opened a can of tuna and ate some lunch.

After that, she went through the envelope the attorney had left for her. It was a bunch of paperwork showing the property was now hers. There were a couple things she needed to sign and return. She read through everything thoroughly and happily learned that since the property was not located within the borough, she would not have to worry about paying property taxes, which meant her money would stretch a lot further. Everything else looked pretty straightforward, so she signed the papers and stuffed them in the return envelope the attorney had provided. That took about a half-hour and left her wondering, once again, what to do with herself.

When the fire started to die down in the afternoon she carried a couple armloads of wood from the woodpile to the house. The woodpile was still substantial, and every bit of wood burned meant Nora would have less wood for the winter, but she didn't care about that right now. She was still settling in to her new home. There would be plenty of time later to restock the woodpile.

She spent the evening flipping through Pete's journal. Nora was surprised to find it wasn't just lists of supplies. There were actual journal entries where Pete had shared his thoughts and feelings, little bits of himself preserved on paper. As she read his entries, the uncle she never knew became a little more real to her. His journal spoke of dreams he'd once had, a lost love from long ago, and a child he wished he could have known.

Two days into Nora's solitude, Willie stopped by again, probably to make sure she was still alive. Nora was certain that was the only reason for his visit.

"If you still have that Scotch, I thought I'd take you up on it," he said when Nora answered the door.

Nora smiled and invited him inside. After two days completely alone, it was nice to see another person.

He held in one hand a canister of smoked salmon he'd caught

and smoked himself. In the other hand, he held a pair of used rubber boots. "I brought some stuff to trade for it, fair and square."

They were brown and ugly, with small spikes on the sole for traction, and they looked exactly like the pair Willie was wearing.

A month earlier she never would have considered wearing them, not even for practical purposes. Heck, even a week earlier she probably would have turned them down. But Nora knew better now and she accepted them graciously. They would keep her feet dry getting in and out of the boat, and that was a good thing, even if they were hideous to look at and might be uncomfortable to wear.

"Willie, have you been reading my mind?" she asked, grinning at the boots. They were exactly what she needed. She reached onto a shelf and pulled down the still unopened bottle of Scotch, offering it to him in exchange for the boots.

"Oh, no," he said, chuckling as he sat down at the table. "These old boots ain't worth that much. I was thinkin' I'd just have a small glass for now."

"Okay, then," she said, grabbing a glass off the shelf and sitting it in front of the old man. She had a feeling she was getting the better end of the deal, but she didn't push the issue.

Willie poured a small amount of Scotch into the glass, Nora sat down at the table across from him, and he launched into a story about the first time he met Pete.

By the time the story was told, the glass of Scotch was empty. Nora offered him a second glass, but he politely refused. Not the kind to wear out his welcome, Willie stood up, said goodbye, and left.

His visit was short but Nora was glad for the company, as fleeting as it was. She now understood why Lily had given her the Scotch, as well. In the bush, it was almost as valuable as currency, maybe even more so.

CHAPTER

6

"I figured you'd be here," Willie said as he approached the log home tucked back in the woods. Jake was perched on the log bench next to Willie's front door. He'd been waiting there for a half-hour. "You know, I've seen more of you in the past week than I usually do in a month."

Jake ignored Willie's comment.

"How is she?" he asked.

"Why you askin' me?"

"Well, you've been checking in on her every day, which means you're the only one who knows how she's really doing out there."

"You almost sound a little jealous, you know that?" Willie said. "She's been in that cabin for, what, five or six days now? And you've been out here almost every day this week askin' about her. That's not like you at all, especially this time of year when you're usually out on the water. If you're so concerned about her, you ought to go out and see for yourself, sometime."

"She doesn't want me around."

"What makes you think that? She's a nice little lady. Always been pretty welcomin' toward me. She even gave me some of Pete's old things today," he said, holding up a bag to show him. "Good stuff, too. The one pair of pants looks like he hadn't even worn 'em yet."

"I know she doesn't want me around because she flat out told me the day I brought her the boat and showed her how to use it. We got to talking about the road leading out of town and she got her panties in a bunch when I told her she shouldn't try to drive that old trail. Said I was being a 'typical dominant male.' Then she asked me to leave. Told me she'd return the boat as soon as she got Pete's old one repaired and I didn't need to bother trying to help her out anymore."

Willie chuckled. "Sounds like you may have gotten on her bad side."

"No kidding," he said dryly. "Look, I just want to make sure she's okay, that she's not in over her head."

"I think you want a little more than that. Otherwise you wouldn't be out here askin' 'bout her all the time."

Jake couldn't believe he was having this conversation. First his sister and now Willie. Why did everyone think he had a romantic interest in Nora?

"Like I said before, I'm not interested in getting involved with a woman like her. She seems a little high-maintenance for my tastes. And besides, she'll probably be gone by winter."

Winters in Heron were always the hardest on his mom. She couldn't get out, she always complained. The ferry only came once a month and she felt trapped. It's what eventually drove her away. Jake was exactly like his dad, the kind of man who wouldn't give up on the woman he loved. If he allowed himself to get involved with someone like Nora, someone who would eventually leave, it would tear him to pieces.

"I'm not so sure," said Willie. "Now that I've been gettin' to know her, I think she's gonna stick around."

"You still haven't answered my question," Jake persisted.

"She's doin' just fine." Willie looked at him hard and long, then. "There is one thing I noticed, though."

"What?"

"Her woodpile's been gettin' smaller and smaller," said Willie. "Now, I would help her out if I wasn't gettin' so old, but my bones ache when I start swingin' an ax. That's why I put the heat in the floors last year. Seems to me, you oughta go out there and drop a tree or two for her. I'm sure she'll really appreciate it, seein' as how she's gonna be out of wood before winter rolls around at the rate she's burnin' through it."

"Don't try to play matchmaker," said Jake.

Willie looked at him with a raised eyebrow and shook his head. "I'm no cupid, that's for sure. Just tryin' to keep her alive. Besides, you're the one who keeps askin' 'bout her."

CHAPTER

7

Nora unwrapped a Little Debbie cupcake and set it on a small plate. She didn't have a candle to stick in the top, so she just pretended she did. Closing her eyes and making a wish, she blew out the imaginary candle.

"Happy birthday to me," she said aloud before taking a big bite out of the chocolate cupcake. The white filling oozed out from the center and Nora caught it on her finger and then licked it off. Chocolate was an indulgence Nora rarely allowed herself. But the rules she'd stuck to in Los Angeles didn't seem as important here. It's not like she needed to fit into those unrealistically small size 0 dresses anymore. There were no important dinner parties or social functions to attend. There were no watchful eyes to make her feel guilty for occasionally cheating on her diet. There was no controlling boyfriend to chastise her for each and every little indulgence. So when Nora finished eating her cupcake, she opened another one for the heck of it, smiling with satisfaction because she could do whatever she pleased and there was no one around to remind her otherwise.

Nora was actually celebrating two things that day. It was her 25th birthday, which she supposed was reason enough to celebrate, but it was also her seventh day in Alaska. She had survived on her own for a full week. It wasn't a huge achievement, but it meant something to her. She had shrugged off the chains of her old life and was starting anew. She felt alive and free. So free that when Nora spotted her scrapbook sitting on the shelf, she decided to put it away for good. She didn't need any reminders of her old life any more. It held photos of her time with Conner and newspaper clippings detailing the social events they'd been seen at, with speculations about their relationship. It seemed unreal now. Like it had been someone else's life. Not Nora's.

Uncle Pete hadn't left her much, just some land with a rustic old cabin and a little money, but he'd given her so much more than he probably ever could have guessed. His gift had given Nora the courage to leave Conner and the means to start over fresh. That's exactly what she was going to do.

A cardboard box still sat on the floor next to the table. It was half-full with things she'd accidentally brought out to the cabin, the electric coffee grinder and a few other small electronic devices.

Nora tossed the scrapbook into the box and then pulled her cell phone out of her pocket. There really was no point in carrying it around anymore. For the heck of it, Nora turned it on and browsed through the photos one more time. There were a few pictures of Conner, which she promptly deleted, along with a slew of photos she'd taken on the ferry on the trip north. Most of those were scenes of mountains, islands, and water. It all looked the same. From the southern coast of British Columbia all the way to Juneau, there was practically no way to distinguish where you were at.

And then there were the photos she'd taken of the inlet and of

Jake. Nora lingered on those photos the longest, noticing the intensity of Jake's gaze as he stared off into the beauty of the inlet. He knew the land and the waters intimately. Nora could tell he loved this place and everything about it. He would never leave it. She wondered if someday she would feel the same way.

The last photo was the one Jake had taken of the two of them in the boat. They were both smiling as Jake leaned in so close to take the photo. Nora had definitely felt something, a surge of blood pumping through her veins, a spark of electricity, at his closeness. How could she not? He was attractive and ever so masculine. Everything about Jake was appealing. Well, almost everything. Nora couldn't forget the unmistakable air of authority in his voice when he'd told her to stay away from that trail.

Turning the phone off, Nora tossed it into the box with the scrapbook and the other electronics. Then she shoved the last bit of cupcake in her mouth, picked up the box and climbed the ladder to the loft. She picked up the two framed photographs that sat on the dresser and placed them in the box, as well. One was of her in a ball gown, at the entrance to a museum charity event. She had looked stunning in the form-fitted white silk and had captured the eye of the photographer, who spent half the night photographing her. The other was a portrait of her and Conner. It had been taken for what was going to be their official engagement announcement, but Nora had broken it off before the engagement had been made public. When Nora had left Los Angeles, she'd taken both photographs because she'd wanted a few mementos of that part of her life. Even though Conner had been overbearing and domineering, it had been a spectacular life. She'd been surrounded by such luxury and she'd grown comfortable with the finer things in life. But that wasn't her life anymore. And even if she could get it back, she didn't want it.

Nora closed the box and pushed it under the bed with her foot.

The box only went a few inches under when it stopped. It hit something.

Kneeling down, Nora pushed the box aside to see what was under the bed. Grabbing a handle, she pulled out an old, hard-shelled suitcase. It was covered in dust and heavier than Nora had expected. She flipped up each of the four clasps that held the case shut, and carefully opened it up. Inside, she found an assortment of books and something else. It was an old VHF radio. Nothing more than a lightweight hand-held unit. Nora smiled. It was like a birthday present. Maybe the best birthday present she'd ever received.

Shoving the box of photos and electronics under the bed, Nora closed the suitcase and then hauled it down the ladder. At the table, she opened it back up. She pulled the books out and stacked them on the shelf. Then she turned her attention to the radio. She carefully studied all the knobs and controls. When she opened up the battery compartment, she found it empty. Nora grabbed the bucket of batteries Pete had left at the cabin and began searching for the right size. It took some time, but eventually she found batteries that still held a charge. She actually squealed with delight and clapped her hands when the red power light finally came on.

Fumbling with the knobs, Nora turned the radio to the first station and tried it out.

"Anyone there?" she asked, holding the button while she spoke and then releasing it in hopes of receiving a response.

There was none. The radio was silent, except for the faint crackle of dead air. She pushed the button again.

"Hello?"

There was still no answer, so Nora flipped the switch to the next channel and tried again. On the fifth channel, she heard voices. There were two people talking back and forth. But they couldn't hear her, she realized quickly enough. She turned the knob again and again, trying each channel to find someone, anyone, who could hear her.

At channel 16, Nora got lucky.

"Hello? Is anyone there?" she called out over the static. There was no response, so she tried again, just like she had on every other channel. Her fingers rested on the knob, ready to flip to the next channel, when she heard a reply.

"This is the Lil Pelican," the voice said. "Do you need assistance?"

"Oh... uh," Nora wasn't sure what to say. She didn't need help. She had simply wanted someone to talk to.

"Who is this?" the voice on the other end asked impatiently.

Suddenly shy about talking over the radio, Nora didn't answer. She thought about turning the radio off right then. After all, she had no business messing around with the radio. She didn't know what she was doing, and it showed.

"Identify yourself," the male voice came back over the radio authoritatively.

His voice sounded so official, Nora abruptly set the radio down on the table in front of her and stared at it, unsure what to do. *I should just switch the radio off,* she thought again. But it was so nice to hear another voice, she couldn't do it. Hesitantly, Nora picked the radio back up and held down the button to talk. But she still didn't know what to say, so she released the button after a few seconds.

"Look, this isn't a toy," came the voice on the other end, frustrated now. "If you don't need help, get off this channel."

Nora had to respond, she decided. "Sorry," she said. "I was just... I don't know what I'm doing. I'll get off now. I'm really sorry."

There was silence on the radio for a few seconds as the man on the other end thought he recognized the voice. Wondering if he was right, Jake stood in the tiny cabin of the Lil Pelican with the radio in one hand. With the other hand, he cut the engine so he'd be able to hear the radio more clearly. Was it her?

"Who is this?" he asked again, much less harshly this time as the boat rose and fell with the swells of the water where he'd been trolling the inlet.

Nora recognized the change in his voice, and even though she was still hesitant about using the radio, she answered.

"My name is Nora," she said.

It was her. Jake smiled, picturing her in the cabin talking on Pete's old radio.

"I... I'm new here and I was just looking for someone to talk to," she continued. "I found this old radio and I'm still figuring out how to use it." Jake enjoyed the sound of her voice over the airwaves, even if she was babbling now. "I really don't know what I'm doing. I've been switching through the channels trying to find someone..."

"Listen, this channel isn't for small-talk," he interrupted her. "Switch over to channel 71, okay? I'll meet you there."

"Okay," Nora agreed uncertainly. She turned the knob until it read 71. There was only static on that channel, so she waited.

"Are you there, Nora?" she heard his voice a few seconds later.

"Yes, I'm here." She didn't know what else to say. "Um, you said you were the Little Pelican, right? What's that mean?"

Jake chuckled. She really didn't have a clue, did she?

"It's the Lil Pelican," he explained. "And that's the name of my boat."

"Oh, so you're the captain?"

He chuckled again and Nora heard the humor in his voice when he replied. "Yeah, captain of a one-man vessel. At the most, the Lil Pelican can hold two or three people, but it's easier to run this thing alone."

Jake briefly considered telling Nora it was him she was talking to, but she seemed content to talk to the anonymous fisherman, a stranger whose name she hadn't bothered to ask. Besides, the last time they'd spoken, they hadn't parted on good terms. Jake had a feeling Nora wouldn't be interested in talking to him if she knew who it really was on the other end of the radio.

As he told her about his boat, Nora closed her eyes, listening to the anonymous voice on the other end and imagining what he looked like. His voice was deep and masculine, revealing no hint of his age. But if he was like any of the other fishermen she'd seen on the docks of Heron, he probably had a big, bushy beard to ward off the biting wind of the open seas and worn, weathered hands from years of working the fishing lines or nets or whatever they used out there. She pictured him in a big, heavy raincoat and tall rubber boots, pulling in fish in the light misty rain. And the sound of his laugh made her think of the nice old man who'd served as the groundskeeper at the Bradshaw family estate, so the face Nora imagined in her head looked like a grandfatherly type with a balding head and a friendly smile.

"So, how is everything? You're not running into any problems out there alone, are you?"

Nora laughed then. It warmed Jake's heart to hear that sound.

"No," she said. "No problems. Just bored out of my mind. Going crazy, pacing back and forth. That counts as an emergency, right?"

"I suppose it could," Jake said, strangely relieved she was alright. "So, you're settling in all right?" He wanted to keep her talking. He liked the sound of her voice.

"Um... yeah. I guess so. I've only been here a week, but... yeah, I'm settling in all right."

"You're not convincing me."

Nora laughed. "I'm not convincing myself very well, either. I keep telling myself all this peace and quiet is a good thing and I should be thankful I don't have a busy schedule and a bunch of people stopping by to visit all the time."

"Is it really that bad?"

"I don't know. I guess not. Someone recently told me I'm being overly dramatic about my situation. Do you know Lily? Of course you know Lily. It's a small town, right? She called me a drama queen the other day and then she proceeded to make fun of me."

Yeah, that sounded like his sister, always ready to poke a little fun at someone else's expense. "So you don't like Lily?" Jake asked, a little concerned his sister had unintentionally alienated the newest member of the community.

"Oh, I love Lily. So far I've met a total of three people, and they've all been nice enough, but Lily's the best." Talking to the fisherman felt comfortable, like they were old friends who talked on the radio every day. "She's the first person I met in town and she's been so friendly and welcoming. I think we could become friends."

"So who else have you met?" Jake was curious what Nora thought of him.

"Just Lily's brother, Jake, and my neighbor, Willie." Nora chuckled, slightly embarrassed at the way she'd met Willie. "Willie actually walked up on me when I was half naked."

Half naked? Willie failed to mention that fact.

"I think it startled him more than me, though," Nora continued. "I didn't know what to think of him at first, but he's a great neighbor. He keeps stopping by to check up on me. It's kind of sweet."

Nora realized, then, she was monopolizing the conversation. She knew nothing about the fisherman on the other end of the radio except the name of his boat.

"I'm sorry. I've been babbling. Tell me a little about yourself. What's it like being a fisherman?" she prompted.

Jake chuckled at her question. Nobody had ever asked him that before. Everybody in Heron fished, either commercially or, at the very least, to feed their families. "Well, it's like any other job, I suppose. It can be frustrating at times. Sometimes I put in a lot of hours out here and don't catch much of anything. But there's something to be said for getting out on the water and away from everybody for a while. At least I have my own boat. I can fish at my own pace. It's peaceful. The rise and fall of the boat on the swells is calming for me. Keeps me centered."

"What about in the winter? Lily told me the waters can get pretty rough."

"Oh, I don't usually fish in the winter, unless I'm in the mood for a winter king salmon. No, in the off season, there's plenty of other stuff to keep me busy."

"Like what?"

"You name it. Chopping and hauling wood. Repairing the house. Foraging." Jake figured the portrait of life he was portraying sounded a bit daunting to Nora. At least he hoped it sounded daunting. That way she'd know what she'd be in for if she stayed. "There's a never-ending list of work to be done."

Nora sighed, looking around the ramshackle cabin. There were gaps between some of the logs that let a cool draft into the house and the woodpile outside was getting low. She had a lot of work to do if she was going to live there for any length of time.

When Jake heard only silence on the other end of the radio, he decided to change the subject. As much as he wanted to know whether she really had it in her to stick it out in the harsh Alaskan wilderness, he didn't want to scare Nora away. There were plenty of good things about living in Heron, too. Things you couldn't find anywhere else but the Alaskan bush.

"You know, people tend to visit Alaska in the summer, when everything is warm and beautiful, but the best time to be here is in the winter, when there's not much to do but settle in and wait for spring. It's so much more relaxed. If you stick around, you'll see what I mean."

"If I stick around," Nora repeated absentmindedly. That was the question, wasn't it? Even though she'd placed the ad, she still hadn't decided whether she really wanted to sell the property. So far, living in the cabin wasn't nearly bad as she had originally thought. Sure, the place needed some work, but it was cozy and it was starting to feel like a home. The more she thought about it, the more Nora realized she might not want to sell it, after all. So, she didn't have a job or any source of income. Did she really need it? She had a place to live and absolutely no debt. She didn't have to worry about electric bills or heating bills, or even property taxes, for that matter. Her only real expense was groceries and gasoline for the skiff. Oh, and more suitable clothing. Her small savings would cover those expenses for months, maybe even years. All she needed to do was learn to live off the land and she'd be fine.

Of course, there was the isolation to deal with, but she might learn to live with that, especially if she had someone like Jake to cuddle up next to at night. Nora caught herself smiling at the thought, in spite of the fact she considered Jake an overbearing, control freak. If only he were more like the man on the radio. Then he would be perfect.

She returned her attention to the fisherman on the radio, imagining she was talking to Jake instead of some old brawny fisherman. "Tell me what I can look forward to," she said eagerly.

"Well," Jake thought about it for a moment. "For one thing, almost everyone around here is musical, in one way or another. There'll be impromptu jam sessions where people get together to play or just listen to the music. There's really a sense of community here. Everyone helps everyone else out and they don't really expect anything in return. People get together for the holidays and birthdays and sometimes just for the heck of it. When there's a party, everyone is invited, and I mean everyone. There's a real closeness you can't find on the mainland."

"Mmm. That's sounds nice. Tell me more."

Jake smiled, happy to tell Nora why he loved living in Heron and why he'd never, ever leave. It was the only place in the world he ever wanted to live. He hoped she'd come to love it as much as he did.

"I'm really glad you answered my call," Nora said nearly an hour later.

"Me, too. Remember, if you need anything, call for the Lil Pelican. My radio is always on."

By the time Nora turned the radio off, all thoughts of selling the property had slipped away, replaced by a sense of gladness that Pete had left her his cabin and she had taken the huge leap of moving to Alaska. Now more than ever, Nora felt like she could actually build a life there.

Nora stood up and placed the radio on the shelf behind the table. She had a feeling she was going to use it quite a bit, now that she had someone on the other end to talk to.

She turned and glanced out the window. The waters of the inlet had grown dark, a reflection of the gathering clouds overhead. A drop of rain splashed down on the windowsill. Then another.

For nearly a week straight after that, it rained constantly. The rain started out as a light sprinkle on the first day. The wind picked up the second day and it turned to a downpour. That's when Willie's visits ceased, since the trail connecting them was becoming too treacherous. By the third day, the path from the cabin to the woodpile was nothing but slippery mud. The rainwater coming down from the mountainside dug deep trenches into the earth as the water made its way toward the inlet.

Nora stayed indoors the entire time, venturing out only for firewood once a day. She paced the floors, cleaned everything twice, and nearly drove herself mad with boredom. With the heavy rains outside, Nora felt trapped. She couldn't go into town. She couldn't do much outside. She was stuck in the tiny cabin, whose walls seemed to be closing in more and more each day.

The radio, and the fisherman's voice on the other end, was the only thing that helped her keep her sanity through what was becoming the longest period of isolation in her life.

CHAPTER

8

After being cooped up for more than a week in the cabin, Nora was glad when the rain let up a little. It didn't quit raining completely, but it had diminished to a fine mist and the waters were calm enough for Nora to venture a trip into town.

Just as clumsily as before, Nora maneuvered the skiff through the inlet toward Heron. She absolutely had to buy more supplies. She couldn't get by with the impractical clothes she'd brought with her and she was tired of eating food out of cans. She needed something fresh, something real. Not to mention, she needed to get out of the cabin and be around other people.

Motoring past the harbor, Nora surveyed the boats moored at the docks, curious to see if the Lil Pelican was there. She hoped to catch a glimpse of the man whose soothing voice had brought comfort to her during the past week. It had been the only thing keeping Nora from pulling her hair out and going crazy. She wasn't accustomed to being alone and she wanted to thank him for keeping her company on those rainy days when she'd been shut in. And she wanted a face to put with the voice. As she eased past the harbor, Nora spotted the Lil Pelican moored to the dock. It looked empty. There was no sign of anyone around. *Oh, well,* she thought. Maybe next time she'd get to meet the fisherman.

A minute later, Nora pulled up to the dock at the store and tied the boat off. She recognized the man working there. It was the same man she'd met on the dock her first day in town. As she awkwardly climbed out of the boat and onto the dock, he grinned his toothless grin at her and Nora couldn't help but smile back.

"You heading back south?" he asked.

Nora looked at him curiously. "No," she answered. "Why do you ask?"

"Just figured. You showing up here and the ferry coming today. Thought you'd be getting on it."

"Nope," she said politely. "Not this time."

"Humph," was the man's only reply. Picking up another crate, he turned and loaded it onto a boat.

Nora walked up the plank toward The General Store, wondering about that brief conversation. She didn't know what to think of it as she headed toward the store.

Opening the door to walk in, Nora stepped into a long hallway that ran the length of the store. It wasn't one large store, as she had expected, but rather a series of small, separate rooms for each type of merchandise. On the left was a tiny room that served as the liquor store, followed by another larger room that served as the hardware store. Nora walked past the hardware section, noticing it was filled mostly with boots. There were two long shelves of the ugly, brown Xtra-Tuf boots she now realized everyone wore, followed by a couple aisles of fishing gear and another aisle of tools, nuts, and bolts. The next door opened up into a Laundromat.

At the end of the hall, on the right, there was a door to the grocery section of the store. It was a small space, lined with refrigerated foods along one wall and three short aisles of dry goods. Nora's bedroom back home had been bigger than the grocery store, she mused, as she grabbed some coffee, a couple boxes of dried pasta, a bag of rice, and a basket full of canned goods. She also picked up a dozen eggs, a pound of butter, and a pound of hamburger. Since she didn't have electricity, she had to be careful not to buy too much food that could spoil. One of the many hazards of living in the bush, she was learning.

There weren't any other customers in the store, so Nora left her groceries at the check-out counter and then wandered up to the second level, where she found a small clothing section. There were a few items that were obviously for tourists, mostly sweaters and t-shirts that read, "Heron, Alaska," on them. Nora picked out three sweat shirts that looked like they would keep her fairly warm, as well as a couple t-shirts. Then she found a raincoat, and in spite of the hefty price tag, decided she needed to buy it. As it was, Nora's clothes were already damp from the misty weather and if the rain kept up, she was going to need that raincoat.

When she got back downstairs, Nate was waiting for her at the check-out counter. He was loading the food into a small cardboard box when she approached the counter.

"You know you can't cook on the ferry," said Nate as he tallied up the price of her purchase. Even though this was Nora's first time in The General Store and they hadn't met yet, he knew who she was. "You might be able to heat up these canned goods in the dining room's microwave, but the rest of this is going to spoil by the time you get back south."

"I... I'm not getting on the ferry," stammered Nora.

"Sticking around for a while, then?" he asked, looking up at her. He didn't even try to conceal the surprise in his voice.

"Yeah," Nora said, handing him the money. That was the second person who had assumed she'd be getting on the ferry and leaving... and she'd only seen two people in town so far. She put the raincoat on, picked up the box, and left. Outside, she walked down the plank, loaded the box into her skiff, and covered it with a canvas tarp to keep the food dry. But she wasn't ready to head back home yet. Instead, she found herself walking down the boardwalk in the direction of the ferry dock. She watched as the ferry made its way to port. The deckhands scurried around, docking the vessel and preparing the gangplank for walk-on travelers to exit the ship. She realized there were no vehicles exiting the ship this time. Nora had to chuckle a little at the absurdity of her own arrival in Heron two weeks earlier. If only she had known. She never would have brought her car. She could have saved herself a lot of embarrassment, not to mention a fair amount of expense. But it was too late now.

As the few passengers began to disembark the vessel, Nora turned and walked back up the boardwalk. On a whim, she stopped at the Pub & Grub. Instead of sitting at the busy bar, Nora found a table next to the window, where she could watch the ferry. It would remain in port for two hours, she knew. That was the schedule.

A young man she'd never seen before came over and handed her a menu. Nora ordered a soda and handed the menu back. She sat there, sipping her drink, and watched the others in the restaurant for a while. But her attention kept wandering back to the ferry. It was the only way out of town for most people, and Nora almost wished she could jump on the ferry and ride away. But where would she go? She was definitely better off there in Heron than she would be back in Los Angeles. No, Nora wasn't going to leave. At least not yet. She'd decided to give Heron a chance and that's exactly what she was going to do.

For a long time after her drink was gone, Nora sat there thinking. Everyone thought she was going to fail, that she was going to go running back to wherever she'd come from. That's why the man on the dock had assumed she'd be leaving on the ferry. Nate had asked the same thing. Heck, everyone in the pub probably thought she'd be leaving. Well, they were wrong. The more she thought about it, the more determined she became to prove she could make it out there on her own.

"You heading out soon?"

It was Lily. Nora hadn't even noticed her approach. That simple question was the last straw. "Why does everyone keep asking me that? Yes, the ferry is in town. No, I'm not going anywhere," she said, not even trying to hide her frustration. "I'm staying right here."

"I know you're not leaving town," said Lily gently, pointing toward the window that overlooked the inlet. "Ferry's already pulled away from the dock. I was asking if you were heading back to your place anytime soon."

"Oh," said Nora, feeling a little foolish then. "Sorry. It's just that every single person I've met today has assumed I'd be on that boat... and honestly, I almost wish I was."

Lily smiled genuinely. "I, for one, am glad you aren't," she said softly. "If you're not in a hurry to get back home, I thought maybe you'd like the grand tour of town." Lily looked at her expectantly and Nora decided she didn't want to turn down this invitation. It would be her first real chance to get to know the town and its residents.

Nora smiled back. "Sure," she said.

Turned out, the grand tour didn't take long. Nora had already seen most of Heron simply by walking from the ferry dock to the store, but Lily pointed out each of the buildings and told Nora who lived where. She showed Nora the post office, a small area tucked into the rear of The General Store, and introduced her to Barbara, who sorted the mail when it came in off the float plane each day.

And Lily formally introduced her to Lars, the toothless man who worked the dock, along with half-a-dozen other people they met along the way. Halfway through the tour, the light mist turned to a steady rain and Nora zipped up her new raincoat.

"When do you think the rain is going to let up?"

Lily laughed. "Probably around August," she said. "It rains almost constantly this time of year. Those few days of sun we had a while back were just a fluke." The look on Nora's face was priceless and Lily laughed some more. "Don't worry. You'll get used to the rain. It's what makes everything here so lush and beautiful. Whenever I start to feel the gloom of the cloudy days, I just think about all the life this rain brings. I think it's worth it."

"I'll have to take your word for it."

"You'll see," Lily said. "Come on. Let's get out of the rain. We're not far from home. You can meet my dad." Lily led Nora away from town, down a narrower wooden walkway branching off the main boardwalk, jutting inland as far as the mountain would permit. Along the way, they passed several houses tucked into the forest and Lily pointed out a community garden planted near the school, a small round building also used for public events. Just past the school, they stepped off the boardwalk and followed a worn footpath down a gradual slope until a pretty white two-story house appeared. It sat near the shore of a small cove, tucked into the hillside. The tall pines of the forest enveloped it, wrapping around the yard so tightly it was completely hidden from the rest of town.

"You live here with your dad?"

"Yeah. We all do. Me, Jake, and Dad," Lily explained.

"It's beautiful, but it looks so out of place here." Unlike most of the houses in town that had taken on a dingy hue from years of moist weather and the ongoing battle against mold, the house looked like it had been painstakingly maintained over the years.

"I know. Dad insists on repainting it every year so it always looks fresh. He's just as meticulous about the inside, too. Not a loose nail or broken hinge. He keeps it that way for Mom." Then she added, almost as an afterthought, "Mom lives in Juneau."

"Oh, so they're divorced?" asked Nora, confused.

Lily shook her head. "No. They never got divorced. I used to wish they would so Dad could move on with his life. But he loves her. He won't give up on her." It had been 12 years since Madeline had left town, but she'd never really left Samuel. As much as she loved her husband and her children, she'd never been happy living so far removed from everything and eventually she had reached her breaking point. One day, she packed a bag and boarded the ferry. She couldn't handle living in the bush for another minute.

"That had to be hard," Nora said sympathetically.

"It was. I was 14 when she left. Jake was 16. Mom wanted us to come with her, but neither one of us wanted to leave Heron." Samuel had thought about selling the fishing boat and following Madeline, but he had the kids to think about. Heron was their home. So, Samuel had stayed put, waiting for the day when Madeline might change her mind and return to them... and to him. "Come on," said Lily, changing the subject. "Smells like dinner's cooking."

Nora followed Lily in through the back door, which led directly into the kitchen. Sure enough, a pot of clam chowder sat on the stove, steaming hot and filling the room with a delicious aroma that made Nora's mouth water instantly. The kitchen looked well used. Heavy stainless steel pots hung from hooks on the walls and the sink was half-full with dirty dishes. A round wooden table sat in the center of the room, already set for dinner.

"You didn't tell me you were bringing company home, Lil." The voice was deep and friendly, a perfect match to the tall, well-built man walking into the kitchen. His hair was gray, the only thing betraying his age. His eyes were lively and cheerful. His muscles still strong in spite of the fact that he'd just celebrated his 51st birthday.

"Hey, Dad. This is Nora. Nora, this is my dad, Samuel."

"It's nice to meet you," said Nora politely.

Nora stretched out her hand and Samuel took it in his own. "The pleasure's all mine. It's not too often I get to entertain a beautiful young woman like yourself."

"Thank you," Nora blushed. She liked Samuel immediately. He had a cheerful demeanor and a good-humored way about him that made her feel instantly at ease.

"You're staying for dinner, right?" asked Samuel.

"If that's an invitation, then I accept."

"Good," he said. "The chowder's ready and since Jake won't be back until later, we might as well eat. You hungry?"

"Starving," Nora grinned.

As they sat down to eat, Nora turned to Lily. "Oh, yeah. I forgot to bring back your casserole dish, Lily. It was delicious, by the way."

"What casserole dish?" She took a sip of the hot soup and looked curiously at Nora.

"The chicken casserole. From my second day here. Jake brought it along with the box of goodies you sent."

Lily grinned, amused. "That wasn't from me. The casserole, I mean," she said. "You might want to thank Jake for that one."

Nora didn't know what to say. "Oh," she said. "I assumed…"

"No worries," Lily cut in. "We all cook around here. I'm obviously the better cook," she looked over at her dad playfully, "but Dad and Jake can both hold their own."

"You learned from the best," Samuel teased.

They joked with each other so easily, so comfortably. Nora could see the love between the father and daughter and wished she'd had that with her own dad.

"Are you sure you're Lily's dad?" Nora cut in. "You don't look old enough."

Samuel laughed heartily. "We married young, Madeline and I. We were only 23 when Jake came along. And Lil followed right behind two years later. I don't know what's taking these kids so long to settle down," he said, winking at Lily. "By the time I was their age I had a family and a business to run. Taking their sweet time, they are."

Lily snorted back a laugh. "Here we go again. He acts like I'm an old maid... at the ripe old age of 26."

"I just want you to be happy, Lil. You're young. You should be out having fun, dating. Not spending all your time working. You spend too much time at the pub."

"That place couldn't run without me."

"See what I mean? Too focused on work." Then Samuel turned to Nora. "So, Nora. Tell me what you do."

The question caught her off guard. *What did she do? Like, for a living?* She took in a deep breath and let it out slowly, trying to think of something good-sounding. She was rather embarrassed she couldn't think of anything, so she avoided making eye contact with either of them when she answered, focusing instead on the pattern of the dinnerware. "Honestly," she said, "I don't know. My last boyfriend didn't want me to work, so I didn't. He believed my job was to look pretty, so that's what I tried to do."

When she looked up, she expected to see judgment. Instead, they were both looking at her encouragingly. "Well, I'm sure there's something you're good at, other than looking pretty," Samuel said.

"The restaurant already hired on some extra help for the summer, but if you're interested in a job we could probably take you on next year," Lily offered. "We always need help during the tourist season."

"That's a very nice offer," said Nora. "You might regret it once you see how bad my waitressing skills are. In the meantime, I suppose I should try to find some way to earn a living."

"Don't you have a lot of things in your car?" asked Lily. "If you don't need them, Nate could probably help you get rid of a few things. He sometimes sells stuff on consignment at the store."

Sell her possessions? Nora didn't want to do that. There was a good chance she'd need those things again. But she did have a lot of clothes and accessories she didn't need anymore. They were mostly designer items that might fetch a substantial amount of money anywhere else... but probably not in Heron, where the women didn't seem too tuned in to the latest fashions.

"Do you really think anyone would want to buy my stuff?" Nora asked skeptically.

"Sure. It's cheaper than having things shipped all the way out here. Dad, tell her about the time you tried to buy Mom that watch from the catalog."

Samuel laughed and eagerly launched into the story, with Lily frequently cutting in to insert some minor detail he'd forgotten. It was endearing to watch them together. The remainder of the dinner flew by, with Samuel telling anecdotes about life in Heron and Lily urging him on.

After dinner, as Nora said her goodbyes and got ready to leave, something caught her attention. On the wall hung a framed photograph of a boat, a narrow vessel equipped with long trolling rods for fishing. On the side of the boat were the words, painted on in neat white writing, Lil Pelican. Standing on the deck was a much younger looking Jake, grinning with the day's catch.

Nora turned to Lily. "Is this your dad's boat?"

"Yeah. Well, it was Dad's. He named it after me. Did you notice how he calls me Lil instead of Lily? He used to call me his

Lil Pelican. Thank God he doesn't anymore," Lily added emphatically. "Anyway, Jake bought it off him a few years ago when Dad decided to retire from fishing."

"So Jake is a fisherman?"

"Yeah," Lily giggled at her question. "Don't sound so surprised. Just about everyone around here fishes."

So, Jake was the fisherman she'd been talking to on the radio. The last time she'd seen Jake he had been domineering. Bossy. Overbearing. Everything she didn't like in a man. The man on the radio had been so easy to talk to. Understanding. Considerate. Thoughtful. Were they really the same man? Had she gotten the wrong impression of Jake?

As Nora pulled on her raincoat, she realized she hadn't seen Jake anywhere. She'd spent the entire day in town, but she hadn't gotten one glimpse of him. Now, knowing Jake was the man on the other end of the radio, she was actually a little disappointed not to see him.

"Are you sure you can find your way back to the dock?" Lily asked Nora at the door.

"Yes," Nora reassured her. "I'm sure I won't get lost. Just follow the boardwalk, right?"

It seemed easy enough, until she got back to the boardwalk and couldn't remember which direction they'd come from. Tucked back in the woods, she couldn't even see the water. But the sight of the school and the community garden off to the right helped jog Nora's memory and she turned in that direction.

As she walked, she thought of Jake. They had talked so easily over the radio, so openly. If she'd known it was him all along, would she have let her guard down? Probably not. She was actually glad she hadn't known it was him, glad because those preconceived notions she had about him weren't able to get in the way when they talked over the radio.

"Hey, there," came a voice out of nowhere. Nora looked around and saw no one. "Up here." Nora's gaze turned upward, toward the voice. There he was. Jake sat perched on the edge of the roof. He swung one leg over onto a ladder to climb down and a few seconds later he was on the ground next to her.

For the past hour he'd been waiting for Nora. He was working on the roof of the community building when she and Lily walked by on their way to the house. Seeing her in town, on the day the ferry was in port, he'd been sure she was saying goodbye to Lily, that she'd be boarding the ferry and leaving for good. But the ferry had departed. Nora hadn't left, after all.

"Not the best day for building repairs," Nora said, looking him over. The rain was still coming down and, in spite of the raincoat, Jake was soaking wet.

"No, it's not," Jake chuckled. "But we can't exactly wait around for sunny days, now can we?"

"Apparently not."

Jake laughed then. "Try not to sound too enthusiastic about it," he said cheerfully.

"Sorry. I'm just not looking forward to a half-hour boat ride in the rain." Nora started to walk away. Since she found out Jake was the mysterious fisherman, she'd been hoping to see him. Now that he was there in front of her, she didn't know what to do or say.

To Nora's surprise, Jake immediately fell into step beside her. They followed the boardwalk through the forest toward town. The wooden planks were slick from the rain, so they walked slowly to avoid slipping.

"I wasn't sure you'd be staying," he said.

"You and everyone else, it seems."

"I'm glad you did."

Nora stopped and looked at him, then. "Really?" she asked.

"Yes."

"You know, I saw a picture of you with your boat," Nora said casually. "It was hanging on the wall at your dad's house. Why didn't you tell me it was you on the radio? You let me go on and on. Not once did you bother to mention your name."

"You never asked."

"You're right." Nora shrugged. "Maybe I liked the mystery of not knowing who was on the other end of the radio."

"And now that you know?"

Nora smiled at him. "Well, I'm not disappointed."

"That's good," said Jake, relieved. "Look, I'd like to take you out sometime. On a date."

Nora started to laugh, but then stopped herself. "A date? In Heron? What on earth would we do?"

Jake's smile disappeared. "It was a bad idea. Never mind."

"No," said Nora. "I'm sorry. I didn't mean it that way. I just... I'm sorry."

"So, you'd like to go out sometime?"

Nora liked him, that much she knew. There was no other explanation for why he kept popping into her thoughts. She wasn't sure about starting a serious relationship, but that didn't mean she couldn't at least try and enjoy her time in Alaska. Jake could turn out to be the perfect distraction.

"Yes. I'd like to go out with you," she decided. "I just don't know where we'd go."

"I'll figure something out," Jake said, his smile returning. "I'm heading to Juneau for a few days, but I'll get in touch with you when I get back. We'll make plans then."

"You're a busy man, aren't you?"

"Yes, but I make time for the important people in my life." *Was Jake saying she was important to him? Surely not. They barely knew each other.* But when Jake took her hand in his own and squeezed it lightly, excitement coursed through her body. "I really am glad you decided to stay," he said.

Nora felt a sudden pang of guilt. Sure, she had decided to give Heron a chance, but she hadn't really decided to stay for good. At least not yet.

CHAPTER

9

A helicopter circled the mountaintop, making at least its fourth or fifth trip around the peak that still held a few patches of snow from the previous winter.

Nora first noticed the aircraft hovering over a clearing on the northwest side of the mountain while she maneuvered her skiff toward the store dock. She continued watching the helicopter, even as she cut the throttle and let the boat drift the rest of the way to the mooring. As she pulled up to the floating dock and looped the rope around a post, securing the boat, she glanced toward the mountain again. That time she spotted the helicopter slowly moving around to the other side of the peak. She grabbed her tote bag and a cooler out of the skiff, sitting them beside her on the wooden platform, and turned her attention back toward the mountain. The helicopter turned again, moving back toward the northwest side of the mountain, hovering around the summit a little over 3,000 feet above sea level.

"It's Mark," she heard someone say behind her. "Mark Nelson.

Went up yesterday morning and didn't come back down."

"By himself?" she asked, turning around to see Lars loading a couple boxes onto a float plane tied up on the other side of the dock.

"Humph," he grunted. "Told his wife he was going to check his traps."

Nora didn't know Mark at all, except by name and reputation. He was a local, one of the few that were born and raised there, and his furs were sold at the store. Lily had told her that much during their grand tour of town a few days earlier.

"He knows the mountain pretty well, though, doesn't he?" she asked. "Lily told me he leads hiking excursions or something."

"Doesn't matter. Anything can happen out there. You need help?" he asked, nodding at the dirty, old Coleman cooler by her feet.

"No. I can get this," she said, picking it up and walking toward the ramp to the store.

"Tide's low and the ramp is steep," was all he said as he took the cooler from her, propped it up on one shoulder, and climbed the ramp.

About halfway up the ramp, she was glad Lars was carrying the cooler for her. Trudging up at such a steep incline wasn't easy. Nora was winded before she reached the top, where Lars had already set the cooler down outside the store. Without a word, he turned and trotted back down the ramp to finish loading the plane.

"Thanks," Nora hollered at him after she caught her breath. He looked up and waved casually to her from the floating platform below.

Leaving the cooler right where Lars had left it, Nora walked around the wooden deck encircling The General Store to get one more look at the search mission on the mountaintop. As she watched the helicopter make another pass toward the southwest before it disappeared from view, she wondered what the likelihood was of finding Mark and what condition he would be in if they did find him. *At least the weather is on his side*, Nora thought as she stepped through the open door into the store. For mid-June, she had been told the temperature was unusually warm – it was in the high-60s. And for the first time in almost two weeks, the rain had stopped completely.

Inside the store, the boards under Nora's feet creaked with each step she took. She liked that about this place, the creaking floorboards. Everything felt old and weathered, but not falling-apart old, more like standing-the-test-of-time old. There was a sense of history in the timeworn building. It was one of the first structures built in the town when it was settled more than a hundred years earlier, as evidenced by the old photographs of the town hanging on the wall, and it still felt like the pioneer spirit was fresh and young and alive there.

"You hear about Mark?" Barbara asked Nora as she approached a small counter at one end of the store that served as the post office. The mail had just come in off the float plane, and Barbara was still sorting through it. Hunched over the small stack of mail, the older woman held her long black hair in one hand at the nape of her neck to keep it out of the way and quickly tossed the mail into small piles with her free hand. Nora found it remarkable how efficiently Barbara was able to sort the mail one-handed. She stopped sorting for a second, thinking, then turned around and pulled an envelope out from under a pile stacked on the shelf behind her. "This came for you yesterday," she said, handing a catalog and an envelope to Nora and then going back to her sorting.

"Um, yeah. I saw the helicopter out there looking for him," Nora responded absentmindedly, looking at the envelope for a return address. Seeing none, she checked the postmark. Los

Angeles.

A warm breeze drifted in through the propped-open door, bringing with it the smell of salt water and fish, and Nora looked up from the envelope. Barbara had stopped sorting the mail and was staring at her. "I hope they find him," Nora said lamely before stuffing the envelope into the catalog and shoving them both in her tote bag.

"It's just like Jerry and his two buddies last winter," Barbara said, filling in the silence, and going back to sorting the mail. "Oh, you wouldn't know them, now would you? Jerry was my brother-in-law. Him and Cal Lawrence and Finny Larson used to go across the inlet to hunt all the time. Last winter, they were on their way back, crossing over a pond, and they all three fell through the ice. Finny's the only one that made it out of the water. They found his body almost a week later near the edge of the pond, but they never did find the others." Barbara stopped talking long enough to gauge Nora's reaction. Nora didn't know what to say, so she only nodded sympathetically, and Barbara continued. "But that's the way it is. Live here long enough and you're bound to know someone who went out into the wilderness and never came back. We all have stories like that. You will, too, someday."

"Or maybe I'll be the one to disappear," Nora said with a smile, trying to lighten the mood. Her joke fell flat and Barbara stared at her. As Nora turned to leave, she thought she heard Barbara say something under her breath, but she couldn't quite tell.

Nora made her way back through the store toward the grocery section, where she grabbed some ground coffee, a box of dried milk, and cereal. Two days earlier, Willie promised to start bringing her homemade bread and eggs once a week, so she didn't need to buy either of those. But she still had a craving for a good old-fashioned hamburger, so she picked up a pound of ground beef and some cheese.

Then she made her way to the checkout counter. On a shelf behind the counter sat a small collection of Nora's only slightly-used designer handbags. Not surprisingly, none of them had sold yet, but then again it had only been three days since she'd handed them over to Nate to sell. She'd briefly thought about selling some of her electronics, but she was hesitant to get rid of those things. The designer handbags, on the other hand, she'd never need again. They were merely a reminder of the superficial life she'd left behind.

After she paid for her groceries, Nora took them outside and put the perishables in the cooler. Then she went back inside, to the separate area that served as the liquor store. She bought a box of wine. As an afterthought, she grabbed a case of beer and a bottle of Scotch for Willie, something she could give him in return for the fresh bread and eggs. As she walked out the door, she ran into Lily.

"Having a party?" asked Lily, eying up the box of wine, the beer, and the liquor. "Because if you are, then I expect an invite."

"Does a party of one count?"

"I suppose it could," Lily grinned. "Speaking of parties, the town is having its Summer Solstice Festival in a week. It's a big deal. There's a huge potluck and a ton of games. Everyone stays up all night, listening to music, playing music, singing, dancing. You have to come."

"When is it?" asked Nora.

"The 21st, of course. For some people, it starts the night before. But most people start gathering at sunrise and party right on through until morning on the 22nd... if they can stay awake that long." Lily grinned mischievously. "Everyone will be there. Even Jake."

"What's that supposed to mean?"

"Nothing." Lily enjoyed playing matchmaker, and she had a

pretty good hunch it wouldn't take much to get Jake and Nora together. "Just that it would be the perfect opportunity for the two of you to get to know each other a little better. I think you two would make a cute couple."

Nora chuckled awkwardly and shook her head. "Uh, uh. I agreed to a date, but that's all."

"A date, huh? Jake didn't tell me that." Lily looked pleased. "Give me the scoop. When are you two going out?"

Nora didn't know the answer to that question. He'd asked her out, but they hadn't actually made any plans. And Nora hadn't seen or heard from him since then. Of course, it had only been three days, and Jake did say he was going to be in Juneau for a few days.

"What about you?" Nora asked, evading Lily's question. "I've never seen you with a guy. There seem to be a lot more men around here than women, as far as I can tell."

Lily laughed loudly. "Have you ever heard the old expression? The odds are good, but the goods are odd." Nora laughed then, too. "So you know what I'm talking about," Lily continued. "You've seen the men around here. Don't get me wrong, I like 'em a little wild and wooly, but they are definitely a little too odd… except for my brother. Maybe it's because he got out for a few years, but he's a lot more level-headed than most of the guys in Heron."

"What do you mean he got out?"

"Oh, he spent three years in Portland. Did fairly well for himself down there, but I guess he missed the island. He came back home about a year ago. At first, I was a little disappointed he came back alone. I was hoping he'd bring back a sister for me. But now that you're here…"

"Quit it." Nora laughed. "It's just one date. We're not getting married."

"We'll see about that. Look, I gotta go," said Lily, giving her a quick hug. "Don't forget about the solstice festival. I expect to see you there."

"I think I can squeeze it into my schedule."

By the time Nora finished saying goodbye to Lily, Lars had already grabbed her now-full cooler and was loading it back onto her boat. The tide had risen slightly and the ramp wasn't quite so steep going down as it had been when she arrived earlier, but she still thought it was nice of him to help her out.

"Here, let me help you with that," he said as Nora approached the boat with the case of beer and box of wine. He took them and placed them in the stern of the boat. "I can keep an eye on this stuff if you still have more stuff to do in town."

"Thanks, Lars. But I'm finished here." Nora smiled. "Heading home now."

He nodded and watched her climb into the skiff. When she turned to start the motor, Lars blurted out, "So, the cabin is 'home' now? You're going to stay?"

Nora turned and looked up at him, smiling. She nodded her head. "I think so," she said.

Lars smiled back encouragingly. "Well, be careful out there."

His last remark reminded Nora of the missing man up on the mountaintop. "I'll try," she said as she stole one more glance up at the mountain. *It will take a miracle for them to find him*, she thought to herself as she started the outboard motor and pulled away from the dock.

The mountain towered over the inlet, and for several miles she had a hard time pulling her gaze away from the spec of a helicopter, hovering around the peak. Nora was thankful when the mountain disappeared from view, as she rounded Tailor's Point on her way deeper into the inlet, and her mind was free to wander away from the search mission.

She loved this inlet. She realized at that moment she actually loved it there. As new as it still was to her, it already felt like home. The deep, cold waters held so many mysteries, probably as many mysteries as the never-ending forest that surrounded it. But what she liked best about the inlet was the point where the water collided with the land, the shoreline where huge pieces of shale met lush, towering pines. The cool air felt cleaner and smelled sweeter than anywhere she'd ever been.

When the cabin came into view, Nora turned the skiff toward an opening in the rocky shore, a long section of tidal flats mostly underwater at that point, and coasted toward the shore until the bottom of the skiff scraped the ground, digging into the pebbled waterbed. Jumping out of the skiff, she grabbed the front and pulled it onto the shore. She unloaded her goods and then pulled the skiff further up onto dry land, safely away from the still-rising tide.

Inside the tiny cabin, Nora unloaded her supplies onto the shelves. She left the meat, eggs, and butter in the cooler next to the table and the box of wine on the table. She put the bottle of Scotch on the bottom shelf along with her growing collection of beverages she was stockpiling for guests, assuming anyone ever stopped by. The case of beer, she took outside. Walking a short distance to the creek, she stooped down and pulled a fish net out of the water, placed the cans of beer in the net, then lowered the net back into the chilly creek. *At least the fish net is getting some use*, she thought.

Back inside the cabin, Nora looked at the clock. Only 2 o'clock in the afternoon and such a beautiful day. The perfect day to get outside and try to chop some wood. Or, even better, the perfect day to ignore the dwindling woodpile and soak up some sun.

Nora picked up the catalog she'd received in the mail, along with the box of wine and a plastic cup off the shelf. Then she went outside. She sat down on the ground, leaning against one of the large pine trees next to the cabin, and poured a cup of the sweet concord wine. It tasted good. She took a long drink, closed her eyes, and listened to the sounds of the water and the forest around her, basking in the warmth of the sun on her skin.

She'd been sitting there for a long time, enjoying the outdoors, when an unfamiliar sound in the water caught her attention. Sitting up straight, Nora turned her attention toward the water. To her delight, she watched as a whale surfaced briefly a few yards from the shore. *Finally!* It was the one thing she'd been hoping to see for weeks.

She set the cup of wine down on the ground and stood up to get a better view. To her surprise, there was not one whale but several of them. Their slick bodies moved under the water, skimming the surface ever so lightly. At first, Nora thought they were playing. Then she realized they were actually working together to find food.

The water swirled, as the whales dove under and swam in circles, maneuvering a school of fish into position. The surface of the water rippled with air bubbles and, above the water, birds swarmed around the disturbance. Suddenly two whales rose up out of the water, their mouths agape, catching hundreds of fish. Then, as quickly as they'd leapt out of the water, the whales leaned to the side and splashed back down, disappearing under the surface.

It was the single most amazing thing Nora had ever seen in her life. Scanning the water, she hoped to catch another glimpse of it. A short distance away, the scene repeated itself, culminating once again in a glorious display as the whales lunged out of the water and crashed back down. Nora saw them surface once more, off in the distance, and then they were gone.

Disappointed when the show ended, she sat back down against the tree and picked up the catalog. She flipped through the pages, looking at outdoor clothing and hand tools, when something fell out into her lap.

Glancing down, Nora saw the envelope. She set the empty cup down next to her, picked up the envelope and opened it. It was from the publication in Los Angeles, confirmation that her ad had been placed. She had almost forgotten about the ad. Now it seemed silly she'd ever wasted the time placing it. Her mind made up, Nora made a mental note to call the publication the next time she went into town. She needed to cancel the ad.

At some point in the past few days, without even realizing it, Nora had made her decision. She was going to stay in Heron. It may have been when she gave her things to Nate to sell on consignment or maybe it was on the long ride from town to the cabin, but she'd definitely made her choice. Especially after the show she had just seen, Nora knew for certain she couldn't sell the property.

"This is home," she said quietly to herself. "I'm not going anywhere."

* * *

At first, Nora couldn't wait to tell someone about her decision. She was going to stay. It was exciting, exhilarating. But the more she thought about it, the more she realized she'd already been telling people she was staying. Even though she hadn't made up her mind at the time, she'd let Lily believe she was going to stay in Heron. Jake, too.

A day passed. Then another and another. She tried calling Jake on the radio, eager to talk to him, to tell him about the whales and how she was finally able to understand why he loved this place so much. But there was no answer on the other end. Just radio silence.

It didn't surprise her. After all, Jake had said he was going to Juneau for a while and he never did say when he'd be back. But she was still a little disappointed.

Picking up a can of tuna, Nora debated whether she wanted to subject herself to a meal from a can. The hamburger she'd bought in town had already been used up. The eggs and bread Willie had brought over a few days earlier were gone. Oh, how she wished for electricity and a refrigerator so she could buy more fresh food and not worry about it spoiling.

She tossed the canned tuna back on the shelf, grabbed a light jacket and one of Pete's old fishing poles, and went outside instead. She didn't know the first thing about fishing, but she did have a can of worms she'd collected a week earlier after a heavy rain. She'd left the can sitting outside the cabin, right next to the door. Stooping down, Nora picked it up and headed south toward the creek. Now seemed like a good time to learn how to fish.

Nora stepped up onto a large, flat rock and surveyed the stream. She was looking for a good place to drop her line. The creek bed was filled with smooth, round rocks, many of them covered with a green, slimy coating. The water was fast-flowing, but not very deep. At its shallowest point, the creek was about 6 inches deep, but there were areas of the creek where the depth plunged to three or four feet.

Sitting down on the rock, Nora decided any spot in the creek was a good spot to start. She didn't have the slightest clue whether to cast her line into the deeper waters or the shallow waters, but she figured she would learn eventually. Even if it meant she'd have to learn by trial and error.

Pete's collection of old books had included one about fishing. Out of boredom, Nora had read through it several times and thought she had figured out the process of how to tie a hook to the end of the line. With a little concentration, she managed to fumble her way through it. Satisfied with her knot, Nora gave it a slight tug to make sure the hook was secure. The knot came loose instantly. She untied the knot and tried it again, making sure she did it exactly as she'd seen it in the book. When she tested it again, the knot held, surprisingly. Tying a hook to a fishing line was one more thing to add to the long list of things she needed to practice. But she'd have plenty of time for that.

Nora reached over and grabbed the can of worms sitting next to her on the rock. She opened up the lid and sifted through the dry dirt. She lifted out a dead worm, dry and crusty, and wrinkled her nose in disgust at it. She didn't know much about fishing, but she did know the worm was supposed to be alive and wiggling when she put it on the hook. Nora tossed the dead worm into the water and pulled out another worm. Dead. Tossing the fishing rod aside, she took the can of worms in both hands and frantically searched through the dirt looking for any worms that might have survived the slow death she had unknowingly subjected them to by leaving the can out in the sun. At the bottom, she found one that was not dead yet. But it didn't look very alive, either. She picked it up and looked at it closely. It would have to do. She didn't have any other bait to use. Taking the hook in one hand, Nora slowly forced the tip of the hook through the worm, impaling it from end to end. If the worm had been alive, it was definitely dead now.

Instead of attempting to cast the line out into the stream, Nora let a little line out of the reel and dropped the hook into the water directly below her. She set the rod on the rock next to her and then laid down on her belly alongside the rod. Her head hung over the edge of the rock so she could look down at the worm on the end of her line. The water was so clear, Nora could see every detail of the rocks just a couple feet under water. The worm lay there on the creek bed, lifeless but swaying gently with the motion of the water.

The odds Nora would actually catch a fish were slim, she knew. Looking around, she didn't see any fish in the stream. But fishing took time. *Eventually, something will swim up this creek*, she thought.

Rolling over onto her back, Nora stared up at the blue sky that barely peeked through the heavy canopy of trees. Not a bad life, she told herself. She had wasted too much time with Conner, trying to become someone she wasn't. Now, she was free to rediscover herself, and that felt good. Sure, it was taking time for her to get into the swing of things, but at least she was trying. Out there, by the creek, she found it a little easier to forget about her past and really focus on the present. As for the future, well, that would take care of itself.

Nora closed her eyes, enjoying the sound of the water running over the rocks. When she really listened, she could hear the sound of rushing water off in the distance. Somewhere nearby there was a waterfall. She hadn't gone looking for it yet, but she knew it was there. According to the topographical map hanging on the wall of her cabin, the creek flowed down from a small mountain directly east of her property and drained into the inlet south of her cabin. The mountain was unnamed on the map, and its elevation was only around 2,000 feet. The peak had still been covered in snow when she'd arrived at the property in the last week of May and her first view of her new home had been breathtaking, even if she was extremely disappointed the cabin wasn't exactly what she'd expected. The beauty of the mountain and the inlet definitely overshadowed the derelict old cabin she'd inherited. The cabin might be falling apart, but her surroundings made it all worthwhile. In fact, everything she'd seen in Southeast Alaska had been stunning. It was so astoundingly different from anything she'd known back home. Sure, California was a beautiful state, but it was nothing compared to the splendor and remoteness of the inlet.

Nora rolled over and looked into the water. The water-logged worm still lay on the bottom of the creek, untouched. She reeled in the line and decided to cast the line out a little toward the middle of the stream. Awkwardly, she swung the rod and released the line. The end of the line landed about four feet away from her. Not exactly what she'd been trying to do, but good enough for now. She sat up and kept her eye on the line this time, enjoying the sunny day. As much as it rained there, Nora knew these days were something to be treasured and she wanted to make sure she didn't take them for granted.

She closed her eyes again. Aside from the sounds of the stream, everything was silent. No birds chirping. Nothing. That was odd. *It's almost too quiet out here sometimes*, Nora thought as she watched her line float downstream with the current. She'd come from a life that revolved around social networks. She had constantly been surrounded by other people in Los Angeles, and now there wasn't another person for at least a mile. The solitude was nice, but it was taking time to get used to it.

Standing up, Nora reeled in her line. She decided to walk up stream a bit, thinking maybe she'd have better luck there. She wasn't giving up hope of catching something. In spite of her limited cooking skills, she hoped she'd be able to batter-fry some fish for dinner.

She walked carefully along the bank of the stream, unconcerned about getting lost. No matter how far she ventured, she would be able to follow the stream back to her cabin.

The forest was thick with moss and fallen trees and other obstacles, so she stayed close to the edge of the water, where it was only slightly easier to walk. When the bank of the stream became impassable, Nora stepped out into the water and made her way further upstream, walking carefully over slippery rocks and struggling to maintain her balance as she moved against the current. She'd left the boundaries of her five-acre property, and she had no idea whose land she was on, but nobody was going to care, she figured. There was nobody out there but her.

Standing in the middle of the stream, Nora cast her line into the water. More determined this time, and definitely more vigilant, Nora kept her eyes on the water, looking for a fish, any fish. About an hour went by before she spotted one. Not large, it swam along a crevice in a large boulder near the middle of the stream. Her line was more than a few feet away, so she reeled the line in a little, trying to maneuver her bait a little closer to the fish, battling its way against the current and barely moving in spite of its efforts to swim upstream. *It would have to be a seriously desperate fish*, Nora thought, *for it to take the miserable bait on my hook*. Surprisingly, the fish took the bait at the end of her line. In her excitement, Nora mistakenly jerked the rod just enough to pull the bait away from the fish. But the fish was hungry and it found the bait again.

With a bit of dumb luck, Nora hooked the fish and began reeling it in. It didn't put up much of a struggle. It was already tired out from battling the current on its way upstream, she guessed, as she pulled the fish out of the water and laid it down on a nearby rock.

Its tail flapped and its eyes bulged as the small fish gasped for oxygen. Not sure what to do, Nora held it down with one hand and tried to dislodge the hook. She'd never done this before. Grasping the hook, she gave it a tug and tore it out of the fish's mouth. *Oh, I didn't expect it to be like this. The poor fish.* She held the fish up, holding tight so it wouldn't wiggle out of her hands, unsure what to do next. She hadn't brought anything to carry it in, so she'd have to carry it in her hands and hope it didn't slip away.

With a tight grip on the fish, she tucked the fishing rod under one arm and turned back to head downstream. As she turned, though, something caught her eye. She spotted specks of bright red and yellow a little further upstream, partially hidden from view behind a tree that had grown out over the edge of the bank of the stream. Clutching the fish and her rod, Nora waded through the water toward it.

"Is anybody there?" she called, realizing it was a person sitting on the bank of the stream, maybe the person who owned this land she'd been fishing on. "If I wandered onto your land, I'm sorry. I live just down the way and…"

Nora stopped when the man came into view. He looked like he'd been there a while. His clothes were dirty and torn. He sat upright with his knees curled up to his chest and his arms wrapped around his legs. His head was tucked down toward his knees, and it looked like he had fallen asleep there. Except, he wasn't asleep. Nora took a step closer, just to be sure. Yeah, the man was definitely dead.

Stepping back, a little caught off guard at the realization she'd just found a dead body, Nora slipped and fell backward into the cold water. In an attempt to catch herself, she let go of the fish and the rod. Her reflexes were too slow. She landed solidly on her back on a large rock lying a few inches under the surface of the water. Nora lay there for a moment, stunned, as the pain shot up her spine. The force of the water gently pushed her sideways.

A little dazed, she turned her head and saw the fish floating near the surface of the water downstream from her. The fish was motionless for a few seconds, and then the water seemed to revive it and it took off downstream, getting as far away from Nora as it could. *Probably better that way*, she thought. She would have likely hacked the thing to pieces trying to clean it. No fish deserved that.

Nora slowly pushed herself up to a sitting position, looked around for her fishing pole, and carefully stood up. The pole had floated downstream a few dozen feet and was caught between a couple large rocks jutting up over the surface of the water. She had landed hard on that rock and it hurt to stand, but the pain was the least of her worries right now. Nora retrieved the pole and then glanced back over at the man. She had a dead body to deal with.

CHAPTER

10

The initial shock of finding a dead body wore off quickly for Nora. She told herself there was nothing to be afraid of. This wasn't the first dead person she'd seen.

"Get a grip, Nora," she said out loud as she stepped toward the man's body. She'd been to a couple funerals, seen people in caskets, caked with makeup in a sad attempt to make them look like they were sleeping. "This is nothing. I've been around dead people before," she told herself, still hesitant to get close to the dead man.

Gathering her courage, she leaned over and quickly rummaged through the man's pockets, looking for a wallet or any type of identification. She went through the pockets on the heavy wool coat first. She found only a few empty candy bar wrappers. Under that, the man wore a fleece jacket. Those pockets were completely empty. Nora unzipped the fleece to check the inside pockets, which were also empty. Not wanting to disturb the body too much, she decided against rolling him over to check for a wallet in his back pockets. She'd leave that to the professionals. If he did have a wallet, maybe they would find it, she decided as she zipped the man's fleece jacket back up and re-buttoned his wool coat.

Standing up, she briefly thought about what to do next. The body was too big for her to move. She wasn't even going to attempt to haul it to her skiff and take it into town. No, she'd have to go into town and report it. That's all she could do.

Nora took one last look at the man, turned and left. So sad to see someone cut off in his prime like that, she thought as she walked downstream through the water. She wondered how he had died. Probably hypothermia. The temperature had dropped pretty low the last few nights. Nora was no expert, but to her it looked like he had been trying to keep warm, all huddled up like that. Nora only had three neighbors she knew of and she'd only met one. If the man had lived out there, he would have been her second closest neighbor, and she hadn't even known him. Or maybe he didn't live out there at all. He could have gone for a long hike and gotten lost. That would be pretty easy to do out there. If he had gotten lost, he may have been following the stream, hoping it would lead him to the inlet. Or maybe he had fallen and sprained an ankle. If something had crippled him, then he would have been helpless, unable to go any further. Perhaps he had spent days by the creek, waiting for someone to find him, with no way to call for help. Who knew how long he'd been there before he succumbed to the cold temperatures? So many questions ran through Nora's head as she made her way out of the creek and onto solid ground. The walking got easier from there, but she was still a long way from the cabin.

Nora hadn't realized how far she'd wandered upstream. Maybe the man had done the same thing, gone farther than he had planned and didn't have time to get back before nightfall set in. He could have been alone in the woods all night long, hoping someone would find him or he'd make it through until morning. If the temperatures had dropped down far enough, one night in the forest could easily claim a man's life. Then Nora thought about all the wild animals lurking in the forest. It was a wonder his body hadn't been picked apart by wolves or bears or who knows what. The possibilities were endless.

A large growth of some kind of thorny bush made the bank of the creek impassable up ahead, Nora saw, so she stepped back into the water, preparing to go around it. The thought of wild animals eating away at the man's body put Nora a little on edge. She hadn't been paying much attention to her surroundings, she realized. Out there, that could be a fatal mistake if she wandered upon a wild animal. Just as the thought popped into her head, Nora abruptly stopped. Maybe she was letting her imagination get the better of her, but she thought she noticed something moving in quickly from her left.

Out of the corner of her eye, it was a big brown blur, and before she even turned her head to look, she already had a good idea of what it was. Definitely not her imagination, she realized, as time seemed to slow to a crawl.

The enormous brown bear was interested in a fish that had just jumped out of the water directly between them. Nora watched as the bear moved toward the middle of the stream, a mere 20 yards away from where she stood. She closed her eyes for a moment, hoping the bear wasn't real and praying that if it was, it would be content to take the fish and leave her alone. She opened her eyes again. Terrified, she took a step backwards and felt her foot slip on the rocks below the surface of the water. Leaning to the right to catch herself, she grabbed hold of a large boulder and tried to steady herself as she took another step away from the bear. But Nora's sudden movement was enough to catch bear's attention. The bear, which had been focused solely on the fish, turned its head and looked squarely at Nora. It had spotted her.

Seconds passed while Nora's mind raced with thoughts of what to do in case of a bear attack. She didn't know if she should play dead or stand her ground and let it know she wasn't going to back down. The only thing Nora knew for sure was she wanted to get out of there. She took another step back, feeling the soft mud at the edge of the stream, and then another step and she was entirely back on solid ground.

When the bear opened its alarmingly large set of jaws and let out a deep snarl, Nora's heart nearly stopped beating. Her muscles were frozen in place by the intense fear that crept through every ounce of her being. She couldn't do anything but watch as the bear swung its head from side to side, an eerie growling noise coming from deep within.

Quickly glancing around at her surroundings, Nora tried to figure out how far she was from her cabin. She spotted a group of large boulders she recognized and she realized the cabin was still quite far away. Running was not an option. Even if the cabin were within sight, she had no doubt in her mind the bear would catch her before she made it halfway there.

Nora stood, frozen in fear, as the bear took a step in her direction, letting out another long snarl of warning. Standing on all fours, the bear stood at least four foot tall by Nora's best guess, an enormous mass of muscle and teeth and claws.

The standoff continued for what seemed like an eternity, though it was really only a matter of seconds. Nora didn't take her eyes off the bear as she tried to figure a way out of the situation. But when the bear slanted its ears back and began making a woofing noise, she realized there was no way out.

Unbelievably, she stood her ground as the bear started to charge, hoping the bear would see she wasn't going to back down. But her courage wavered at the sight of the enormous animal rapidly closing the distance between them. Instinctively, she took a step back. Her ankle struck something and she tripped, landing hard on her tailbone.

This is it. I'm going to die. Right here. Right now.

Then, as quickly as it had started charging, the bear abruptly stopped. Just a few feet away from where Nora lay on the ground, the bear opened its jaws again and let out another growl. It was so close, she could feel the warmth of its breath on her skin.

She wasn't going to get out of this alive. The icy clear waters of the stream would soon turn to bright red as the blood drained from her mauled body, she imagined. *Death by bear mauling. The absolute worst way to die.*

She closed her eyes and waited for the inevitable. Like the man who had died upstream, she would lie there for days, maybe months, before anyone found her body. Assuming they ever found her. Just a few days earlier, hadn't Barbara told her people disappeared in the wilderness and were never found? *This is why they're never found*, Nora thought. *Because they get eaten.*

The seconds seemed like minutes.

The bear looked at Nora and then back toward the fish and then back toward Nora. It snarled again, taking one step toward her and stopping. *If you're going to kill me, just get it over with. Don't drag this out any longer.*

As the bear stared her down, trying to decide whether Nora was a threat, Nora felt the anger begin to set in. She wasn't angry with the bear, though. She was angry with herself. *How could I have been so naïve? I'm not an idiot. I know not to wander into the woods without anything to protect myself. So, what the hell am I doing here, on my ass, waiting to become dinner for a bear?* She was furious now. It didn't matter how close she was to the perceived safety of the cabin. She should have been on guard the entire time. Instead, she had let herself get lost in thought and never even noticed the bear until it was too late.

The massive beast was still several feet away from Nora, and even though it hadn't attacked her yet, it wasn't backing down. But if she was going to die, Nora decided she wasn't going to die sitting on her ass on the ground.

"You want me, then come and get me," she hollered at the bear as she struggled to stand up.

The bear seemed startled, but didn't move.

Nora's voice cracked, both in fear and in anger. She stretched her arms out in resignation, frustration, defeat.

"No more playing around. Just do it! Tear me to pieces! And then when you're done eating me and that fish over there, you can go raid the cabin. It's full of food. I'm not going to need it anymore, anyway," she said as her eyes welled up with tears.

Yeah, now's a great time to start crying, she thought as she sobbed uncontrollably.

"It's my own fault, anyway," she choked out between sobs. "I shouldn't even be out here. I might as well have been asking to get eaten by bears."

Then the tears stopped, almost as quickly as they'd started, on the roller coaster of emotions sweeping through her. The self-pity was replaced by a resurgence of anger and rage. Nora began chastising herself, yelling at herself for being irresponsible. Her ranting continued and only got louder as she berated herself for being so stupid.

"I don't even know what the hell I'm doing in Alaska," she started rambling. Her frustration was so great, she didn't even notice the bear's reaction.

"Believe me, if I could have gone somewhere else, anywhere else, I would have. But, here I am, in the middle of bear country, and I'm surprised when a bear decides to make me his dinner? I completely deserve this. Yeah, I deserve this."

By that time, the bear had completely lost interest in her. It looked back at the fish and then turned, snatched it up, and started walking across the stream and away from her.

Nora watched, shocked, as the bear lumbered off at a slow gait with the fish in its mouth. She realized then, she was holding her breath and she gulped for air. She still wasn't safe, but if she was going to get herself out of this situation, now was the time to move. Quicker now, Nora backed away from the bear, moving in the direction of the cabin as fast as she could. She never took her eyes off the bear as she backed away. Even when the massive animal disappeared into the brush on the other side of the stream, Nora kept her eyes fixed on that spot, making sure the bear didn't change its mind and decide to come after her, after all.

When she reached the cabin, she stumbled inside and closed the door behind her, latching it shut. She still wasn't convinced she was out of harm's way. She kept backing up, eyes fixed on the door, until her back was up against the wall of the tiny cabin. Her heart was racing. *Take deep breaths*, she told herself. The fast-paced beats of her heart thrummed in her head. She forced herself to take another deep breath in and out, trying to calm herself. She closed her eyes. *Deep breath in, deep breath out.* Nora thought it was working. She opened her eyes and took another deep breath. Her heart rate was still fast, but it was slowing getting back to normal.

Looking down, she noticed her hands were shaking and the enormity of the situation hit her again. Nora felt the overwhelming need to flee, and she couldn't get out of the cabin quickly enough. Swinging open the door, she ran for the skiff about a dozen yards away on the shore. She pushed it out into the water, jumped in, and started up the outboard motor, eager to get as far away from the cabin as possible.

Nora opened up the throttle, barely noticing the blue skies were turning to gray as a cloud cover moved in from the south. The skiff bounced along on the waves as Nora sped toward town. The wind was picking up and the water was becoming choppy, making the trip treacherous in such a small boat. On any other day, Nora would have come to her senses and turned back toward the cabin, not willing to take the risk of capsizing her skiff in the icy waters of the inlet. But there was no chance she was going to turn back this time. A shiver ran though her, and Nora opened up the throttle all the way, eager to get out of the cold wind, away from the wild, and back to some sort of civilization. As the boat crashed into the waves, the cold water sprayed Nora, stinging her face and making her even more determined to reach the small community. When she saw the dock for the Alaska Marine Highway jutting out into the inlet, Nora relaxed a little. The end was in sight. She was safe from the wilds, back among people. What a relief it was.

A few minutes later, Nora pulled up to store's dock, grabbed the rope tied to the bow of the skiff, and tied the other end to a post on the floating dock. The dock was unusually empty, the deck surrounding the store unusually quiet, but Nora didn't even notice as she strode into store, grateful to be out of the bone-chilling wind. Nate was not behind the counter and the store appeared to be empty.

"Nate, are you here?" she called out, hoping to find somebody, anybody, to help her out. There was no answer. This was not what Nora needed right now. She needed to tell somebody about the body so they could call whoever to come and take care of it and then she really wanted to go get a drink. She had never been much of a drinker, other than the occasional glass of wine, but she really needed something to calm her nerves.

Nora paced back and forth in front of the check-out counter, waiting to see if anybody was going to show up and trying to figure out what to do if they didn't.

Her hands were still shaking from the shock. She didn't know if it was the shock of finding a dead body or the shock of having just been charged by a bear. It didn't matter which. Both had been equally disturbing, she realized. The former had been enough to ruin anyone's day. Finding a dead body was not the most pleasant experience. The latter, well, that had just plain scared the crap out of her.

"Hey, there," someone said from behind. Nora jumped at the sound of his voice and turned around to see it was just Nate. "Sorry if I startled you. Didn't mean to sneak up."

Nora shook her head and waved off his remark. She sighed. "It wasn't you, believe me," she said.

He looked at her, a little concerned, but he prided himself on not being the type to meddle into other people's business. Nora noticed he had one big bushy brown eyebrow cocked up suspiciously. No, it wasn't raised in suspicion, she realized. It was naturally that way. She hadn't noticed it before, but all of the features on his face were slightly misplaced. His right eye seemed a fraction higher than his left, and even his smile was a little crooked.

Nate stood there, patiently waiting for Nora to tell him what she needed. He didn't like to pry and he also didn't like to invite people to unload their troubles onto him. So he didn't even bother to ask what was troubling her. Nate was all business and that's the way he liked to keep it.

"Well, what can I do for you," he asked expectantly.

"Got a coffin?" Nora responded flippantly.

He raised an eyebrow, this time on purpose, but didn't say anything. Nora almost chuckled as she saw his eyebrows were actually level with each other. She welcomed the distraction, even if it only took her mind off the day's events for a moment. She actually smiled a little at the thought of Nate's crooked face. Nate thought she was smiling about her last comment, she realized. But she hadn't been joking about the coffin.

"Found a body today not far from my place. I don't suppose you know who I would report it to?"

He nodded and picked up the telephone hanging on the wall behind the counter. He dialed some numbers and then handed the phone to her. "State Troopers," he said.

Nora put the phone up to her ear and listened to it ring once, twice. A woman answered on the third ring. For a man who didn't like to directly pry into other people's business, Nate sure didn't mind listening in. As Nora began telling the woman on the other end of the line about the body, she watched Nate walk into an office behind the counter and pick up a second phone. Nate listened long enough to hear all of the details of how Nora stumbled upon the man and he stayed on the line while the woman asked Nora a series of questions about the body, its exact location, and anything else she might have noticed. As the woman's questions came to a close, Nora noticed the faint click of Nate hanging his phone back up. Then he disappeared through the side door of his office.

Nora stayed on the line for a few more minutes while the woman instructed her to stay in town and wait for the Alaska State Troopers to arrive. A couple of investigators would be flying into town and she needed to lead them to the body.

By the time Nora hung up the phone, Nate had returned. He entered through the same door he'd exited through earlier and immediately took up his post behind the counter. Two other men followed him in through the door and lingered around the counter. Nora recognized the dock workers, but didn't know their names. They both looked to be older men, rugged and worn. The fat one sat down on the wooden folding chair next to the counter and propped his feet up on an empty milk crate. The taller one leaned against the doorway to the office. He looked like he was about 50, Nora thought as she watched him spit into an old coffee can sitting beside the door, then reposition the chewing tobacco in his lower lip. He stood there looking Nora up and down. She felt uncomfortable standing there, the three of them staring at her, and she timidly handed the phone back to Nate. He looked at her expectantly, but didn't ask any questions. Eventually, the tall man spoke.

"You're the one living in the back bay." It wasn't a question. Just a statement.

"Uh, yeah," Nora responded. "I guess." She had never heard it referred to as the 'back bay' before, but she supposed that was the best term for it.

"So, who'd you find?" It was the tall man again.

Nora shrugged, tired of people asking questions she really didn't know the answer to. "I really don't know," she said exasperated. She shook her head. "There was no I.D. and I didn't recognize him."

"Well, what did he look like?" The tall man wanted answers.

"Dead. He looked dead. That's all I know, alright?" Nora hadn't meant to be so short with him, but she wasn't having a very good day and she was really tired of questions at that point.

The man didn't seem the slightest bit fazed by her outburst, though. He spat into the coffee can again and looked at her. That's when the fat one spoke up.

"Sorry, lady," he said. "Harry's just trying to figure out if it's Mark. You know he disappeared, right?" He didn't wait for Nora to answer. "We looked for him for three days, but they went and called the search off last night. We're just wondering if your dead guy is him."

"Um," Nora didn't know what to say. "I... I really don't know. I didn't know Mark. Never met him." It was weird she hadn't thought of Mark when she found the body, Nora realized. She'd known Mark was missing, but she never connected the dots or even considered that the man sitting by the stream might be the guy who disappeared on the mountain. She guessed it was possible. Even though the mountain was a good 10 miles away from her cabin and he would have had to travel through untamed forest with dense, thick undergrowth. Getting lost is one thing, but to travel so far by foot requires purpose and determination. The more she thought about it, the more questionable it seemed.

"That's pretty far for someone to wander by accident," she thought. Then she noticed their faces. All three of them looked at her curiously and Nora realized she had spoken her last thought out loud. The tall man, who Nora now knew was named Harry, and the fat man exchanged concerned glances. Nora immediately regretted having said anything. "Or maybe it's not…" she added lamely.

"No," Harry said. "You might be on to something there."

"Yeah, we were wondering why we hadn't seen any trace of Mark on the mountain trail. It's like he wasn't even there. A person like him doesn't just vanish. But if he intentionally took off, well, that would be another story. He always was more than capable out there…"

"You can't blame him for sneaking off," said Harry. "If I had to live with that wife of his, I'd have taken to the woods a long time ago."

The fat one chuckled at that.

"That's enough, guys," Nate cut in. "Quit talking like that about Mark. He was a good guy. He wouldn't have taken off and left Martha, no matter how miserable a woman she might be to live with. You don't have any facts to go along with all your speculation, and until you do, you should keep your mouths shut."

Nate's words resonated with finality and neither man spoke

after that. The two men turned and went into Nate's office then, leaving Nora awkwardly standing by the counter. She smiled uncomfortably at Nate. It was clear Nate would not have any more talk about the dead guy, and Nora was fine with that. But she did have one other matter that needed to be dealt with.

"Is there anything else you need?" Nate asked abruptly. He didn't like the seed Nora had planted in everyone's minds and he was ready for her to leave.

"Actually, there was one other thing I came here for," she said. "What do you have to keep bears away?"

"Bear spray. Over by the hunting supplies," he said brusquely, nodding in that direction. "Won't necessarily keep 'em away, but if you run into one, that spray'll come in handy, for sure."

"How much?"

"Seventy dollars per canister."

Nora winced at the cost. "They're only fifty in Juneau." She'd seen them for sale after she got off the first ferry and waited for the ferry heading to Heron to arrive, but she hadn't bothered to buy one. Then, she had still been under the illusion the house she had inherited was in town. She didn't think she'd ever need anything like bear spray.

"Then buy some in Juneau next time you're there," Nate said, starting to get irritated with Nora. The one thing he hated the most was people complaining about prices. If they didn't like his prices, then too bad. His was the only store in Heron.

Nora resigned herself to paying the exorbitant price. That's life in the bush, she tried to tell herself, wishing she had bought a canister or two in Juneau when she'd had the chance. "No, I need it now. I'll take one canister," she told Nate. She reached into her pocket for some cash and remembered the mad dash she'd taken out of the cabin. Nora had been so spooked she hadn't grabbed her wallet or anything. "That figures," she cried, throwing her hands up in the air. "I left all my fricking money at the cabin." Nora seriously wondered if her day could possibly get any worse.

Nate looked at her uneasily, but didn't say anything. Completely frustrated, Nora turned around and slid down the front wall of the counter, wrapping her arms around her legs and resting her head on her knees. She sat there, curled up into a ball, wanting to cry or scream... or do both.

"Um, I'll open a tab for you and you can pay for it next time," Nate said nervously. He leaned over the counter and looked down at Nora, whose face was buried in her knees. "Go ahead and grab a canister," he said. "I've already written it down."

She lifted her head and looked up at him, grateful. "Thanks, Nate." But she didn't make any move to get up and leave. Nora buried her face in her arms, wishing the day would end already.

Nate anxiously walked into his office, where the other two men stood watching curiously. He sincerely hoped Nora would come to her senses soon and leave. The last thing he wanted to deal with was some half-crazed woman from the Lower 48 who cracked up in his store.

He shooed the two men out the door, back to work, but Nate remained in his office, looking through the glass window and waiting for Nora to get up and leave. He really hoped he wouldn't have to coax her out the door.

When she still hadn't budged ten minutes later, Nate cautiously walked out of his office and approached her. He took his wallet out of his pocket, opened it, and pulled out a $20 bill. On second thought, he stuffed the $20 back into his wallet and found a $10 bill. Nate crouched down to her level and quietly handed it to her.

"Why don't you go on over to the pub and have a drink? You look like you could use one."

Nora looked up at him.

"I can't take your money."

"Oh, I'm not giving this to you," he said matter-of-factly. "I'm adding it to your tab." Then he stood up and walked back into his office, closing the door behind him. Nora got the picture. He was telling her, in no uncertain terms, it was time to leave. She pulled herself up from the floor, walked over to the hunting supplies, grabbed a can of bear spray, and left the store.

CHAPTER

11

Tourists. A group of them had just arrived on two float planes and already they were doing a good job of being a general nuisance, crowding around The General Store, making it impossible for anyone to get in or out. One couple took turns snapping photos of themselves. Another was pointing excitedly at a pair of bald eagles flying somewhere overhead. They seemed oblivious to the fact that it was raining, excited to be experiencing the "real Alaska" they'd read about in the tour brochure.

At the edge of the group, a tour guide was trying in vain to get everybody's attention, asking them to step aside so they didn't block the boardwalk. It wasn't working.

Squeezing past them, Nora tried to avoid the curious looks of the tourists. They were looking at her like she was a local. *Ha! If they only knew.* Nora was just as green as they were. Less than a month, she'd been in Alaska. *If not for these brown rubber boots I'm wearing, I would blend right in with the rest of the crowd*, Nora thought as she pushed her way through.

When she was free, she hurried down the boardwalk the short distance to the pub. Most of the bar stools were already occupied, but Nora spotted a seat at the opposite end of the bar, and walked over to sit down. She'd put on a brave face in front of Nate, at least she thought she had, but Nora was still shaken from the bear incident. What she really needed was a drink to calm her nerves.

When Lily walked over, Nora didn't bother with pleasantries.

"Give me an amber and a shot of Jack."

Lily nodded and turned around to grab the bottle of whiskey off the shelf along the back wall. She understood exactly why Nora was there and why she so desperately needed a drink. Word traveled fast in Heron, and word was that Nora had found a body. Judging by Nora's ruffled appearance, the rumors were true.

Lily poured the whiskey first and set the shot glass in front of Nora, then walked over to the tap and poured a beer. The shot glass was empty by the time Lily came back with the dark Alaskan brew.

"Rough day?"

"You could say that," Nora answered before taking a long drink from the beer mug. Her whole body was shaking and she tried to calm her nerves.

"Are you okay?" asked Lily. "I heard you found Mark's body... or at least everybody's assuming it's Mark."

"Yeah... no." She was still processing everything. "I don't know."

"Do you want to talk about it?" Lily was genuinely concerned for her. Nora could see it in her eyes.

"I really want to forget about it right now."

"Okay," said Lily. She didn't want to leave Nora alone, but there were other customers waiting to be served. Besides, Nora wasn't going to open up about it right then, anyway. "We're pretty busy right now, but let me know if you need anything, alright?"

Nora shrugged her shoulders and took another drink of the beer, waiting for the buzz to set in. Unfortunately, the only thing she felt was the beginning of a headache. She closed her eyes and rubbed her temples, hoping to alleviate the pain before it got worse.

Lily left her alone, then, and went to the far side of the bar to serve another customer. From behind the bar, she had a perfect vantage point to watch everything. It was one of the best parts of the job. She always knew what was happening. News traveled through the pub first, both good and bad. Relationships began there and, more often than not, ended there. Just about everything interesting that happened in town took place in the pub, and Lily was always there, behind the bar, to see it.

So when Jake walked into the pub and spotted Nora, Lily stopped wiping down the countertop and paid attention. Something was going to happen. She'd seen that same look in the eyes of dozens of other men. It was a look of determination mixed with a bit of anger. It was the look of a man on a mission.

Lily tried to suppress a grin as she watched someone stop Jake to chat, his disinterest in the conversation obvious as he cranked his head around to see Nora. He was worried about her, Lily could tell, as he tried to make his way through the restaurant. She had been right to suspect Jake's interest in Nora was more than he let on.

Nora set her empty beer glass down on the bar and glanced up at Lily to ask for a refill. But Lily wasn't paying any attention. Her eyes were turned toward the other side of the restaurant. Curious, Nora turned to see what she was looking at.

Jake.

How long had it been since Nora had seen him last? It had only been a few days since they'd stood in the rain outside the community building and he'd asked her on a date. No, almost a week. His beard was longer and so was his hair, which was tucked under a black knit cap as well as could be.

He stood near a large round table in the center of the restaurant, talking to a group of older men. For a second, Nora forgot about the bear and the dead body as she watched Jake interact with the fishermen. He really was the picture of the typical Alaskan man, but less worn and tired looking than the other men she'd seen in town. Everyone else was laughing as someone at the table told a story. Jake smiled politely, but looked distracted. His brow was creased and even though his lips were curved up in a grin, his eyes looked dark with emotion. No matter how hard he tried to focus on the man's story, he couldn't. There was something more important he needed to tend to.

Then Nora saw Jake glance up at her, as if he'd known she was there. Their eyes met and the expression on his face changed instantly. He patted one of the men on the back, waved at the others across the table, and strode toward her. He didn't take his eyes off her.

Nora glanced back at Lily, but she was busy. Lily had discreetly moved further down the bar, far enough away to give them the illusion of privacy but close enough to hear them. When Nora turned back, Jake stood right in front of her.

"What were you doing out there all by yourself?" he asked, barely restraining the frustration he felt. Jake was angry with himself. He never should have left Nora alone out there. He'd known it from the start.

Nora opened her mouth to answer, but she didn't know what to say. She looked at him, scrutinizing his face. He was concerned for her, but why? Nora had been out there by herself for a month and Jake hadn't shown much interest in her well-being before. "What do you mean?" she asked, a little more sharply than was necessary. "I live out there. All by myself."

"I heard about the body," Jake said brusquely. "What I want to know is what you were doing out in the woods. You could have ended up just like Mark. Do you want to get lost and freeze to death?"

"Look," said Nora, annoyed that Jake thought he had any say over what she did. "I don't need a lecture from you. I've had a rough day. A lot rougher than you think. So can you cut me some slack and let me drink in peace?"

Jake's face softened then. He saw the wariness in her eyes. "You're right," he said. "I'm sorry." He sat down on the bar stool next to her and tried to get Lily's attention so he could order a drink, but she had her back turned to him and was talking with an older fisherman at the other end of the bar. When he didn't get Lily's attention, he got up from the bar stool and walked around the edge of the bar. He quickly grabbed a couple bottles of beer from one of the coolers under the bar and hurried back to his seat.

"Is it okay for you to do that?" Nora asked.

"Can't wait around forever for Lily to work her way back to this end of the bar," he said, cracking open a bottle and pouring it into Nora's mug. He drank his beer from the bottle.

"Look, I really am sorry if I overreacted." Setting his bottle down, Jake turned to look at her. She really was beautiful, even in her distressed state. And seeing her there, her hands still trembling from the ordeal, all he wanted to do was wrap his arms around her and pull her close. "It's just that something could have happened to you out there, too. I don't like the thought of that."

Nora sighed, then. She hadn't planned to tell anyone about the bear, but she couldn't hold it in any longer. "Actually," she said, "Something did happen." Nora hastily told him about finding the body and then her encounter with the bear. She didn't go into great detail, but Jake could tell the experience had been scary for her. As much as he wanted to lecture her, tell her how stupid she'd been to go traipsing off into the woods, he figured she'd learned her lesson. She didn't need him to tell her so.

She also didn't need to go back to that cabin.

"Do you want to stay in town?" Jake asked. There was a spare room at home and if she didn't want to stay there, he knew of a couple cabins in town available for rent. "You could stay the night... or longer."

Of course she wanted to stay in town. The last thing she wanted to do was go back to the cabin alone. But she had to go back. "I can't. I have to wait for the Alaska State Troopers to get here and then show them where the body is."

Jake nodded, deep in thought. "Well, then I'll go with you," he said resolutely. "I want to make sure you're going to be safe out there."

Nora didn't argue. She was actually relieved.

She took a sip of her beer and then looked in the mirror stretching the length of the wall behind the bar. She barely recognized the woman she saw. Nora had to admit her image had taken on a bit of a rustic look in the past few weeks she'd spent in the Alaskan bush. Her hair seemed to be perpetually in a ponytail to keep it out of the way, and the clothes she wore were chosen purely for function, not for fashion. Like everybody else, she even wore the Xtra-Tuf boots instead of the heels that used to be her mainstay. The big brown rubber boots made sense out there, where she had to crawl in and out of a boat on a regular basis. Wet feet were no good in the wilderness, and the water was awfully cold. Nora was more than willing to wear the gaudy-looking boots if it meant staying dry and warm. No, that woman in the mirror definitely wasn't the same woman that had arrived there a little over a month ago on the ferry. Not even close.

"Ugh. What am I doing here?" Nora asked in frustration, burying her face in her hands. She wasn't accustomed to drinking

– the shot of whiskey and the two beers had loosened her tongue. She didn't care what she said, even if it meant she was openly admitting defeat. "I don't know what I'm doing, Jake. Not about anything. I don't know how to live in the wilderness. I don't know how to catch crab... or anything, for that matter. I can't even catch a fish. Not to mention, I almost ended up as dinner for some bear."

Jake didn't say anything. He just sat there, studying her, listening to her.

"I'm out there, all by myself just about all the time. I don't even know if I can handle being alone like that. Why do you think I make so many trips into town? I can't go for weeks without seeing anybody. I can't even go for a few days all alone out there. I need the interaction. It's driving me crazy being out there by myself."

Finally, he spoke. "Well, why did you come here in the first place, then?"

Nora shook her head. She really didn't know anymore. "I had no choice," she answered weakly.

"Sure you did," Jake said. "So your uncle left you some land. You didn't have to come live here. You chose that."

"My uncle," said Nora sarcastically. "Now that's a laugh."

"What do you mean?"

"Nothing. And it's not like I really had a choice about coming here." Nora hadn't told anyone her real reason for coming to Alaska, but if anyone should know, it was Jake.

"What do you mean?" he asked.

Nora held back the tears. "I didn't have anywhere else to go. I needed to get away from my life. Anywhere would have been better than where I was. And then I got this letter in the mail saying I had inherited a house. I thought it would be a fresh start in a new town. Something good, right? I didn't expect this... a cabin in the woods with no electricity, a half-hour boat ride from town."

"Give yourself a break. So, it's not what you expected, but at least you're making the best of it. You're in Alaska now. Be tough. Hang in there and prove everybody wrong."

"Prove everybody wrong? So, everybody thinks I'm going to fail, is that it?"

"Everybody always thinks the newcomer is going to fail. But that's because most of them do. Most. Not all," Jake said. "You know, it's all very exhilarating on the way up. You meet new people and everyone's excited. And then the boat docks and everyone heads their separate ways and they never see each other again. They eventually realize life is tough here. Either they can't find a job or they can't handle the winters or they can't stand being so isolated from everything. Alaska isn't what they expected. Most of them end up going back to America before they've even been here a year. It happens all the time."

"That's something that bothers me," Nora interrupted, her speech beginning to slur. "Why do you call it America? Alaska is part of America, you know."

"Fine. The Lower 48, then," he said, deciding she'd had enough to drink. "Come on. Let's go wait for the Troopers at the store."

Jake stood up and helped her off the bar stool. When Nora stood up, she felt the full effect of the alcohol. She felt quite tipsy and a little sick, but at least she had Jake to lean on.

Outside, the smell of salt water mingled with the aroma of wild irises and fireweed growing alongside the restaurant, a normally comforting scent but one that made Nora nauseous almost immediately after she walked out of the pub. Her eyes had yet to adjust from the darkness of the bar and she squinted at the daylight, clinging tightly to Jake's arm as he led her down the boardwalk.

* * *

The boat ride back to the cabin didn't help Nora's nausea. Only made it worse. The headache wasn't any better, either, especially after a half-hour with the sound of an outboard motor roaring just a few feet away.

Jake cut the throttle as the skiff neared the rocky shore at the north end of Nora's property, letting the motor idle and the skiff drift on the current. The cabin sat close to the beach, a few hundred feet away from them. Surveying the surroundings, Jake couldn't see any sign the bear was still in the vicinity.

"I'm going to go a little further so we can see the other side of the cabin before we pull up to the shore," Jake hollered over the hum of the motor. The Troopers, who had followed behind in Jake's skiff, nodded in agreement. Nora had told them about the bear lurking nearby and they didn't want to take any chances, either.

As they rounded the south side of the cabin, they visually scanned the property for anything out of the ordinary. Everything looked normal.

Jake was the first to step out onto solid ground. The Troopers confidently followed. Nora was a little shakier getting out of the boat.

They walked toward the cabin, listening for any sounds to indicate the bear was still nearby. Jake got to the cabin first, and used his rifle to push open the door, which was shut but not latched. In Nora's haste to get away from the bear, she hadn't bothered to secure the cabin, and she knew the food in her pantry could have lured the bear inside. There was only one small window in the cabin, so it was dark inside, but Jake walked in without hesitation. A few seconds later, he stuck his head back out the door to let everyone know the cabin was empty. *That was a relief, at least.*

Next, Nora led Jake and the two Troopers toward the creek. All of them remained on high alert for the bear as they followed Nora to the spot where she had found the body. The body was exactly where she'd left it, surprisingly undisturbed by the wildlife. Jake recognized him instantly. It was definitely Mark, the man who had gone missing on the mountain.

"He must have gotten disoriented and walked the wrong way," Nora said, thinking aloud. "Ten miles in the wrong direction."

"Not necessarily. It's ten miles by water, because the inlet curves around," Jake explained. "But only three miles by land." He pointed toward the mountain. "He could have easily gotten disoriented and came down the wrong side. It happens more often than you'd think. Even to the unlikeliest of people."

The Troopers took over from there. Nora and Jake waited nearby while they took photos and called in a helicopter to lift the body out of the woods. A couple hours later, both Troopers left in the helicopter while Jake and Nora made their way back to the cabin. The sun had begun its descent behind the mountains to the west and darkness was beginning to set in.

Back at the cabin, Jake lingered for a long time to make sure Nora really was okay. Her nausea had subsided, but the headache lingered, a dull throbbing that only seemed to be getting worse in spite of the three aspirin she'd taken.

Neither one of them said anything as Jake lit the oil lantern and started a fire in the wood stove. He put some water on the stove for coffee. Nora sat on the couch, her legs tucked up underneath her, uninterested in conversation of any kind. It hurt to even think about talking.

Jake was the one to break the silence. "You're shaking," he said, sitting down next to her on the couch and taking her hands in his.

Nora didn't want to admit it, but she was still rather troubled about the day's events. In fact, she was on the verge of panic... terrified the bear would return, that she would be lost to the wilderness, that someday someone else would find her own body beside the creek. Her entire body trembled at the thought.

But Jake was there. She had to hold it together, to show him she was a survivor. She could do this.

Nora turned to him and gave him a brave, unconvincing smile. "I'm fine."

"No, you're not," Jake said, looking her straight in the eye.

She tried to pull her hands away from his. He held on. He wasn't going to let her go. And he wasn't going to let her off the hook, either.

"Really," she said. "I'm just tired. It's been a long day."

"Don't do that," he pleaded softly.

"Don't do what?"

"Don't act like nothing's wrong."

He was right. She couldn't pretend like she was fine when every ounce of her being screamed exactly the opposite. Her insides were an emotional turmoil, and for good reason. She had almost died. If the bear hadn't stopped, she could have been torn to pieces. The end.

She was barely holding it together. Why was she fighting it?

"You're right," she said, as the tears began to fall. She couldn't hold it in any longer. She was in over her head and her own stupidity had almost gotten her killed. "I don't know what I'm doing. I don't know the first thing about survival."

She let it all out. Like a mad woman, she rattled off all her anxieties and her fears of living alone in the woods, all of her frustrations and worries.

"I'm barely hanging on here," she cried.

When her hysteria quieted and the tears began to dry up, Nora realized she was in Jake's arms. Her head rested on his chest, his arms held her tight against him. He'd been cradling her through it all, comforting her, calming her.

"I'm sorry," she said, lifting her head and looking at him. His face was so close to hers, his scent so strong. For a second, she hoped he might kiss her. But then she recognized the look on his face. It was one of sympathy. He felt sorry for her. He was just being nice, trying to comfort her. And his shirt was soaking wet from her tears, she realized.

"Wow. This is embarrassing," Nora said, pulling away from him abruptly. "Sorry about your shirt." She scooted over on the couch, intentionally putting some distance between them.

The second she pulled away, Jake regretted he hadn't kissed her. She'd been so close to him, her eyes inviting him, her lips tempting him. But he hadn't wanted to take advantage of the situation. She was in an emotional state. It wouldn't have been right to kiss her when she was so vulnerable.

"This doesn't count as our first date, does it?" Jake asked jokingly to lighten the mood.

"I certainly hope not," she said dryly, feeling a little awkward now that she'd poured out her heart to him and gotten practically no response back.

"Good," he said. "Looks like the water's hot. How about some coffee?"

Nora wiped a stray tear off her face and nodded her head. Jake smiled warmly at her.

He poured two cups of coffee and handed one to Nora. He could tell she was still shook up, even though she tried to conceal it. The slight tremor in her hands when she took the cup of coffee was enough to betray her.

"Are you sure you don't want to spend the night in town?" Jake asked for the second time that day. "There's a spare room…"

"No," Nora cut him off. "I'll be fine here." She was trying to convince herself as much as Jake. Now that three other people had been out there looking for it, she told herself the bear was probably long gone by now.

"Well, I could stay out here for the night… just to keep an eye on things," he added, still not convinced he should leave Nora alone.

"Really, you should go. Sleep in a real bed, not on some lumpy couch." Nora insisted. She gave him a small smile to prove she was fine with being left alone.

"You're sure?" he asked reluctantly.

"I am."

Jake turned to leave, but before he did, Nora leaned up and kissed his cheek. "Thanks for everything," she said softly.

Nora quickly turned and walked into the cabin, leaving Jake gawking at her. The kiss, as innocent as it had been, surprised him. In all honesty, even Nora was a little surprised she had been so forward.

She watched from the window as Jake headed toward his skiff. He turned back around once and waved at her. Then he jumped into his boat and disappeared into the darkness.

Feeling alone, Nora sunk down onto the couch. She still couldn't get the dead man out of her mind… or the sound of the bear snarling at her. She curled up on the couch with a blanket and lay there for a long time, watching the door and listening for any sounds that might indicate the bear had returned. She eventually fell into a restless sleep.

CHAPTER

12

A strange noise outside awoke Nora shortly after midnight. It was a scratching sound. Paws, or maybe claws, scraping against wood. Scratching, digging, clawing.

At the first sound of it, Nora bolted upright. When she heard the noise again, she jumped up off the couch and lunged for the door to make sure the latch was secured. It was, but she still didn't feel very safe.

Through the window, all Nora saw was darkness. The moon was hidden behind cloud cover and a pitch black void enveloped everything.

She heard the scratching sound a third time, and another noise she couldn't quite put a finger on. Whatever it was, it was close to the cabin. Very close.

The fire in the stove was almost out and the cabin was beginning to take on a chill. Nora hurriedly tossed two more logs into the stove then looked around for something, anything, she could put in front of the door. The handmade wooden latch wouldn't hold up if someone, or something, tried to force their way in. She briefly thought about moving the couch in front of the door, but that would put it too close to the wood stove. The last thing she needed was to start a fire in the cabin. Either she would end up trapped inside, or if she did make it out alive, she'd be forced to watch helplessly as her home burned to the ground. Not to mention, she'd be alone outside with whatever kept making that scratching sound.

Instinctively, Nora grabbed the old rifle Pete had left hanging on the wall. She didn't know what kind of rifle it was or what caliber shell it took. Nora didn't know anything about guns at all. She clumsily pulled back the bolt-action lever and found two shells already in the rifle. Pushing the bolt slowly back into place, she saw one of the shells automatically slide up into the chamber and she assumed the rifle was ready to fire. Television and movies had at least ingrained into Nora's head that there was always a safety switch on guns. She eventually found it and flicked the safety switch on. Guns made Nora nervous, so she double-checked it a second later to ensure the safety was definitely in the "on" position.

She heard the scratching sound again, along with a familiar woofing she'd heard earlier in the day. The hairs on Nora's arms stood up as she recognized the sound the bear had made just before it had charged her by the stream.

The bear. It was back.

Nora quickly grabbed the lantern and scurried up the ladder to the loft. Feeling only slightly safer due to her higher vantage point, she sat down cross-legged at the edge of the loft. She placed the lantern off to her side and pulled the rifle up into her lap. The can of bear spray sat beside her.

Nora looked the rifle over one more time. She flicked the safety switch into the "off" position and aimed the rifle at the door. Then she sat there and waited. She had never fired a shot before in her entire life, but if it came down to it, Nora wouldn't hesitate. She hoped two shells would be enough for whatever might come through the door. She also hoped her aim would be accurate. She sat there on alert for what seemed like an eternity. Her arms ached from holding the rifle for so long. The scratching sound had grown quieter. Nora glanced at the clock. It was 1 o'clock. Even though the noises had quieted, she kept the rifle aimed at the door. When another hour passed and all she could hear was the stillness of night, Nora relaxed a bit. She flicked the safety back on and set the rifle on the floor next to her.

Whatever had been lurking around outside seemed to be gone, but she wasn't ready to give up her watch on the door. Not yet. Sleep was out of the question. As tired as Nora was, she was too scared to let down her guard. She would be up all night watching that door.

She should have stayed in town, like Jake had suggested. Nora knew that now.

I wonder if he's still awake.

Nora leaned over the edge of the loft and looked down at the radio. She was going to be up all night and she needed something to distract her from the bear outside, a friendly voice to help calm her nerves. Talking to Jake over the radio always helped her relax.

No. It's late. I shouldn't bother him. He's probably sleeping. Besides, he'll know why I'm calling. Yes, she should have stayed in town. But she wasn't about to admit that to Jake.

Next to the radio sat Pete's brown leather journal. That could be a good distraction, Nora thought. Quickly climbing down the ladder, she snatched up the journal and then hurried back up into the loft.

Resuming her perch on the edge of the loft, where she could keep an eye on the door and window, Nora pulled the silver ink pen out of Pete's journal and opened it up. The words that filled its pages spoke of Pete's life in the cabin and, oddly, the fondness he felt for his niece. Some of his journal entries were sadly reflective:

> *Once I'm gone, there will be nothing left of me on this Earth. No children to remember me, no wife to mourn my passing. No one will care. Not my brother. Not his daughter. I'm not part of their lives and they probably never even think of me.*

> *Sometimes I wish Nora were my child. It's foolish, I know. She's growing up and I wish I was there to see it. I see the young folks in town starting families and I wonder if I missed out on something by choosing this life. The wilderness always called to me, but maybe I should have ignored it.*

There were plenty of other things in the journal, too. Entries about his hopes and plans, as well as some sketches of what he called his homestead. He had plenty of improvements planned but he never got around to doing any of them.

Nora had read the journal many times over the past few weeks, taking comfort in the fact Pete had experienced many of the same feelings of isolation and loneliness as Nora. It was only three-quarters of the way full. There would have been plenty of room for many more entries, if Pete had lived longer.

Nora flipped through the pages and read Pete's final entry one more time. It was a mundane entry recording the day's salmon catch. He had measured and weighed each of the fish and estimated the profit he would earn if he sold them to Nate.

She smiled as she envisioned Pete sitting down at the table, meticulously recording the information. Planning ahead. The one thing Nora had learned about her uncle was that he planned for every contingency.

In that respect, they were complete opposites. Nora had never given much thought to what lay ahead. Someone else had always told her what to do, and she had always obediently followed the rules. Even as an adult, after she met Conner. He had taken care of the details, planned their entire lives out. Every detail fit into a perfectly arranged schedule, right down to when they would announce their engagement, when they would get married, and when they would start a family.

But she wasn't letting someone else call the shots anymore. Her life had taken her to the wilds of Alaska, and that was where she was going to stay. She wasn't Conner's trophy anymore, either. Nora was in charge of her own life now. She would have to start planning things out in advance, like how much food to stockpile for the winter.

At least she had Pete's records, written out in detail to the point Nora knew what he'd eaten every day, how much he'd eaten, and how much food it had taken for the single man to get through the winter. He'd been just as detailed in his records of fish caught, game killed, and wood chopped. In addition to the journal, he'd left behind twenty-one record books, one for each year he'd spent in the cabin. Yeah, Pete had definitely been a thorough record keeper.

Nora wondered what else she might have learned from him, if she'd grown up knowing Pete. All she had left of him was his journal, and while it provided her with a small peek into his daily life, it really didn't help her understand who he was. What had brought him to Alaska? Why hadn't he been a part of her life? She would never know the answers to those questions. She would never truly understand her uncle.

Nora turned to the next page in the journal. It was blank.

The ink pen sat on the floor beside Nora. Without thinking, she picked it up and began writing.

June 16 - Somewhere south of Heron, Alaska
My uncle left me a cabin in the Alaskan wilderness.

It was weird. She'd only heard his name a handful of times in her life, and yet, he'd left her everything he owned. She only wished she could have known him, understood him. If he'd wanted a family of his own and if he'd wanted to know his niece better, then why did he hide himself away in the Alaskan bush? With Pete gone, Nora would never find the answer to that question. Whatever his reason, it was ancient history now, lost forever.

Nora turned her focus back to the present and resumed her journal entry.

So, like Pete, I'm going to (at least attempt to) keep a record of my life in the bush.

I get up in the morning and I throw a piece of wood on the smoldering coals in the wood stove. I go outside and start pumping water. I fill a large bucket first and then I fill a small kettle. I carry both back into the cabin and set them on the stove to heat up. The small kettle always comes to a boil first. I pour some of the water into the French press, but since I don't have electricity I can't grind fresh coffee beans. I have to use the ground stuff. It's nowhere near as good as the latte I used to have every morning, but it's better than nothing. I use the rest of the water in the kettle to make some oatmeal, which I eat plain. It's not very satisfying. By the time I get done eating, the bucket of water is usually pretty hot. I use that to wash up. I can't believe I haven't had a shower in more than a month. If there's one thing I miss, it's a hot shower.

All these weeks I've sat around the cabin doing nothing. Starting tomorrow I'm going to try and spend at least two hours each day chopping wood. I have no choice. The wood pile is getting smaller by the day. I think I might stack the wood next to the house. Pete built a wood shed a ways away from the cabin, and I'm tired of hauling it so far every day. Willie said I'll need to have the shed full before winter if I don't want to freeze to death. I think he's exaggerating. He does have a point, though. I've been burning up a lot of wood. If I don't start replenishing it now, I'll probably be out chopping wood in the middle of winter. I really hope not.

It's been difficult being alone. Conner always took care of everything, including me. At first, I thought that was a good thing, but near the end I knew I couldn't take it anymore. It was all so fake. I couldn't pretend to be the perfect girlfriend anymore, and I'm definitely not cut out to be the perfect wife, at least not the kind of wife he wanted. If I would have stayed with him, I would have let him become my entire life. I would have become someone else entirely. Never again will I let my life revolve around a man the way I did with Conner. Two years with him, and I don't know how to do anything for myself. But I'm learning.

Nora read what she'd written. She wasn't good with words. Maybe she would get better as time went on.

So far, I have three friends... Lily, Willie, and Jake.

That brought a smile to her face. She considered them friends, and she was pretty sure they considered her a friend, too.

Lily is about the same age as me (maybe a little older) and she's hilarious. Whenever I'm around her, it seems like I can't stop laughing. I'm kind of glad Lily's the first person I met in town. If not for her, I might have turned right around and hopped back on the ferry.

Willie is my neighbor and he's constantly checking in on me to make sure I'm still alive. He keeps bringing me food. Jerky, eggs, fresh bread, goat cheese. Says he's trying to fatten me up for the winter. I don't think he's kidding, either. He has a good heart, I think. It's a shame he's all alone out here.

And then there was Jake. He was still a bit of a mystery. Sometimes a little bossy and overbearing. But other times the perfect gentleman. Kind. Considerate. Masculine. Oh, so masculine.

I have a date with Jake. I'm not sure when, or where he's going to take me, but I'm actually looking forward to it. We've been getting to know each other over the radio and I think I like him.

When Nora looked up from the journal, she saw the skies outside weren't as dark. Morning had come. Through the window, she saw a ray of sunshine beaming down through a gap in the clouds, lighting up the waters of the inlet. She turned her attention back to the journal, letting her thoughts flow more freely now.

It's morning now. The sun is trying its hardest to peek through the clouds. Where it does, the water lights up with a golden hue. I've never in all my life seen anything more beautiful. I can't believe I ever thought about selling this place. Even after everything that happened yesterday, for the first time in my life I feel like I belong somewhere.

That reminded her. She'd forgotten to cancel the ad. Of course, she would have forgotten. The last time she was in town, she'd just been charged by a bear and found a dead body. She wasn't in her right mind. But in spite of the dead body, in spite of the bear, Nora knew without a doubt she was going to stay in Heron. She owed to her Uncle Pete. She owed it to herself.

CHAPTER

13

Rain gathered in the center of the tarp canopy, forming an ever deepening puddle over Nora's head as she pulled the ax out of a stump and attempted to chop the wood into several smaller pieces that would fit in the stove. She was having a difficult time of it, too. Every swing of the ax was a reminder of how inept she was at this whole survival thing. Either she didn't swing the ax with enough force to get through the wood or her aim was so far off she caught just the edge of the stump and sliced off only a long sliver of wood.

Disappointed with how little progress she was making, Nora bent down and picked up the few slivers of wood she'd managed to produce, pieces that weren't good for much, other than kindling. She tossed them through the open door of the wood shed, onto drier ground. If the wood shed were a little larger, and not quite so dark inside, she would have rolled the large pieces of wood inside. But there wasn't enough room to swing an ax in the narrow structure. It was barely large enough to house three long rows of firewood, so she had no choice but to work outside, under the tarp. Overhead, the ropes holding each of the four corners of the tarp to several trees around her were stretched taut from the added weight of the rainwater. Her raincoat kept her dry, but the tarp canopy was the only thing keeping the wood from getting completely waterlogged.

Nora grabbed a long stick and pushed it up in the center of the tarp where it sagged the most, trying to get the puddle of rainwater to drain off the side of the canopy. She jammed one end of the stick into the ground to prop up the center of the canopy and keep the rain from gathering there. It worked for the most part, but smaller puddles started to form along the edge of the tarp. She wasn't too worried about them.

It was still early in the morning. The clouds blocked out most of the sun, except for a few stray rays of sunshine sneaking through between the mountain peaks and the heavy clouds, offering enough illumination for Nora to work outdoors.

After spending a sleepless night on the edge of the loft, keeping vigil on the door to make sure a rogue bear didn't pound it down, Nora was tired. Chopping wood was the last thing in the world she wanted to be doing. But firewood was a necessity, since it was the only thing that kept the cold of night from creeping into the cabin. She'd told herself she should start chopping wood now instead of waiting for the chill of fall.

Besides, Nora was restless after the previous day's events.

She'd been cautious, going outside that morning, even though there were no signs of the bear. No tracks or anything else to indicate it had been there the night before. Maybe Nora imagined the scratching noise, convinced herself something was there. Imagination or not, it had kept her up all night.

Even though she was still a little spooked by it all, she was determined to get over her fears. If she was going to stay at the cabin, she couldn't live in constant fear. And she definitely couldn't keep herself holed up in the cabin. She needed to be able to walk outside, knowing the dangers that might be out there, and willing to take them on. That's what she told herself, anyway.

What she really needed that morning was to clear her mind, and she was hoping hard work would do the trick. So far it was working. With splinters in her hands and a pile of wood that didn't seem to be getting any smaller, Nora's attention was focused solely on swinging the ax hard enough to actually get through a piece of timber.

After an hour of hacking away at the wood, the heavy rain diminished to a fine mist. Nora stopped to assess her progress. She had a small pile of usable fire wood and the start of at least two blisters on her hands. Stretching the muscles on her arms, she decided to get something to drink before resuming her work.

The rifle leaned against the nearest tree. Never again would Nora be caught unprepared. After the run-in with the bear, the rifle was going to be by her side anytime she ventured outside, even if she was just going to the outhouse.

Grabbing the rifle, Nora walked the short distance to the stream. She knelt down and rinsed her aching hands in the cold water. Then she found the rope she had tied to a stump, and pulled the fish net out of the water. She had stowed a couple cans of soda in the bag to keep them chilled, along with a case of beer she kept around for Willie, and it worked perfectly. It was the closest thing to refrigeration she was going to get, at least for the time being.

Inside the cabin, Nora opened the window and propped the door wide open to let the air flow through. Then she sat down on the couch. In spite of the lumps in the cushions, it felt rather comfortable after spending the morning hacking away at the wood pile. She settled in and rested her head on the back of the couch, enjoying the feel of the soda's bubbles in her mouth.

She sat there a lot longer than she had originally planned, staring at the ceiling and daydreaming about the house she'd like to build eventually. Willie had started out in a small cabin about the same size as this one, he'd told her. Over the years, he'd added on until it was a decent-sized modern home. If he could do it, so could Nora.

She didn't want anything large, but she was itching to have more space than the 140 square foot cabin she was living in. The design she had in her head was simple. The home would have a small kitchen, a proper living room, a bedroom, and a bathroom downstairs. She envisioned a large loft upstairs, substantially larger than the one she had now, where she could spend her time painting and doing crafty projects. Nora hadn't painted anything since grade school, but the scenery inspired her and she wanted a space where she could test her talents, limited as they may be.

Outside, she wanted a large covered porch with a small seating area and an outdoor fireplace she could cozy up to on those chilly nights. Nora dreamed of long nights curled up in front of the fireplace, watching the stars glisten over the snow-capped peaks on the opposite side of the inlet, with a cup of hot chocolate to warm her hands.

She was looking forward to the day when she would eventually get electricity and running water set up out there. Hopefully, that day would come sooner rather than later. She'd already requested a catalog from a company that specialized in solar and wind power equipment, and she was anxiously waiting for it to come in the mail.

A snapping sound outside brought Nora back to the present and she sat up straight, on high alert. Thoughts of the bear's return were the first thing that entered her mind. She looked around for the rifle and saw it leaning against the wall, next to the door.

That's good. At least I didn't leave it outside.

Quickly, Nora stood up, closed the door, and latched it tight. She had only a limited view of the yard through the small window on the side of the cabin. With the door closed, she couldn't see a large majority of the property, including the inlet in front of the cabin. Through the window, she saw the rain had completely stopped, with only a few drops falling here and there, dripping from the branches overhead.

Taking a deep breath to steady herself, she picked the rifle up, checked to make sure there was a shell in the chamber, and turned the safety off.

Slowly, cautiously, she opened the door a few inches and peeked through the slit of the barely open door. Seeing nothing out of the ordinary, Nora opened the door all the way, stepped out, and surveyed her surroundings. The branches of the trees swayed in the gentle breeze, and she spied a black squirrel scurrying along the damp earth, running toward the nearest tree. Around the side and back of the cabin, everything looked to be in its place, with no sign of bears, thankfully.

Nora let out a long sigh, laughing at herself for being so jumpy. Clearly, everything was fine. Like the night before, she was overreacting.

Deciding she should get back to work, she went inside to grab her unfinished can of soda and then walked back over to the log she had been working on. Leaning the rifle against a tree, she picked up the ax and swung it hard. She grinned. She actually hit her target and sliced the piece right in half.

She reached down and turned one of the pieces, positioning it so she could cut it in half again. Then she hefted the ax up, over her shoulder. Mid-swing, a movement to her left startled her and she missed the log completely. The memory of the bear charging toward her flashed through Nora's mind. *Oh, no. Not again.* Her thoughts immediately went to the rifle, leaning against a tree three feet away, and she reached for it. When Jake stepped out from behind the wood shed, Nora sighed with relief and leaned the rifle back against the tree.

"Looks like you're getting the hang of it," he said, looking down at her smile pile of wood. "Kind of."

She smiled, trying not to show how startled she was. Her heart pounded a million beats per minute. Maybe it was the memory of the bear charging her... or maybe it was the sight of Jake. Either way, her heart was racing.

"Where'd you come from? I didn't hear your skiff," she asked, trying to sound as casual as possible.

With his thumb, he pointed over his shoulder, toward the forest.

"From over there." The look on Nora's face indicated she expected more of an explanation. People didn't just appear out of the forest, at least not in her experience. "I went down to the Baker's float house to help Tom replace a support log. One side was sinking in the water."

"Oh. Was it flooded?"

"Yeah. The water was about two feet deep in the bedroom when I got there. We managed to get one log under and fastened to the house, but it looks like it'll need at least one more to support it."

"That didn't really answer my question, though," she said, still wondering how he managed to get there without her hearing his boat approach.

"Oh, on my way back, the motor quit. I couldn't get it started again. I was only about a mile south of here, so I rowed to shore and walked the rest of the way." Jake tried to sound as if the stalled motor had thrown a real monkey-wrench into his day. But actually it turned out to be the perfect excuse to stop in and check on Nora. He hadn't liked the idea of leaving her out there by herself the day before, not after she had just found a body and had a run-in with a bear. He needed to know she was okay. The stalled motor, while inconvenient, gave him a plausible excuse for showing up, without making him seem like some kind of 'dominant male,' as Nora had once accused him of being.

"I don't suppose you have a spare outboard motor I could borrow?" His lips turned up at the edges, the beginning of a smile. The night before, he had the same expression on his face after Nora kissed him on the cheek. It reminded her of how she had wanted him to kiss her for real.

"I only have the one on my skiff... I mean, your skiff," Nora said, suddenly feeling a little shy around Jake. "I'm just borrowing it..."

Jake laughed. "I know. I was kidding."

"Go ahead and take it if you need it. I'll manage fine."

"Or you could tow me into town."

"Alright, let me grab a couple things and we'll get going."

"There's no rush. I'm tired and I could use a little rest first. It's been a long morning."

Nora smiled, glad he wasn't in a hurry to leave.

"Well, come inside then. This gives me a reason to take a break from working for a while," Nora said, turning and walking toward the cabin. She heard the heavy footfall of his boots and knew he was following. *As heavy as his steps are,* Nora thought, *it's a wonder I didn't hear him coming a mile away.* She couldn't imagine how he'd gotten so close to the cabin without her hearing him.

Nora turned back to look at him as she reached the doorway.

"You hungry?"

"Not hungry. Thirsty."

Nora knew what he needed, something to warm him up inside and get rid of that waterlogged feeling. Pete's journal, thankfully,

172

included a log of every drink he served to his visitors. It's why she stocked the bottom shelf with drinks just for guests, hidden neatly behind Pete's old ugly curtains. She had a little bit of everything: tea, soda, juice, cider. And for those who liked their drinks a little stronger, there was an assortment of whiskey, rum, vodka, tequila, Irish cream, brandy, and a variety of schnapps. A light layer of dust was accumulating on the pint-sized bottles. The bottle of Scotch was the only one that had been opened, and only because Willie liked a little glass of it now and then when he visited. Somehow, she felt like she knew her neighbors because she knew what they drank, even though the only neighbor she'd met so far was Willie. If memory served her right, Jake liked hot chocolate with a hint of peppermint schnapps.

She pulled two mugs off the shelf above the table and, noticing bits of dirt on the outside of the rim, grabbed the towel that hung over the back of a chair to wipe the mug clean. She checked the other mug over, too, just to make sure it was clean. Without proper running water, it was difficult to wash dishes. And with the wood stove, dust was constantly deposited onto everything in the cabin.

"Do you mind starting a fire?"

"Sure," he said, as he knelt down and opened the door to the stove. Nora had seen how quickly he could build a roaring fire, so she turned back to the task at hand, confident she would have a hot stove to cook over in a matter of minutes.

She pulled a can of condensed milk off one of the upper shelves, along with some cocoa powder, sugar, and a small bottle of homemade vanilla extract Willie had given her. Then she grabbed a small kettle and measured out what she estimated to be the appropriate amounts. It was a recipe she knew well. Drinking hot chocolate had practically become a nightly ritual.

She saw Jake had the fire roaring and had seated himself on the couch, with his legs stretched out comfortably in front of him and his hands clasped behind his head.

"Make yourself at home," she said with a smile as she stirred to contents of the kettle with a wooden spoon.

Jake opened his eyes and lifted his head slightly, just long enough to respond.

"Oh, I am." Then he leaned his head back in that restful position and closed his eyes again. "This couch feels heavenly right now."

Nora took the kettle over to the stove. She picked up a metal rod and used it to open the burner cover enough to give her a medium heat, and set the kettle down. Over the past few weeks, she'd gotten used to cooking on the wood stove. That's something she never thought she'd be able to say. Then again, she'd never exactly envisioned herself living in a rustic cabin, either. And, yet, there she was.

"I know what you mean. It's not much to look at, but that couch has got to be the most comfortable one I've ever had, even with those huge lumps in the cushions," she said, still stirring the mixture. The sugar and cocoa were completely dissolved in the milk. As the chocolate warmed, it took on a deeper brown color. When a heavy steam began emanating from the chocolate, she knew it was ready. Nora picked up the kettle and moved it over to the table, and set it down on a hot pad.

She pulled a ladle off one of the nails in the wall and used it to scoop the hot chocolate out of the kettle and into each of the mugs, filling them about three-quarters of the way full. Then, she reached down to the bottom shelf, moved a few bottles out of the way, and found the unopened bottle of peppermint schnapps. Nora poured a smidge of the schnapps into Jake's cup, hoping she didn't add too much. She left her hot chocolate plain.

Jake sat up as Nora walked over with his drink and handed it to him.

"Thanks. Smells good."

He took a sip, to test how hot it was, then opened his throat and poured half the mug down his gullet.

"Mmm. You made it exactly the way I like it."

"You sound surprised."

"Well, I am. You and Pete are more alike than I thought," he said, as he took another long drink and drained his mug.

Nora still stood in front of him, holding her full mug. She chuckled at how quickly he had polished off the steaming hot liquid.

"Good thing I made a kettle full. Another?" she asked, holding out her hand to take the mug back from him. But he didn't pass the mug to her. Instead, he stood up.

"I can help myself. You sit down and relax."

Nora obeyed, taking a seat at the far end of the couch. She settled in and watched him make another drink, noticing that he poured less of the hot chocolate into his mug and more of the peppermint schnapps.

Nora curled her legs up on the couch and sipped the hot chocolate. It was nice having Jake there. He looked like he belonged in a log cabin in the woods. He was handsomely rugged. But he was so much more than that, too. Nora couldn't quite put her finger on it, but there was something about him. Something intriguing.

Still standing by the table, Jake turned around and leaned against the wall. He took another drink of the hot chocolate, savoring it a little more this time.

"I love this stuff. I could drink it all day," he said.

"You talking about the hot chocolate or the peppermint schnapps?" Nora asked teasingly.

"Yes," he said with a smile. "By the way, the place looks good. I meant to tell you yesterday. Looks like you've settled in nicely.

Doesn't even look like Pete's place anymore, except for those awful curtains on the shelves." He chuckled, remembering. The fabric was old and dingy. It featured a maritime theme. "The old man sewed those curtains himself. Even though they're crooked as hell, he was pretty proud of himself."

Nora glanced over at the ugly curtains with the sailboat pattern. She had hated them from the start, but hadn't bothered to replace them. For a while, she considered taking the curtains down, but they helped hide the clutter of the shelves, so she had left them hanging there. Now, she thought maybe she would keep them as a reminder of the uncle who had given her a new start in life. She'd never known Pete, but she was thankful he'd left the house to her, even if it wasn't what she'd expected. It was a shelter from the craziness of the world.

"Did you know him well?" she couldn't resist asking. She knew so little of her uncle. She'd barely even known he existed before she received that letter in the mail from Mallow.

"Yeah," he said with a look of sadness in his eyes. "He saved my life." He chuckled a little as he recalled the first time he'd met Pete. "I was probably ten years old and I was grounded for plucking half the feathers out of one of my mom's chickens. So I decided to run away. I stole my parents' skiff and decided to go to Juneau. Didn't know what direction it was, though, and I ended up down here in the back bay. I didn't know how to recognize the wake from the rocks below the surface, and I got the boat hung up a good 20 yards out from the shore. I was still pretty determined to get to Juneau and I didn't want my dad to find me before I got there, so I decided to swim for the shore. It was the most stupid thing I've ever done and I realized it right away. But the current had me and I couldn't get back to the boat. Thought for sure I was a goner, but then Pete appeared out of nowhere and plucked me up out of the water. He brought me back here, warmed me up, fed me. Asked me what the hell I was doing out there and nearly threw me back in the water when I gave him some smart-assed response." Jake's smile reflected the fondness he'd felt for the old man. "Anyway, we had a good talk before he radioed my parents. He straightened me out and convinced my parents to go easy on me."

Nora smiled. Pete was a good guy. That's what she'd learned about him so far. She wished she knew more about him.

"Did Pete ever talk about his past? I mean, before he came to Alaska?"

"Not really. Why do you ask?"

"I don't know." She shrugged her shoulders. "Remember that picture you told me about? The one of me and Pete when I was really little?"

"What about it?"

"I've gone through all of Pete's stuff and I never ran across it."

"He was buried with it," Jake said quietly. "It was the one thing he asked for."

The enormity of Jake's words sunk in slowly. The photo really had meant something to Pete, then. She had meant something to him.

"You know, Pete might have been a hermit, but he was a very level-headed person," he said, sensing Nora needed to know more about the man. "It wasn't unusual for him to stay out here for months at a time without seeing another soul. That would drive some people crazy, but I think it kept him sane."

Nora chuckled then. "I think I teeter back and forth between the two," she said. If there wasn't so much truth to her statement, it may have been funny.

"It's a hard life out here, Nora," said Jake reassuringly, "but I can tell you're a survivor. You just need to find a balance."

She nodded, thinking about his words. Balance. Seemed like

Nora's entire life had been off balance. Things had been out of focus for so long, but each day she spent there in her cabin, everything became a little clearer. She could survive there, and she believed she could even love it there. She already had begun to love the beauty of the mountains and the water that surrounded her. In spite of how much Nora had grown to love the Alaskan wilderness, she still found the isolation overwhelming. She was a little too separated from the outside world. Sure, she was starting to like the seclusion and she didn't mind being alone quite so much anymore. It was the sheer inaccessibility she still had problems adapting to. Travel from one town to the next, which was only 80 miles away, would require half a day on the ferry and needed to be planned well in advance due to the limited ferry schedule. Nora occasionally missed being able to hop on the freeway and drive wherever she pleased. The inadequate inventory at The General Store meant she needed to order certain supplies, which in turn would require a significant wait for it to be delivered, not to mention the increased cost to have it shipped to the remote town. Even ordinary mail took three times longer to receive there than it had back in California. Maybe Jake was right. When Nora found a way to balance the isolation, the solitude, and her own happiness, maybe she would truly feel at home in the wilderness.

Nora took another sip of her hot chocolate. There something she'd been wondering about for a while, ever since Lily mentioned that Jake had once left Alaska. As she watched him leaning against the wall, she considered whether she should ask him. Since they were being so open with each other, Nora decided to go for it.

"What made you leave here?" she asked. "All those years ago, I mean?"

He looked a little caught off guard by her question at first, but immediately relaxed.

"I guess it was the isolation. I was 24 and I wanted to see what else was out there, just like anyone else."

"So, what brought you back here, then?"

"That's simple. I realized what I had here was special. Very few people get to live like this, surrounded by all this beauty. I wake up to the sight of the morning sun reflecting off the snow on the mountains. The last thing I see before I go to bed is the moon reflecting off the water. Life's harder here, but it just feels right."

Nora didn't say anything, but nodded her agreement. She was only now beginning to appreciate the raw beauty and harshness of the Alaskan wilderness. Even though this wasn't what she had expected, this is where life had led her. Every day she spent surviving the wilderness, she found things felt a little more right than the day before. Even though everyday could be a struggle for survival, she actually felt like she could one day belong there.

She looked down at the mug in her hand, still half full of hot chocolate, if it could still be called hot chocolate. The concoction barely held any warmth. She drank it down in two long swallows and thought about refilling her mug. She always did have a weakness for chocolate.

When she looked up, she noticed Jake was watching her intently, his lips turned up slightly at the corners. He was still standing by the table and held the ladle in one hand and the schnapps in the other, fully equipped to replenish her cup.

"You're right on top of things, aren't you," Nora said.

He grinned at that comment and a slight gleam lit up his eyes as a thought popped into his head – *there's something else I wouldn't mind being on top of.* "Refill?" he asked politely, repressing the urge to say what he was really thinking.

"Yes, but just hot chocolate. No schnapps for me."

"Me, too," he said, capping the bottle of schnapps and putting it back on the shelf. He poured them each one more cup of hot chocolate, emptying the kettle.

Then he walked over to where she sat on the couch. He leaned down toward her, closer than was necessary, to hand her the mug. His hand fleetingly caressed Nora's, lingered for a second longer than was necessary. When he sat down next to her, Nora breathed in his scent and felt giddy at his nearness.

The fire crackled as the log inside the potbelly stove broke in half, and Nora noticed how warm the small room was. *Is it just me, or is it getting hot in here?*

She glanced out the window. Although it was still quite cloudy, the sun was high in the mid-day sky. The rain was still holding off and she felt mildly guilty that she was wasting the day inside, especially since the forecast called for rain the rest of the week. But the guilt didn't last long, as her thoughts turned back to the man sitting next to her, sipping his drink. Nora smiled at him.

"You looked lost in thought there for a minute," he said, watching her intently.

"Just thinking about how good this drink tastes," Nora lied. Her stomach grumbled, then, and they both laughed.

"You like salmon? I happen to have a humpy on a line in the water back at my skiff. It would make a great dinner, if you're up for it."

Nora grinned. "I thought you weren't hungry."

"Well, it sounds like you are. Besides, I think I'll be pretty hungry by the time we get that fish cleaned and cooked. How about it? Shall we hop in your skiff and tow my boat back here, then make some dinner?"

"Okay," Nora agreed.

A few minutes later, they were on their way to the small cove where Jake had left his boat. He sat at the stern of Nora's small skiff, operating the motor, since he knew where they were going.

When they got to the boat, he jumped out and waded over to his own boat. He had left it on the shore, but the tide had come in and the boat, which was tied to a tree, was now floating in about a foot of water. He untied the boat and tied it to Nora's skiff, then reached into the water and pulled a line out. A good sized salmon on the end of the line struggled fiercely to get away as Jake held it up for Nora to see. The fish must have been almost 24 inches long from head to tail, enough to feed an entire family.

"What do you think?"

"Looks good."

He nodded, pulled a bucket out of his skiff, filled it with water, and put the fish in the bucket for the ride back to the cabin.

* * *

The salmon tasted delicious. They ate side by side at the small kitchen table, sipping red wine and chatting. By the time they finished, only a quarter of the fish remained. Nora had never realized how good salmon could taste, nor how much she could enjoy just being with another person.

"That was amazing. Thank you," she said after eating the last bite of fish on her plate.

"More wine?" Jake held the bottle up, ready to top off her glass. She really did look amazing, sitting across from him at the table. He liked everything about her. The way she cut the food on her plate into tiny pieces. The way she took her time drinking a small glass of wine, one little sip at a time. The way she pulled her long hair back to keep it out of the way and, even better, the way her hair rested on her shoulders when she wore it down. The way she wrinkled her nose at his bad jokes, but laughed at them anyway. There were a thousand other little things about her that drove him mad with desire. A thousand little quirks that made it very difficult for him to restrain himself around her.

"No, thanks."

"You sure?" He knew she would say no, that she preferred to keep her mind clear. He liked that about her, too.

"You know, I think you might be trying to get me drunk," said Nora flirtatiously as she picked up the dinner dishes, turned, and set them in a washbasin on the shelf. "Any decent man..."

Jake stood up then, too. He couldn't restrain himself any longer. He needed to touch her, to feel her lips on his.

The cabin felt smaller than it ever had before as Nora realized how close he was to her.

"No one's ever accused me of being decent," he said as he moved in behind her, trapping Nora in the corner. "And if there's any question about my intentions, we can get that out of the way right now, if you'd like."

His scent was more intoxicating than the alcohol and Nora closed her eyes. He was so close she could feel his breath on the back of her neck. She took a deep breath to steady herself and then opened her eyes again. Yes. He was still there. No. She wasn't imagining it.

"I love long hair on a woman," Jake whispered, reaching up and pulling the rubber band out of Nora's hair and losing the long tendrils onto her shoulders and back.

Nora turned toward him, but she couldn't bring herself to look up into his eyes. Afraid of what she might see in his eyes, Nora kept her own eyes down. Already, she found herself short of breath and her entire body tingled at the slightest touch. Making eye contact with him would be too much for her.

"Jake..."

She made the mistake of looking up at him and completely forgot what she had been planning to say. Her breath caught in her throat as Jake moved closer to her and his lips touched hers, so warm and urgent. Nora realized she had been waiting for this moment all day, maybe since the moment she first saw Jake. Her pulse quickened as she gave in to the kiss, let herself get lost in it. When the kiss ended, she didn't pull away. She wanted more.

"There. That's out of the way," Jake said huskily, looking down at her. He still held her close, afraid she might pull away from him if he gave her the chance. "Now, what were you going to say?"

"Hmm... nothing."

"No objections?" he asked cautiously, hoping she wanted him as much as he wanted her.

"No."

"Good," he replied. His mouth was mere inches from hers, inviting her to kiss him back. She did, savoring the taste of his lips. Her arms moved up around his neck, her hands pulling him closer. When they came up for air, Nora felt lightheaded.

"I think the bear may have come back last night," she said unexpectedly. She hadn't meant to tell him. She just blurted it out without thinking. "I heard a scratching sound outside and another noise that I've only ever heard when I had the encounter with the bear. It scared the crap out of me and I didn't sleep at all last night."

"Why didn't you tell me sooner?" Jake looked worried.

"I don't know," Nora stammered. "I don't even know for sure if it was the bear. I might have been imagining it. It's pretty easy for me to get spooked out here."

"Well, in that case, I insist on spending the night tonight... just to keep an eye on things," he said.

"That's silly," Nora argued. "I'll be fine."

"I'll sleep outside, if you'd be more comfortable. But I'm not leaving you here alone tonight," he said, tucking a stray hair behind her ear. The look in his eyes said he was serious.

Nora didn't argue any further. Honestly, she was glad she didn't have to spend the night alone again. Glad that Jake would be there to take care of her.

CHAPTER

14

Jake awoke early, with the sun. Nora was still asleep in the loft, and he didn't want to wake her, so he went outside.

She can't do this all on her own, Jake thought, surveying the property.

The wood pile was already half what it was when he'd first dropped her off at the cabin. That was less than a month earlier. He'd witnessed her feeble attempts at chopping wood the day before. As hard as she tried, she hadn't accomplished much. She'd managed to slice off a few slivers of wood from one log. Who knew how long she'd been hacking away at that one piece?

She just couldn't do it on her own. There was too much heavy work that needed to be done and Nora wasn't built for that kind of work.

She needed help, whether she was willing to admit it or not.

* * *

Fresh brewed coffee. The smell was quite possibly the best thing to wake up to in the morning. Especially when someone else got up first and took the liberty of brewing a pot.

The scent wafted up from the wood stove below, filling the loft with the roasted nutty aroma of the coffee. It looked like a scene from a Folgers commercial, Nora waking up, stretching, taking in the heavenly aroma, and smiling contentedly. It really was a great way to wake up.

The only thing that might have made it better would be waking up next to Jake. But he was already gone from the cabin. The only trace he'd left behind was the fresh pot of coffee sitting on the stove.

Nora ran a brush through her hair and then climbed down from the loft, hoping Jake hadn't left without saying goodbye. The night before, he'd proven himself a perfect gentleman and slept on the couch, but not before he'd made his intentions toward her perfectly clear.

She poured herself a cup of coffee before venturing outside to see where he'd gone and what he was up to. She found him by the woodpile. His back was turned to her, so he didn't see her approach. Nora smiled to herself. A flannel shirt lay draped over a stump. He wore only a pair of blue jeans, fitted perfectly to his lean form, accentuating his masculinity. He didn't know she was there, which gave her the perfect opportunity to watch him, to observe him in the wild, in his purest form.

The ax swung back. Then forward with a swift force, slicing easily into the piece of wood, splitting it perfectly down the center. The pieces fell off the chopping block, onto the ground that was already littered with dozens of other split logs.

Jake bent forward and positioned another piece of wood on end on the chopping block. Again, the ax swung back, his powerful arms an extension of the rudimentary tool. They were one, he and the ax, working like a fine tuned machine, both hard and strong.

In spite of the cool temperature, beads of sweat were beginning to form on his skin. They glistened in the sun, dripping down his back as his muscles worked in perfect unity. Muscles defined so clearly. Tensing, pulling, swinging the ax again and again.

A red handkerchief hung part way out of his back pocket. He rested the blade of the ax on the ground long enough to grab the handkerchief, wipe his brow, and stuff it back into his pocket.

Then he went back to work. He split another dozen logs before he leaned the ax against a tree and straightened up, stretching his back. The muscles rippled as he stretched his shoulders one way and then the other.

Nora wondered what it would feel like to run her hands over those muscles, to feel them stretched taut. Solid.

Instinctively, she moved toward him.

Jake heard her and turned around.

"Good morning," she said, stopping a few feet away from him.

"It is a good morning, isn't it?" he responded, looking her over. She was wearing a pair of pajama shorts and an oversized t-shirt, sipping from a mug of hot coffee. Her hair was down, flowing over her shoulders in a just-got-out-of-bed way. It was the sexiest thing he'd ever seen.

"Yeah," Nora smiled, realizing how nice it was to wake up and have someone there with her. "I'm glad you stayed the night," she said genuinely.

"Me, too," Jake said, reaching for his shirt and pulling it over his shoulders. He fastened three of the buttons, leaving the rest open.

"You know, you don't have to do this." Nora gestured toward the woodpile. "I can chop more wood anytime."

Jake chuckled and that adorable dimple in his cheek appeared. "I think I do. I saw how long it took for you to split that one piece yesterday."

Nora smiled, knowing all too well that he was right.

"Well, did you want me to run you into town, so you can get that motor fixed?"

"Trying to get rid of me already?"

"No," Nora said. "I thought you might have things to do. Work. Fishing."

"Being here with you right now is a little more important than fishing, and a lot more fun," he said, as he took her hand, pulled her close to him, and lightly kissed her. "Besides, I fixed the motor first thing this morning. It was just a clogged fuel line."

"How early did you get up?"

"A lot earlier than you," he said, leaning down and kissing her again. This time, his kiss left her breathless, dazed.

"Well, what would you like to do today, then?" she asked, willing to do almost anything he asked in that moment.

"You know, I never did get the chance to take you crabbing."

Nora grinned, thinking back to the day when he'd taught her to operate the boat. She'd gotten angry with him and cut the boating lesson short. Oh, how wrong she'd been. She had misjudged him in so many ways.

"You're right," she said. Crabbing wasn't exactly what she had in mind when she asked what he wanted to do, but she didn't care. She just wanted to be with him.

Jake grinned back at her. "I have everything we need in my boat."

An hour later, they were on the other side of the inlet, near the edge of a large cove.

"This looks like a good place to drop a trap," Jake said, cutting the throttle and letting the boat drift on the current. He reached behind his seat and grabbed one of the traps. Then he reached into a cooler, pulled out some bait, and hooked it into the trap. He tied a buoy to the line and dropped the crab cage into the water. Over the course of an hour, they dropped four crab cages in a circular pattern around the cove. By the time they were finished dropping the last one, they were nearly back to the first trap. The buoy marking its location was a few feet away.

At Jake's direction, Nora pulled the line until the trap reached the surface. She was surprised to see two crabs wriggling around in the wire cage.

"Looks like a couple Dungeness crabs," Jake grinned. "Those are my favorite."

Nora looked into the cage, unsure of what to do. It was exciting to pull in her first catch, but she was reluctant to pick a crab out of the cage. She was a little scared one of them would grab hold of her with its pincers. Jake saw her hesitancy and quickly reached in and pulled out the smaller crab. Then he held it out to Nora.

"Here, hold it like this, so it won't pinch you."

She cautiously took it and watched as he picked up the other larger crab. Using both hands, he grabbed the crab's legs in each hand and slammed it hard against the edge of the cooler, knocking off its head. The legs still wiggled as he turned it over and pulled off its genitals and tossed them in the water. Grabbing each side of the crab, he broke it in half down the middle, leaned over the edge of the boat, and shook out each piece to make sure they were clean.

"Your turn," he said.

An amused smile lit up his face as he watched Nora's futile attempts at knocking the crab's head off. She slammed it into the cooler three times without success. After patiently watching, Jake took Nora's hands in his and moved the crab into an angled position, so when she hit it against the edge of the cooler the fourth time, its head popped off easily.

"There," he said. "Now you can see the lungs. We need to pull those out too." Nora watched as he finished cleaning the crab for her. Then he handed it back to her so she could break it in half, just as he'd done with the other one.

"You want to do the next one?"

"Not really," said Nora, feeling squeamish at the idea of pulling the organs and genitals out of a crab with her bare hands. "But I'll give it a try," she added bravely.

The second trap was empty, but the third trap held a large king crab. This time, she pulled it out of the trap on her own. Doing as she had done the first time, she popped its head off. Then she cleaned the crab exactly how Jake had instructed her. *This isn't so bad after all*, she thought, as she tossed the two halves of the crab into the cooler.

Her growing confidence betrayed her on the final trap, though. Just like the other traps, Nora leaned over the edge of the boat and pulled in the line. But this time, the trap caught on something on the way up. Leaning further over the edge, she gave it a firm tug to try and free it. When she did, though, she rocked the boat enough to lose her balance. Jake, focused on keeping the boat from capsizing, didn't have a chance to catch her. Nora let go of the trap line and flailed in an attempt to grab hold of the boat. Her hands found only air before she plunged below the surface of the frigid waters. A second later, she came up gasping for air, her body reeling from the shock of the sudden cold.

Jake acted quickly. He moved to the rear of the boat and grabbed Nora's arm as soon as she resurfaced. Bracing himself in the boat and shifting his weight to keep it steady, he quickly pulled her up out of the water and over the edge of the boat. Before she even sat down, Jake had his jacket off. He wrapped it around her and checked to make sure she was okay, silently cursing himself for letting her pull the last trap in.

Nora shivered. The cold was setting in.

Jake quickly pulled up the empty trap and tossed it into the boat. He took the seat at the rear of the skiff and fired up the motor. The crabbing fun was over. He pointed the boat in the direction of Nora's cabin and opened up the throttle all the way. As soon as the boat struck the sandy bottom of the tidal flats, Jake jumped out and pulled the boat up onto solid ground. He helped Nora out of the boat and took her inside. She was still shivering when Jake helped her up the ladder to the loft. She disappeared behind the curtain and Jake turned toward the wood stove, tossing a few pieces of wood into the stove to get the fire burning hotter.

Up in the loft, Nora stripped off her wet clothes. She quickly dried herself and then put on a warm sweater and a pair of jeans.

"I'm really sorry about that back there," Jake said when Nora crawled down from the loft a few minutes later. He was devastated he'd let something happen to Nora. He was supposed to be teaching her how to survive out there, not how to get herself killed.

Nora moved toward the warmth of the fire. "It's not your fault," she said, embarrassed at how stupid she'd been. She held her hands out over the top of the stove, trying to absorb the heat. "I should have known better than to lean over the edge so far."

"No. I should have been the one pulling the trap in," Jake said, moving closer to Nora. "You just looked like you were having so much fun. I was enjoying watching you and I got careless." He reached up, then, and gently touched her face. "I'm really sorry," he said a second before he brushed his lips lightly against hers.

The touch of his lips against hers sent heat coursing through Nora's body. "Don't worry about it," she whispered, unable to think about anything but the feel of his mouth on hers. His scent was intoxicating. Nora pulled away to catch her breath, to regain her senses. "Can you believe it? A minute ago I was freezing and now I'm starting to sweat. This stove sure heats up the cabin fast."

"Yeah, it does," Jake said, sensing she needed a little space. "I'll go get some water and we can get those crabs cooking."

"I can help..."

"You stay here and get warmed up." He kissed her gently on the forehead, then he pulled a large pot off a hook on the wall above the stove and went outside. From the doorway, she watched him walk toward the water pump. He slung the handle of the pot over the spout and then pumped the lever a few times until the water started flowing.

Nora didn't want him to see her watching him, so she went back inside and began clearing the table. She didn't know what else to do with herself, so she grabbed a stick of butter off the shelf and pulled a small pan off the wall. The pan was a bit dusty, but Nora wiped it with her hands and then set it down on the table. She pulled the paper off the butter, which was already softened from the heat of the stove, and dropped the butter into the pan. She set the pan next to the stove, knowing full well it would melt without the direct heat of the stove.

A moment later, Jake returned and placed the pot of water on top of the cook stove. He set the cooler with the crabs down just inside the door.

"Once the water boils, we'll toss these babies in. Then lunch will be ready in no time."

Nora smiled back at him. "Good," she said. "Because I'm hungry."

Twenty minutes later, Jake announced the crab was ready. Using tongs, he pulled the crabs from the boiling water and dropped them into a large bowl.

Nora washed a couple plates and set the table. Then she looked for something to drink with their lunch.

"Do you think this will go alright with crab?" Nora asked, holding up the bottle of Scotch.

Jake set the plate of crabs down on the table and then looked at the label. When he realized what Nora was holding, he let out a soft whistle. "That will go good with just about anything," he said, taking the bottle from her hands. "Are you sure you want to drink this?"

"Why not?" Nora said, feeling adventurous. "That's what it's made for."

Jake smiled at her and opened the bottle. He held it under his nose for a second to take in the aroma.

"Let's hope this tastes as good as it smells," Jake said. He reached over and pulled two small cups off the shelf then poured a small amount of the dark, amber liquid into each of the cups. He offered one to Nora as he sat down at the table across from her.

Nora took it and looked down into the cup, considering whether she really wanted to try it. She looked to Jake for encouragement. He raised his cup and Nora followed suit.

"To living free," he said. "And surviving the wilderness," he added, taking a drink of the Scotch. She raised the cup to her lips, but took only a tiny sip of the liquid. When it burned on her lips and tongue, the look on Nora's face made Jake laugh.

"I think I'll save this stuff for guests," she said, setting the cup back down on the table.

"You mean all the neighbors that won't leave you alone?"

"Yeah," Nora said, playing along. "I can't seem to find any peace and quiet out here."

They both laughed.

Jake set his glass down on the table and reached for Nora's hand. "So, what did you think of our first date?" he asked sincerely.

"That was a date?"

"It's what passes for dating around here."

"Jake, if you think crabbing is a date, you need to get out more often," she said.

"Well, then, how about a real date next time?"

"What did you have in mind?"

"The Summer Solstice Festival. It's a few days away. Come with me."

Nora thought about it for a second. "Can I wear heels and leave these ugly brown boots at home?"

"Sorry. The rubber boots are part of the deal," he said.

"Well, how can I say no to that?"

"Don't even try," he said, leaning in and kissing her softly.

CHAPTER

15

It was strange how Nora's daily life had shifted so dramatically. Everything she did now was dictated by the tides instead of a clock. Before hopping in the skiff for a run into town, she always consulted the little red booklet sitting on her table to see when the tide would be high. She'd quickly learned most things were easier at high tide, when there was less chance of getting hung up on the rocks that lurked below the surface of the water, posing a risk to someone like Nora, who still had a lot to learn about the nuances of the inlet. It also helped that the ramp to the store's dock had a less steep incline at high tide.

But Nora wasn't going to the store. She was headed to a small beach a few hundred yards past Heron Bay, to the site of the Summer Solstice Festival. She intentionally timed her arrival in town with the low tide, when the beach would be exposed and she could easily unload her boat.

She was early. It was a little past 8 o'clock in the morning and the festival wasn't set to officially begin for another hour.

Because of the low tide, she made her way up the inlet cautiously. She made sure to keep the boat in the deepest part of the water, where she knew there were no rocks under the surface waiting to tear a gash into the aging aluminum of the tiny boat. Right around the halfway mark on her way into town, the waterway made a sharp twist to the right. As she maneuvered the boat, keeping it along the center of the channel, she looked back at the wake she had created behind her and turned the throttle slightly. She knew this area of the inlet better, and had no worries about underwater obstacles. As she turned her attention back toward the stern, though, she caught a glimpse of black skimming the surface. *A massive rock*, she thought, *and only a couple feet away from the boat.* Nora had been certain this area was deep and clear, but as she quickly turned the boat away from its collision course with the rock, it disappeared. Not a rock, she realized, but a whale. She'd seen a few in the inlet, but always from the shore. Never had she been that close to one. The sight left her in awe, but also unnerved her. She nervously secured the clips on her life jacket and increased the throttle, anxious to reach town and get out of the water.

A few short minutes later, the town came into view. Nora motored past the harbor and turned into a small cove on the north side of the community. She cut the engine and let the boat drift up to the shore.

When the bottom of the skiff scraped the sandy ground, Nora jumped out. She quickly grabbed her supplies out of the skiff, placing them on the damp rocky beach that would be covered in several feet of water in a few hours. She hadn't brought much into town with her, only a tote bag filled with a throw blanket and extra clothes, a folding chair, and a small cooler.

There wasn't a dock on the beach, but there was something she'd heard other people call an "out-haul." Two other small boats were already hooked up to the out-haul system, which consisted of a long rope connected to two pulleys, one on land and one further out in the water. Picking up the heavy rope off the ground, Nora pulled the two other skiffs toward land. Then she tied her boat to the rope next to one of the other skiffs. Gripping the rope of the out-haul, she used the pulley system to tow the skiff, and the other two boats, back out into deeper waters.

It was a simple system. It kept the boats in deep water so they never ended up stranded on the beach. And no matter how high or low the tide was, the boats were always within reach, by pulling the rope and hauling them in.

With that task complete, Nora stood up and stretched her back muscles. They ached after the half-hour skiff ride. But she completely forgot about her minor aches and pains as she watched the boats bob up and down on the waves. The clouds had started to scatter and rays of sunlight shot down onto the water. On the other side of the inlet, the sun was starting to illuminate the mountains, some of which still sparkled white at the peaks with mounds of winter snow that had yet to melt. Nora smiled at the pure beauty that always surrounded her, thankful to be there.

The water lapping at her feet reminded Nora the tide was starting to come in and she needed to get her stuff to solid ground. She turned around and slung the tote bag over her shoulder. Then she tucked the folding chair under one arm and carried the cooler in her other hand toward the festival grounds, which were already buzzing with activity.

Not far from where she moored her boat, Nora saw a stone stage, freshly built. She set her folding chair up a few feet from the stage, tossed her tote bag in the chair, and left her cooler sitting on the ground next to it. Only a few days before, the area had been overrun with blueberry bushes and forest undergrowth. Up close, she couldn't help but appreciate the skill and effort that went into building the stage. Those stones weren't brought in by boat. Those stones were hewn on the island. It absolutely amazed Nora that volunteers had not only cut and hauled those rocks a few days before, but they also did such an expert job of fitting them together. But when a few determined people got together in the bush, they could accomplish almost anything, Nora had come to realize.

Distracted by the beautiful stone platform, she barely even noticed the guitarist sitting on the edge, tuning up his guitar and getting ready to perform. So it startled her when he started playing an original piece a few seconds later. Lily had said this festival was a big deal, but Nora hadn't expected things to get underway quite so soon. She thought she'd gotten there early, but she quickly realized the town had already been celebrating for a couple hours. A chalkboard next to the stage listed the schedule of events – the young guitarist was actually the third performer of the morning.

She looked around for a familiar face and it didn't take her long to realize they were all familiar. Even though she still couldn't remember all of their names, Nora recognized every single person there and they all greeted her with smiles and waves.

Already, she got the feeling festivals in the bush played a much more important role than the ones she had attended back home. Those ones from the past were always crammed with thousands of people, complete strangers. All those people, nameless faces, wandering around from one booth to the next, eating cotton candy from vendors and leaving trash everywhere. Those festivals held a certain feeling of anonymity. Nora had always been just a face in the crowd and everyone had seemed to be having a better time than her. But in Heron, a festival really was an occasion. And it looked like almost everyone turned out for the Summer Solstice festivities.

As the young musician wrapped up his performance, Nora

walked around the stage, toward a long table set up alongside a grill. The table was quickly being filled with food. It looked like everyone brought a dish to pass – actually most brought several dishes to pass – and Nora realized she'd completely forgotten to bring something to share. The buffet table held platters of smoked salmon, fresh salmon, shrimp, Dungeness crab, crab cakes, and clams. It was all fresh out of the inlet. So fresh that a couple buckets of live crabs sat near the table, right next to a pot of boiling water, ready to be cooked up on demand. Another table overflowed with side dishes and desserts of all kinds.

These people know how to eat, and eat well, Nora thought, surveying everything as she walked past the buffet table. Given that it was still quite early in the day, only a handful of people had started eating off the buffet.

She spotted Lars, the dockworker, a few feet away digging a trench. When he saw Nora, he stopped digging and stuck the end of his shovel into the ground so it stood upright. He wiped the sweat off his forehead with his arm sleeve as he walked toward her with a smile.

"So, you found the place, eh?"

"Not hard to find, really," Nora responded with a smile. "I just followed the smell of all this food. I'm not even hungry, but I'm thinking about digging in right now. It all looks and smells so good."

As Nora talked with Lars, she realized she couldn't stop smiling. It wasn't Lars that made her smile, but everything going on around her. The sights, the sounds, the smells, the constant activity, warmed her inside. The smile on her face came without any effort. She was genuinely happy there, among the people of Heron.

"Hey, Lars, we need some help with this," someone called from the other side of the trench, interrupting their conversation.

"Well, I gotta get this hole dug. Tug-o'-war is the most popular event," Lars said, gesturing toward what was to become a mud pit.

Barbara from the post office approached as Lars walked away. She introduced Nora to her daughter, Aspen, who had flown in that morning on the float plane with the mail. Before she knew it, Barbara left the two of them alone and went off to visit with someone else nearby. Nora stood there awkwardly for a moment, looking around and wondering what to do or say. Aspen, it turned out, had plenty to say. After only a moment's hesitation she started jabbering about how much she loved visiting the little town.

"I'm so glad to be back here. It's like I haven't even been gone." Within a matter of minutes, Nora found out her political views, which tended toward Republican, and her religious views, which she described as Mother Earth-oriented. Even though Aspen monopolized the conversation, Nora didn't really mind. She liked her, right from the beginning.

"I was born here, if you can believe that. No hospital or anything. Born in my parents' bed, probably on the same mattress they still use. God, I hope they've replaced that old mattress by now, but knowing them…" she trailed off. "Anyway, I moved away not too long after high school. Couldn't stand to stay here for one more minute. Now, it's hard to believe I ever wanted to leave this place. Just look at it."

Looking around at everyone, Nora had to agree with her. This was really a tight-knit community, the first she'd ever actually witnessed.

"Look," she said, pointing through a small clearing of trees at a small, old shack. "Do you see the little brown building that's falling apart? That's where we lived until I was five. Can you believe both of my parents, my two older brothers, and I all lived in that little thing?"

"But it's not any bigger than my cabin, and I feel like I'm

squeezed into a sardine can most of the time."

"Yeah," she said with a laugh. "I don't know how we did it. Probably helped that us kids were all little. But still, my mom must have been tripping over us constantly." A light filled her eyes as she spoke. "You know, I think those were some of the best times of my life, living in that little shack."

She barely stopped talking long enough to breathe.

"You see the house next to it? The one with the porch? My dad built that house while we were living in the cabin. As soon as he had the floor laid down in the living room we moved into the new house. My mom was so happy to have the extra space, she didn't even care the house wasn't finished. She was thrilled to be getting separate bedrooms.

"I think we lived there for a full two years before my dad actually finished it. For the first few months, there weren't even any walls separating the bedrooms. He had the studs in place, but no actual walls.

"Oh, and it was cold in there, too. The first winter, the house still wasn't insulated so we all wore about three layers of clothes and spent most of the time curled up under blankets. It was terrible. All I wanted was to be back in our old house. Silly, huh?"

Nora smiled at her, thinking about her own little cabin and how much more comfortable it was than the big, sterile-feeling home she'd shared with Conner. She understood exactly what Aspen was talking about. Sometimes smaller was better.

"It sure is good to be back here, though. This town is my absolute favorite place in the world."

"So, why did you leave, if you love it so much here?" Nora asked.

"Oh, you know. The usual stuff. I was young and thought I was smarter than everyone else. Mostly, I wanted to get away and experience new things. Anyway, I got pregnant and didn't want to follow in my parents footsteps, so I left."

Aspen told Nora about her son, who she had left in Juneau with her husband. Apparently the seven-year-old preferred to spend his time with his friends back in "civilization" and had no interest in going out to the bush. She hoped that would change as he got older. And of course, her husband had to work so he couldn't come out for the festival even if he wanted to.

"You know, I don't really regret leaving, but I kind of wish Aaron could grow up here. Can't have it both ways, I guess."

As Aspen jabbered on, Nora let her gaze wander. It stopped on the image of Jake making his way through the crowd. He was smiling. Nora noticed the dimple in his cheek, one of the things she liked most about his smile, as he strode toward them.

"There you are," he said. "I've been looking for you." Aspen assumed he was talking to her and immediately flung herself into his arms.

"Jake," she squealed happily as she gave him a long hug. "I haven't seen you in years. It's been way too long."

Nora stood there, awkwardly watching them. When they pulled apart, she saw the smile on Jake's face as Aspen gave him a peck on the cheek. The two had a history together, she could tell. Truth be told, watching them together made her a little jealous.

"Oh, Jake, I've been showing Nora around, since this is her first Summer Solstice Festival. But I'm sure you two have met before, right?"

Jake answered Aspen by moving to Nora's side and wrapping his arm around her waist, letting everybody know Nora was there with him.

"You could say we've been introduced," Jake said, gazing down at her.

"Oh, I see how it is," Aspen said, looking pleased. Maybe Nora's jealousy had been unwarranted. Aspen, it was clear, had no romantic interest in Jake. "You've been holding back, Nora. We've spent the entire morning together and you never thought to mention Jake?" Aspen winked at her and Nora felt her cheeks warming. She hoped no one noticed her blushing.

Someone else drew Aspen's attention, then. She waved to an older man across the way, hollered, "Hey, Sandman!" and hurried away, leaving the two of them alone.

"And she's off," Jake said, smiling after her. Then he turned toward Nora, still grinning. "She always was like that."

"Like what?"

"On to bigger and better things, I guess. Now, shall we get this date started?" he asked, taking her hand. He smiled that make-your-knees-go-weak smile and Nora nodded her head, forgetting about the jealousy she'd felt when Aspen hugged him. "Good. Let's get some lunch. I'm starving."

* * *

Her plate loaded up with shrimp and crab, Nora followed Jake to a wooden picnic table near the edge of the festival grounds. Lily was already there, sitting across the table from Samuel and a woman Nora hadn't met yet. She had the most beautiful white hair Nora had ever seen. The sides were pulled up in barrettes and the rest flowed down her back in long, loose curls. In spite of the white hair, she looked like a woman in her prime, her skin still remarkably smooth and her eyes bright.

"I thought you said you wouldn't be coming this year." The words sounded unusually abrasive coming out of Jake's mouth.

The woman turned and smiled at Jake in spite of his harsh greeting. "Well, I changed my mind. A woman can do that, can't she?"

Then she looked at Nora.

"Ah, this must be Nora," she said, standing up and taking Nora's hand in hers. She held on, clasping both hands around Nora's in a welcoming gesture. "I've heard so much about you... from Lily and from Jake. I'm Madeline," she explained. "Jacob's mom."

Jake's mom. The woman who had left her family.

"Oh," Nora murmured, a little caught off guard at unexpectedly meeting Jake's mother. "It's nice to meet you," she added politely, unsure of the situation.

Madeline returned to her seat beside Samuel. He took her hand in his, lifted it to his mouth, and lightly kissed the back of her hand. Lily had said they weren't divorced, but Nora had a hard time understanding how Samuel could be so loving toward a woman who had left him years ago, a woman who still refused to come back to him.

Nora sat down next to Jake, whose eyes were cast downward, unwilling to look up at his mother. That's when Nora noticed the chatter around them had died down to nearly complete quiet. Some of the people nearby stared uneasily at them. Nora saw one woman nudge another and point, whispering something inaudible. Samuel and Madeline acted as though they didn't notice the whispers or the stares, though they both picked up on the sudden shift in everyone's attention, as well.

Madeline chuckled quietly. "Well, this is a little uncomfortable, now isn't it?" she whispered to Samuel. "Some things never change, I guess."

Samuel smiled at her, a smile that seemed to be more consoling than anything.

Nora didn't even try to hide the confusion she felt and she couldn't help but ask. "Why is everybody staring?"

Madeline tried to laugh it off, but the uneasiness in her voice betrayed her. "They haven't seen us together in a very long time. Don't worry about it, dear."

The meal passed in an awkward silence, everyone acutely aware they were the center of attention. Nora ate a few bites, noticing Jake seemed to be in a hurry to finish. He didn't look comfortable there, sitting across from his parents, as he quietly shoveled the food into his mouth and swallowed without hardly chewing.

When they were finished, Jake picked up her empty plate and stacked it with the others.

"Come on," Jake said, eager to get away from the spectacle his parents had become. "Let's dance."

He took her hand and led her toward a clearing near the stage.

"Are you going to tell me what that was all about back there?" Nora asked as Jake wrapped his arms around her waist and began leading her in a slow dance. A few others were dancing to the slow melody of a two-man band, letting the soft chords move them. "I thought you got along with your mom. That's why you went to Juneau, right? To spend time with her."

Jake looked away, back in the direction of the picnic table where his parents still sat eating.

"I do," he said. "It's complicated."

"Complicated?" Nora looked him squarely in the eyes, reached up and gently turned his face so he had to look at her, too. "That's not an answer."

He sighed and shook his head. Nora wasn't going to let him off the hook.

"I do get along with her. She's my mom. I love her." He hesitated for a moment, trying to figure out how to explain it. "It's just that when she comes back around, I feel like she's leading him on. She has no intention of staying here. But every time she comes back, he falls into her trap again. It's better if they stay apart."

"Better for who?" Nora asked softly.

"Look, I really don't want to talk about this right now," Jake said. "Can't we just dance?"

"Okay," she said reluctantly. "If that's what you want." She didn't ask any more questions or push him for further explanation. Instead, she closed her eyes and enjoyed the feel of his arms around her. She let the rhythm of the music move her until she forgot about the tension between Jake and his mother, until all she noticed was the way their bodies moved together on the dance floor.

The slow song was followed by a fast-paced duet of two finger-picking guitarists. Then four young men, who looked to be in their teens, got up on the stage with their guitars and started playing something they'd made up the same day. By the time their 15-minute piece ended, Nora needed to take a break.

"I need something to drink," she said, laughing. In spite of the earlier tension, she was having a great time. "Will you excuse me for a minute? I'll be right back."

Nora made her way through the crowd toward the far end of the festival grounds where a drink stand had been set up. The sounds of the festival quieted as she got further away from the music, the dancing, and the games. On the outskirts, the festival was nothing more than a faint noise in the distance.

She stopped when she heard two voices nearby, on the other side of the drink stand. They were voices she recognized.

"Stay here," she heard Samuel plead. "Just for the week."

They didn't know she was there.

"No. I have obligations at home."

"That's not your home. This is your home. It always has been." Nora heard the pain in Samuel's voice.

"Don't, Samuel. We've been through this before. I can't stay here. I won't. This place sucks the life out of me."

She touched his hand then. Smiled at him sadly.

"You could come back with me, you know. The kids are grown. They have their own lives..."

This time it was Samuel who refused. "No. I'm staying here, where I belong. We have a home here, a life. I can't leave it behind."

"Then I guess we're at an impasse, aren't we?"

"Yeah, I guess so."

Madeline walked away, leaving Samuel behind. Exactly as she'd done years before. It broke Nora's heart to see him go through it all over again. Maybe Jake was right. Maybe they should be apart.

Nora waited behind the drink stand until Samuel left, as well. She didn't want to embarrass him by letting him know she'd heard everything. When she was certain he was gone, she discreetly stepped out of the shadows and headed back toward the festival grounds.

The dance floor was busier now. Nora stood on the edge of the dance floor, watching Jake twirl Lily around, when Madeline appeared by her side.

"Come, dear. Walk with me for a while." It wasn't a request, Nora realized, as Madeline took Nora's hand, tucked it around her arm, and led her away from the dance floor.

"It's strange being back here. It's like I haven't even been gone." She didn't sound wistful, the way Aspen had earlier. "This place never changes. It's the same old thing, over and over again. The same people having the same petty arguments. The same routine day in and day out. I think that's why I had to get out."

"Why are you telling me this?" Nora asked.

Madeline stopped walking and turned to look at Nora. "Because I see a bit of me in you."

"But you don't even know me. We met an hour ago and we've

barely spoken to each other."

"I know enough. I know you come from a very different background. I know every day here is a struggle for you. In those respects, we are alike."

"I'm nothing like you." *I would never leave my family behind*, Nora wanted to scream at her.

"You are, in all the ways that matter," she said softly. "You don't know what it's like when the winter sets in, when there's no way out. I'm not sure you'll truly be happy here, and I don't want to see my Jake get hurt. He's been hesitant to trust women in the past. I think that's my fault. I don't want to see you lead him down a path he may never recover from."

Madeline squeezed Nora's hand and then left her there alone. The older woman's words still echoed in Nora's mind when Jake found her a few minutes later.

"There you are," said Jake, grabbing her hand and pulling her close to him. "I thought maybe you'd gotten lost."

"No, not lost." She stood up on her tip-toes and kissed him lightly, trying to force Madeline's words out of her mind. "I'm exactly where I belong." She hoped she was telling the truth.

CHAPTER

16

A bright light shined in Nora's eyes and she briefly opened them before pulling the covers up over her head to block out the sun. She was still tired and didn't want to get up. But then her half-conscious mind started working and she opened her eyes in alarm. Tossing the covers off and sitting upright in the bed, Nora realized she had no idea where she was. She rubbed her eyes, trying to remember where she was and how she had gotten there.

Nothing.

The last thing she remembered was watching the sunrise over the cove. That would have been around 4 a.m. Wait, she remembered having cocktails for breakfast. She drank three of the deliciously sweet drinks before Lily told her there was alcohol in them.

After that, things got a little foggy.

Did she actually get up on the stage and sing? She groaned at the memory, faint as it was. Nora was definitely not a singer. She vaguely recalled she and Jake had danced for a while. But she couldn't remember anything else.

Still feeling disoriented, Nora looked around the room. No clock. She had no idea how long she'd slept. The bright sunshine filtered in through the sheer curtains. Still daylight, so she must not have slept too long.

Then the door opened and Jake walked in, looking remarkably fresh for someone who had been up for almost two days straight. Unless he had slept, as well. Nora quickly surveyed the bed, looking for an indentation that would give her an indication of whether Jake had slept beside her. Of the two pillows on the bed, Nora's was the only one disturbed.

"Good morning," Jake said, looking at her curiously. "Looking for something?"

"Um, no," she said, slightly embarrassed she still couldn't remember how she had gotten there. Thankfully, she was still fully clothed, so that was one less thing she had to wonder about. "Did you say 'morning'?" Nora was sure it had to be afternoon.

He chuckled. "Yeah. You've been sleeping..." he paused to look at his watch, "for about 17 hours."

"You're kidding," she said mortified.

"Nope. I carried you back here right after lunch yesterday."

"Carried?"

"Well, you walked part of the way, but since you were having trouble standing, I picked you up and carried you the rest of the way." She laid back down and pulled the covers over her head, then, completely embarrassed.

"Oh, I'm so sorry," Nora said from beneath the covers. She pulled the covers back slightly to peek out from underneath at him. He was leaning casually against the dresser, sipping a cup of coffee.

"Don't worry about it. We've all been there at one time or another," he said. Then he gestured toward the door. "I made some coffee and toast. Join me for some breakfast?"

She sat back up in bed and smiled weakly at him. "Sure. I'll be right out. Give me a minute, okay?"

"Take your time," he said, turning and leaving the room.

A few minutes later, she found Jake in the kitchen, sitting at the table spreading homemade blueberry jam on a slice of toast. A cup of coffee and a plate sat on the opposite side of the table, waiting for her. Nora sat down across from Jake, hoping she didn't look too dreadful.

"Thank you… for everything," she said as she picked up the coffee cup and tentatively took a sip of the hot liquid. "This is good," she said, sounding more surprised than she intended. Nora took another, longer drink.

"Can't believe I can make a decent cup of coffee? Shocking, isn't it?"

The smile on his face told Nora he was teasing her and she smiled back. "I actually expected a cup of sludge. Are these freshly ground beans?"

"Of course," he said, smiling at her delight in the coffee. "You know, my skills don't end with coffee. I make a mean flat bread pizza. If you stick around for dinner, I might impress you."

"We'll see," was all she said, but the corners of her mouth turned up just a little as she looked at him coyly.

He raised an eyebrow. "We'll see, huh?" Scooting his chair around the table so he sat right next to her, Jake leaned in close. Real close.

"I already know how you feel about the coffee, but you haven't even tried the toast and jam." He was so close Nora could feel his breath on her neck. Her skin broke out in goose bumps and Nora's breath caught in her throat for a moment. That's what Jake wanted. He felt like flirting and he liked seeing Nora squirm.

He was so close to her Nora didn't dare turn her head to look at him. If she did, she knew their lips would touch and she might not be able to control herself. A simple kiss didn't seem like much, but when it came to Jake, she was never content with a single kiss.

Very meticulously, Nora spread the blueberry jam on the toast, trying to ignore Jake's close proximity. As if he wasn't close enough to her, Jake scooted his chair even closer and leaned in to her ear. He whispered ever so quietly, "I have many hidden talents, you know." He said it so seductively, Nora forgot about the toast in her hand. She turned her head to look at him and before she knew it his lips were on hers, kissing her lightly, gently. His lips were strong and commanding and... gone before she knew it. She didn't even have a chance to respond to the kiss before Jake pulled away. "The jam, I mean. That's one of my hidden talents. I made it last fall." He was teasing her, she realized. And, what's more, she liked it.

He stood up, then, and walked over to the sink with his empty plate. Nora turned back to the toast in her hand and took a bite. The jam did taste good. Too good. Just like Jake.

It would be way too easy to fall in love with him, and that might be a bad thing. So far, they had kissed a handful of times and it was fantastic. Nora couldn't deny the attraction she felt toward him. He was everything a man should be. Strong. Masculine. Kind. Gentle. But after her encounter with Madeline, Nora wasn't sure if a relationship was a good idea. What if Madeline was right and Nora really didn't belong in a small bush community?

She glanced up at him. He was standing next to the sink, leaning back against the cabinets, watching her. He looked... content.

"Oh, Nora," said Lily excitedly as she walked into the kitchen. "I didn't realize you spent the night." She went to the sink, slugged Jake playfully on the arm, and filled herself a glass of water. "So, did you have a good time?" she asked, grinning expectantly at

Nora, wanting to hear the juicy details.

Oh, no. Lily thinks we slept together. Everyone is going to think we slept together. Nora was mortified. She needed to leave before Samuel woke up, too.

"Um, I should probably get going," she blurted out awkwardly then. She stood up, without saying anything else, and walked out of the kitchen.

"Was it something I said?" Lily turned to Jake.

"I don't know. I don't think so."

Jake followed Nora through the house and stopped her at the front door.

"What's going on?" he asked, sincerely confused.

"I just need to go," Nora explained. "My stuff... the cooler and chair... do you know...?"

"I brought everything back here," he said before Nora finished her sentence. Then he grabbed a light jacket off a peg on the wall and opened the door. "Come on. I'll carry your things to the boat."

Outside, the cooler and chair sat on the front porch. Jake grabbed them both and started toward the beach. Nora followed in silence a few steps behind him. When they reached the shore, he picked up the heavy rope lying on the ground and hauled her skiff in from the deeper waters, then he loaded her things into the boat and turned to Nora.

"Are you sure you have to go?" he asked. Jake didn't know what had gone wrong, but he wanted the chance to make it right. "I was hoping you'd stick around a little longer."

Nora didn't want to encourage him, but he looked so hopeful. One look at his face and she knew she'd have a hard time denying this man anything he asked of her. That was precisely why she had to stand firm and leave right now. This thing between them shouldn't go any further. It had already gone too far.

But the faint pleading sound in his voice tugged at her heart.

Her resolve wavered.

"I guess I don't have to leave yet." she assented.

He smiled, delighted. "Good. I was hoping you'd say that because I was planning to show you something."

"What?"

"You'll have to wait and see," was all he said, but he took her hand and wrapped it around his arm, then led Nora away from the beach. They stopped back at the house long enough for him to run in and grab a rifle and a small backpack, both of which he slung over his shoulder. Then they followed the boardwalk inland, past about a dozen houses. After about a quarter-mile, the boardwalk ended abruptly. There was nowhere else to go. Nothing but trees all around them.

"Well, that was a nice walk. Shall we turn around?"

"We're not done yet," he responded, climbing over the railing and jumping down about three feet onto the squishy ground below. "Come on. Climb over. I'll help you down."

"Are you kidding?"

"No," he said, holding out a hand to her. "Come on."

Reluctantly, Nora stepped up onto the lower slat of the railing, swung one leg over, and then the other.

"Where are we going?" she asked after she jumped down onto the ground.

He grinned. "Follow me and you'll find out." He took a small round bell out of his pocket and hooked it on the belt loop of his blue jeans. Then he took Nora's hand in his and led her toward a narrow path worn through the forest. The bell jingled and jangled with each step he took.

The trail was only wide enough for one person, but it was obviously used often enough because the ground was well worn. They followed it through thick undergrowth, weaving back and forth, continually upward.

214

As they continued onward, Nora's legs began to ache from the strain of what had become an uphill climb. But she didn't want to admit how out-of-shape she was, so she didn't ask Jake if they could take a break. Her pace slowed, though. Jake noticed she was getting tired, so he stopped and turned to her.

"Let's rest here for a minute," he said. "We're about halfway there, so this is a good spot."

"Where are we going, anyway?" Nora asked as she sat down on a large boulder beside the trail, thankful for the chance to catch her breath.

"Up the mountain," he said matter-of-factly. "I thought that would have been evident by now. Not far up the path there's a clearing with a really nice view of the inlet. I think you'll like it."

"So what's with the bell?" she asked.

"Bear bell," he explained. "Let's 'em know we're coming… so we don't accidentally sneak up on one."

"Does it work?"

Jake shrugged. "Maybe. Maybe not."

The thought of bears alarmed her slightly, bringing back memories of her own encounter with the bear only a week earlier. "Are there a lot of bears up here?"

"I've never seen one on the trail, but you never know," he said, trying to ease her mind. "And if we do run into one," he reached into his pocket and pulled out a canister, "I have bear spray. You can carry it if you want. But be careful you don't spray it at yourself. It burns like you wouldn't believe."

"So, let me get this straight. We've been tromping though bear infested forest and you're just now offering to let me carry the bear spray? What if we'd run into a bear? I was completely defenseless, not to mention oblivious to the fact we might even see a bear."

Jake chuckled at her. "Oblivious? By now you should know

better," he teased.

Nora smiled. Jake had a point. But Nora hadn't known where they were going, either. The entire hike she figured their destination was around the next bend. She certainly didn't think they were going to hike to the top of the mountain.

"You're right," Nora said, standing up. "I should know better. Just like I should know better than to go anywhere with you." She was teasing now.

Nora grinned at him and walked past him.

"Are you sure you want to lead the way? You don't know where you're going."

"We're just following the path, right? Shouldn't be too hard." She tried to sound more confident than she really was. To be honest, the mention of bears had put her on edge, but she didn't want Jake to notice.

"Okay," he said from a few feet behind her. "Lead the way."

Continuing upward, the hike was slower with Nora in the lead. For one thing, she was less sure of her footing and unfamiliar with the trail. More than once, she almost lost the path when they reached a switchback, but thankfully Jake pointed her in the right direction each time.

When she reached a fork in the trail, she stopped and turned to Jake.

"Which way?" she asked.

He smiled. "Hmm?" He was feeling playful again.

"Which way do I go?"

"Which way do you think we should go?" he answered her question with another question, grinning at her with a look of mock innocence. Nora smiled and raised an eyebrow at him, waiting patiently.

"Follow the trail to the right. They join back up with each other near the summit, but this way is easier," he said.

"Thank you," Nora said with over-exaggerated graciousness. Turning back toward the trail, her foot caught on a rock and Nora lost her balance. Jake swiftly jumped forward and caught her in his arms a second before she would have hit the ground. "Are you alright?" he asked. "Does anything hurt?" He still held her, inches from the ground.

"I... I'm fine," Nora said. She was fine, except for the severe embarrassment and wounded pride.

"You're sure?" he asked again as he lifted her back up onto her feet. He still didn't release his grip on her and she didn't try to pull away. She looked up at him and nodded. "Yeah. I'm okay." He held her close, reluctant to release her from his embrace, and brushed a stray hair away from her face.

Nora was still stunned at how quickly he reacted. She could have seriously injured herself if she'd fallen on the jagged rocks along the trail. But he caught her in the nick of time. She gazed up at him.

"Th-thank you." Those were the only words that escaped her lips before Jake covered her mouth with his own. This time, Jake kissed her long and hard. Nora had no choice but to kiss him back. She didn't want to do anything else. She completely forgot her misgivings about getting involved with Jake. She didn't care. His kiss felt so good. Her body responded instinctively and when he pulled away, she found herself wanting more.

And then Jake brought them back to reality.

"Maybe I shouldn't have brought you up here. The trail can be treacherous in some spots," he said. "Do you want to turn back?"

She'd never thought of herself as clumsy before, but it was becoming more and more apparent to her that she had a tendency to trip over rocks, fall out of boats, and slip in creeks. The great outdoors was unforgiving, and Nora seemed to be rather accident-prone. But she didn't want her incompetence to keep her from seeing that view Jake had mentioned.

"No. Let's finish this hike," she said, more determined than ever. "I'm looking forward to the view from up top."

He released her from his embrace then, but kept a tight grip on her hand. Then he smiled at her and resumed the lead position. "The view is great," he said over his shoulder as he started back up the trail. "But that's not what we're going up there for."

"You're not going to tell me, are you?"

"Nope."

Nora followed closely behind him. Jake moved much slower now, making sure she had good footing with each step and holding her hand for support. Even though they were only a short distance from the alpine meadows of the mountaintop, it took nearly a half-hour before they emerged from the forest and the trail opened up to a grassy expanse. Nora turned around to take in the view of the inlet and the other mountains that seemed so much smaller from up there.

"Beautiful, isn't it?" Jake said.

She had no words to describe it. She felt like she was on top of the world. The buildings in the tiny town below were mere specks. Everything looked so peaceful.

"Come on. We're not done yet."

Nora turned to follow him. The peak of the mountain still stood at least another 200 feet above them, by her best guess.

"Are we going all the way to the top?"

"We could if you want, but I had something else in mind," Jake said, veering off the path and heading toward the south side of the peak. He stopped for a second and looked at Nora expectantly, waiting to see if she really did want to hike the rest of the way up.

"This is close enough to the top for me," Nora said, smiling. "I don't need to stand on the summit."

Jake grinned at her. "Alright, then. Follow me."

Nora willingly obeyed, following him off the path and through the tall grass. As she followed him, she found herself looking around, taking in the sweeping views of the inlet and wondering if she would be able to see her own cabin. Of course not, she realized. If she couldn't see this peak from her cabin, then surely she wouldn't be able to see the cabin from the mountaintop.

The sound of an engine caught Nora's attention and she stopped to watch a float plane descend into the inlet. Like a bird, it swooped down toward the water and skimmed the surface until it came to rest on the water next to one of the docks by The General Store. The only way she knew it was the store was because it sat on the far end of town and was surrounded by a large dock. From this distance, the building was nothing more than a small rectangle and the plane really did look like a bird off in the distance. Almost at the same time the first plane landed on the water, a second float plane revved up its engine and took off from the inlet. Looking around, Nora saw at least one other plane in the air, heading toward the small town.

"Tourists," Jake said. He was watching her as she watched the float planes coming and going. "It's that time of year."

"Is it always like this in the summer?" Nora couldn't help but ask. The town was so small, she couldn't imagine it being able to handle hordes of visitors. "The Rainforest Lodge can't possibly be big enough for that many people. Where do they all stay?"

"It doesn't get too bad," Jake said. "There are seven… no, eight… lodges in town. Plus another one a few miles north."

"Eight lodges?" She walked past the Rainforest Lodge almost every time she came into town, but she had no idea there were so many others. "Where are they, hidden in the trees?"

Jake smiled, realizing she still had a lot to learn. "They're all mom-and-pop places. You pass by them all the time. About a quarter of the houses in Heron are technically lodges. It's how a lot of the people here make a living… at least, when they're not fishing."

"But what brings them here? The tourists, I mean." Nora shook her head. "Wait, that didn't sound right. This place is beautiful. It's obvious what brings them here. What I don't understand is, of all places in Alaska, how do they find out about this little town?"

"Well, what brought you here?" Jake asked her in all seriousness.

"But I'm not a tourist."

He chuckled. "For the time being, you are. Everyone in town is still waiting to see how long you'll stick around. Most are betting you'll be gone before autumn."

"That's encouraging," Nora said sourly.

Jake smiled at her again. "Hey, don't worry about it. I'm betting you'll at least make it through the winter." He was teasing her. "The way I figure it, you'll be determined to make a go of it here. By the time you realize you were crazy to spend a winter in the bush, you'll be snowed in and won't be able to leave until spring, anyway."

Nora smiled back at him. "You know, I might surprise everyone and stay here forever."

"I'm counting on it," Jake said sincerely, hoping she wouldn't change her mind further down the road. Then he turned and started walking again. "Come on, it's not much farther now." He sincerely hoped Nora planned to stay for good, but somewhere in the back of his mind he still had his doubts. Not for the first time, Jake wondered how smart it was to fall for the new girl in town. There was no doubt, though, he was falling for her.

When the terrain grew rocky, Jake took Nora's hand again. He led her through a narrow passageway between two large boulders. As they reached the opening, Jake stepped off to the side, affording Nora her first look at a hidden lake. The sight nearly took her breath away and she let out a small gasp. Nestled above the tree-line and surrounded by large boulders, the lake sat perfectly undisturbed. The surface was so smooth and reflected the mountains so clearly that Nora had a hard time distinguishing where one ended and the other began.

Along the northern shore of the lake sat a small cabin, built by the U.S. Forest Service as a recreational cabin for back country hikers.

"This is incredible," Nora said, unable to tear her eyes away from the sight.

Jake agreed. "I know. I've been coming here since I was a kid."

"Is this what we came up here for?" she asked.

"Yep," he said.

He led her to a grassy spot near the lake shore. Then he took his jacket off and spread it out on the ground for Nora to sit on. He laid down on the ground next to her and they spent the early afternoon by the lake. Lying there beside him, Nora felt more content than she ever had in her life. They barely spoke. They were just two people alone on the mountaintop, enjoying the sound of nature around them, listening to each other breathe, basking in the warmth of the sun.

As the afternoon wore on, Nora's stomach grumbled, breaking their silence.

"Listen," Jake said quietly, dramatically. "Did you hear that growl?"

"Umm, hmm."

"Sounds like a bear."

"Very funny." Nora looked over at him and shoved his arm playfully.

"How about a late lunch?" he asked, sitting up. She looked so beautiful, lying there beside the lake. He wanted to stay there, beside her forever. But the day was wearing on and she was obviously getting hungry. So was he. "I did promise you a flat bread pizza if you'd stick around and you definitely held up your end of the bargain."

"It's about time," Nora grinned. "I was beginning to think you were trying to starve me to death."

Jake smiled. "No. I wouldn't want to do that." He grabbed the backpack he'd carried up the mountain and headed toward the USFS cabin. Nora followed him.

The inside of the cabin was primitive, even more so than Nora's cabin, though it was significantly larger. It was one large room with a big wood stove right in the middle of the room. Bunk beds lined one wall. A wooden table and chairs sat along the opposite wall.

"Remind me not to complain about my accommodations when I get back home," Nora said dryly, looking around the cabin.

"It's not so bad." Jake smiled, sitting his backpack down on the table. From the backpack, Jake pulled out a bottle of olive oil, bottled water, and a thermal bag that held a chunk of Parmesan cheese and a chunk of fresh mozzarella.

"You're in for a real treat. This is homemade mozzarella," he said, handing it to Nora. "Go ahead and try it," he encouraged her.

She tore a small piece off and popped it into her mouth. It tasted divine.

"Are you for real? You're not going to tell me you're a closet cheese maker, too, are you? Is there anything you can't do?" she asked incredulously.

He chuckled and shook his head. "No. I can't take credit for that one. Tracy, next door to me, makes it. You've probably seen his goats."

Nora nodded. She had seen them wandering around during the festival.

"I've been buying his cheeses for years. It really pisses Nate off. Cutting into his business, he says. But this is so much better than anything he has at the store."

Jake turned then and opened a cabinet. He pulled out a canister of flour, salt and yeast.

"How did you know that stuff would be there?"

"Everyone keeps the cabin stocked with the essentials. If someone gets stranded up on the mountain, at least they have shelter and some food," he explained. "I brought these up a few weeks ago."

In a matter of minutes, Jake had mixed up some dough and was kneading it on the small wooden table. The muscles in his forearms moved in rhythm and Nora couldn't help but admire his form. He was everything a woman could want... masculine, sexy, and making her dinner.

She watched him, a little envious he was able to make something from scratch without even using a recipe. It seemed to come so naturally to him. Nothing had ever come naturally to Nora. Sure, she had eventually mastered her mother's brownie recipe, but it had taken a lot of trial and error and she still didn't know the recipe by heart. Nora had to work at everything and she still never quite measured up to those around her. But for the first time in her life, when she was around Jake, she felt like she was good enough.

Finished kneading the dough, Jake placed it on a pan, covered it with a towel, and then turned to her. "It'll be a while before I can finish this," he said, looking at her expectantly. "What would you like to do in the meantime?"

Uncontrollably, Nora's thoughts went to the bed on the other side of the room. There were a few things she wouldn't mind doing, but that wouldn't be appropriate, not so early in their relationship. She tried to force those thoughts out of her mind. "I'm not sure," was all she said.

"Well, I was thinking we could go look for some mushrooms for the pizza. There's a ridge not far from here where a small forest fire went through last year. It should be a good spot to find some morels. We'd only need a few."

Nora smiled, happy to have an excuse to get out of the house and away from the temptation of the bed.

Jake grabbed two small canvas bags from one of the cabinets and led her out the back door. Walking away from the cabin, they passed through a stand of tall pine trees as Jake confidently led the way down a small hill and then back up onto a blackened ridge. The cabin was blocked from Nora's view, but she knew it wasn't more than a few hundred yards away.

"Lightning struck over there," he pointed, "and started the fire last summer. Thankfully, the rain put it out before it got too far." Then he smiled. "I'm actually glad the fire came through, though. Gives me a good spot to find morels. For the next couple years, they'll be growing like crazy right here."

Jake showed Nora how to spot the mushrooms and how to tell which ones were good. She had never done anything like this before in her life, but she found it quite fun to search for the elusive fungus. It was exciting each time she found one. As she picked her third morel, Nora felt a drop of rain hit her arm. Jake felt it too, and looked up at the sky, which only moments before was blue and now was covered in rapidly darkening clouds. One thing he knew all too well was that the weather on top of the mountain could change in an instant. "We better get back now," he said, taking Nora's hand and leading the way toward the mountaintop shelter. Seconds later, the skies unleashed a torrent of rain. By the time they reached the cabin, they were both soaked, but Nora was laughing.

"What's so funny?" Jake had to ask.

Nora shook her head, still giggling. "I don't know. I just feel so alive right now." They stood on the covered porch, safe from the downpour, but Nora felt an overwhelming urge to run back down the steps and stand in the rain. Spontaneously taking Jake's hand, she pulled him back out into the rain. He stood there in awe, watching as she spread her arms out and tossed her head back, welcoming the cool rainwater. Jake couldn't help but be amazed by this woman... everything she did and everything she was.

Then the sky filled with lightning and Jake's better sense kicked in. It wasn't safe to stand out there in a thunderstorm.

"C'mon. We gotta get inside." Nora was still smiling, but she heard the urgency in Jake's voice and she quickly followed him back up to the porch. She stayed outside, under the safety of the porch, while Jake darted inside to find something to dry off with. There wasn't much in the cabin, but he did find a blanket under one of the beds.

When he went back out, he found Nora on the porch swing, happily watching the storm. He wrapped the blanket around her and sat down beside her.

Nora sighed. "Looks like it's going to be a while before we can head back down." There was no trace of disappointment in her voice, Jake noticed.

"Might be stuck up here all night," he said, looking at her so he could gauge her reaction.

She glanced at him, smiled coyly, and then turned her attention back toward the heavy rain. Being stuck in a cabin on the mountaintop with Jake would not be a hardship, not by any means.

Nora pulled the blanket tighter around herself. The chill of the rain was setting in and Jake noticed her discomfort. "Let's go inside," he suggested. "You can watch the storm from the warmth of the cabin, if you want."

"That's a good idea."

When Nora stepped inside, she found the stove had been lit and the fire was rapidly warming the cabin. Still dripping wet, in spite of the blanket Jake had given her, Nora went straight for the wood stove. The fire was hot and her clothes began to dry almost immediately.

"Better?"

She nodded her head. "Much."

"Good."

Jake went to the table and began slicing the mushrooms. Nora watched while he topped the dough with olive oil, mushrooms, and slices of the fresh mozzarella. Then he expertly slid the flat bread onto a pan and took it over to the stove.

"Dinner will be ready soon."

"Good," she said. "Because I'm starving. I believe you promised me lunch, but it's a lot closer to dinnertime now."

Jake chuckled. She was right. "Sorry about that," he conceded.

* * *

"Well, now what?" Nora asked after they had eaten dinner. The rain was still coming down and every few seconds the sky lit up with lightening. The heart of the storm was upon them. They were definitely stuck in the cabin.

"That's what I was going to ask you," he said with a mischievous grin. "I guess we'll have to entertain each other."

"It's a good thing I found a deck of cards." She reached up onto a shelf on the wall and picked up a small cardboard box. She had spotted the deck of cards earlier and thought it would be a safe diversion to help them pass the time away while they were stranded. "I play a mean hand of poker," she added, hoping to entice him into a game.

"Well, I play a mean game of strip poker." Jake meant his

comment as a joke, but as soon as the words were out of his mouth, he regretted them. The last thing he wanted to do was force Nora to strip down to nothing. He'd much rather take her clothes off himself, slowly kissing every part of her body.

Feeling certain she could outplay Jake, Nora decided to take the dare. "You got it," she said confidently. *It might be fun*, Nora thought, thinking about how uncomfortable Jake would feel stripped down to his skivvies.

Jake smiled uneasily. He didn't often find himself in this position, feeling unsure of himself and very much out of control of the situation. He never in a million years would have expected Nora to take him up on a game of strip poker. But Nora always had a way of surprising him.

"Let's keep it simple. Five card draw. Nothing wild," she said, taking immediate command of the situation.

Jake couldn't back down now, so he put on his best poker face instead.

Nora sat down at the table and expertly started shuffling the cards while she waited for Jake to take the seat opposite her. As she shuffled the cards from one hand to the other, Jake started to wonder if he stood a chance with this woman… at cards, that is. Either she put on a really good show, or Jake was in for a world of trouble, he realized as he sat down.

Nora swiftly dealt the cards and then looked expectantly at Jake. This was her first time playing strip poker. "So, how does this work? Do we ante up a sock right off the bat or do you only take something off when you lose a hand?"

Jake was dumbfounded. He'd never actually played strip poker before, either. "House rules," he said, acting confident. "The winner gets to choose which article of clothing the loser takes off." That sounded like a good plan, he thought.

"Alright," she said, in complete agreement with that

arrangement. After all, Nora had no intention of removing any of her clothes.

At first, Jake thought he'd let her win the first hand, so she wouldn't be the first to be forced to take something off. As it turned out, he didn't need to be so kind.

Nora's poker skills became evident to him almost immediately. She won the first hand, laying down a full house to easily beat Jake's two pair.

"I'll go easy on you," she said excitedly following her first victory. "You can start with your belt."

Jake stood up and slid the belt off, laying it on the table between them.

His competitive nature was kicking in. As he sat back down, Jake looked at Nora intensely, trying to wear down some of her confidence. He looked her up and down, hoping to make her uncomfortable and throw Nora off her game. "Yep. I think I know what piece of clothing I'm going to make you take off when I win the next hand," he said with certainty.

Nora raised an eyebrow, unaffected by Jake's remark and even more determined to win every hand. "We'll see," was all she said as she handed the deck to Jake for the next deal. Nora won the next hand, as well, laying down four-of-a-kind to beat Jake's straight. As compensation, she kindly requested Jake's button-up flannel shirt. Unfortunately, Nora's hopes of seeing Jake's rock-hard chest evaporated quickly when he began unbuttoning the shirt, revealing a cotton t-shirt underneath.

After five more hands, Jake's confidence was completely shattered. He lost every hand. Nora sat across from him, grinning. Her delight was evident as Jake handed over his t-shirt. Nora added it to the pile of clothes, which now included the belt, both of his shirts, both socks, and a pair of jeans. Jake sat across from her in nothing but a pair of boxer shorts.

"Well, I think I'm the clear winner here," Nora said happily, not wanting to push it too far. "Shall we call it quits?"

"I would appreciate that," Jake said gratefully. He reached out across the table, then, to take his clothes back.

"Uh, uh," Nora cautioned him, teasing. She grabbed the clothes in her arms and stood up. "These are my winnings. You don't get them back."

Naturally, Jake chased after her. Nora squealed when Jake caught her from behind and wrapped her in his arms. Holding the clothes out, she struggled to keep them away from him. "You can't have them," she said, liking this little game. She was determined not to give the clothes back and thoroughly enjoyed Jake's effort to retrieve them.

With Nora in his arms, though, Jake forgot about the clothes. "That's not what I want," he whispered huskily into her ear. Nora stopped struggling, then, and turned to face him. In his eyes, she saw an intense burning desire. She felt it, too. His dark blue eyes captivated her. Lost in his gaze, Nora found herself letting go of her inhibitions and choosing to give herself to Jake.

"What is it you want?" she asked, barely a whisper.

"You," he said as his mouth closed over hers. Distracted, Nora let go of the clothes and they dropped to the floor. The taste of his lips ignited a passion inside Nora she'd never felt before. She wanted him like she'd never wanted any man. And she knew in that moment, if Jake wanted her, too, she would give herself to him completely, right then and there.

The spark between them was intense, maybe too intense. If the kiss lasted even a second longer, he wouldn't be able to control himself. He wouldn't be able to stop. He had to be certain this was what she wanted.

"Are you sure about this?" he asked.

"Yes," she said, deepening the kiss.

It felt so right holding Nora in his arms. Their bodies fit together perfectly, he realized, as he ran his hands through her hair, lightly touching her neck and then tracing the length of her collarbone. She was the most beautiful woman he'd ever known and by far the most intriguing. His lips moved naturally from her mouth to her neck then her shoulder. He wanted to taste her, every bit of her.

When his hands moved down to her waist and gripped the bottom of her blouse, Nora let him pull the shirt up over her head. She heard the sharp intake of Jake's breath as his gaze moved downward and he realized she wasn't wearing a bra. Instinctively, his hands moved toward the soft flesh. He kissed her, hard. He left her breathless and wanting more. Nora moaned from the sensation as a warmth spread throughout her body. An ache, a longing, began to well up inside of her.

"Jake…" His name barely escaped her lips.

"Yes?" he asked, his voice husky with arousal.

"I want you…" she whispered.

"I know."

Nora's heart raced when he picked her up in his arms and carried her to the bed. Laying her down, Jake stripped off the rest of his clothes and stretched out beside her. He needed to touch her and to taste her. He needed to be one with her.

Expertly, Jake brought Nora to her climax. Clinging to Jake, her entire body shuddered as waves of pleasure coursed through her. When Jake found his own release, he collapsed on the bed next to Nora and pulled her in close. He planted a kiss on her forehead and then rested his own head next to hers. In the aftermath of their lovemaking, they fell into a contented sleep while the rain beat steadily down on the roof.

* * *

"Is that the sun?"

"Yeah. The storm let up a couple hours ago."

Nora sat up and looked around the room. Jake stood by the stove, adding another piece of wood to the hot coals. A narrow beam of light streamed in through the window and Nora caught a glimpse of blue skies outside.

"What time is it?" she asked.

"I'd guess somewhere around 4 a.m."

Nora groaned and pulled the covers back over her head. "Ugh. It doesn't get light out this early at my cabin."

"That's because you have a mountain blocking the sun for the first three or four hours of the day," Jake said, chuckling. "Just think how much more wood you could chop with those extra hours of daylight."

Still under the covers, Nora rolled her eyes. "Maybe I'll find me a big, strong lumberjack to do all that stuff," she teased.

"A lumberjack is fine, but what you need is a fisherman. Someone who will put food on the table."

"What good is that if I freeze to death?"

Jake laid down next to Nora and wrapped his arms around her. "I'll keep you warm," he said softly, sincerely.

"I suppose I could settle for a fisherman... if he chops wood on the side. But he'd also have to clean the fish, do all the cooking, and wash the dishes afterwards."

"That sounds perfectly reasonable. And what would you do all day?"

Nora thought about it for a minute. "Hmm. Something completely useless."

"You could learn to knit," Jake suggested.

"No." Nora smiled. "You're missing the point. If I learned to knit, then I could make hats and scarves and things we could use. It has to be something useless."

"You could stay in bed all day and be my sex goddess."

Nora smiled and then shoved him playfully. "Be serious," she said. "I'm thinking I could sit on the shore and draw pictures of whales swimming in the inlet."

"Ah, but that could be useful, too. You'd be a local artist and you could sell your drawings to the tourists in the summer. Tourists love that sort of thing."

Nora laughed then. "You haven't seen me draw. Believe me, nobody's going to buy stick-figure drawings of whales, local artist or not."

Jake laughed, too, and pulled her tighter into his arms.

Nora quickly fell back to sleep, but Jake laid there for a long time watching her. What was it about this woman that he found so irresistible? She was the most incredible woman he'd ever met. He didn't know what had brought her to him, but he knew one thing for certain.

"I'm going to marry you," he whispered softly, lightly kissing her forehead.

As Nora drifted off to sleep, she thought she heard Jake say something. *Did he say he was going to marry her?* No, she couldn't have heard it right. That would be crazy. They'd only known each other for a month. Surely she was dreaming.

CHAPTER

17

"I don't want to leave," she said, looking around the cabin one last time. Their night on the mountaintop had been magical. For Nora, it marked the end of her old life and the beginning of something new with Jake. She wanted to stay up there, where the rest of the world didn't exist, where it was just her and Jake.

"You say that now because the sun is shining and everything looks so beautiful from up here," Jake said. "But don't forget last night. Storms like that make it dangerous."

"I was thinking of last night," Nora said, blushing.

Jake smiled. He understood. While the storm had raged on outside, they had made love for the first time... and the second time.

"And now we have to head back to reality," he said.

Nora's smile disappeared. Jake noticed her changed demeanor instantly.

"What's wrong?" he asked.

"Nothing," she said. It was only when Nora thought of going

back down the mountain, back to her cabin, that she remembered the advertisement listing her property for sale. She'd meant to cancel the ad, but she still hadn't gotten the chance. She would have to take care of it when they got back into town. She smiled at him, then. She was glad she'd decided not to sell the property, happy she would be staying in Heron... with Jake. "I think I'll take a walk down by the lake before we leave."

She turned and walked out the door, leaving Jake to finish cleaning up. The rule for using the cabin was to leave it in better shape than you found it, and that's what he was going to do. The bed was made, the floor swept, and the woodpile restocked. Jake left the remaining olive oil in the pantry, along with the other food, then he shuttered the cabin and made sure everything was secure.

Fifteen minutes later, he emerged from the cabin. He saw Nora down by the lake, walking barefoot along the pebbled shore, dipping her toes in the cool water. She held her shoes in one hand and reached down and touched the surface of the water with the other. Jake leaned against the porch railing and silently watched her, amazed at how beautiful she looked at that moment, not wanting to interrupt her explorations. Intuitively, Nora turned and saw him and she smiled at him. Jake's heart leapt at the sight.

Leaning down, Nora put her shoes back on and then trotted toward the cabin. She was happy there, and it felt great. She walked over to Jake and took him by the hand. "I had a great time last night," she said, standing up on her tiptoes to kiss him.

Jake grinned. "So did I," he said. He turned and closed the final shutter on the cabin. Everything was secure. "Are you ready to go?"

"No," she said with one last longing smile at the lake. "But I guess we have no choice."

Jake understood. They'd spent an incredible night together. For a day, it was as if there was no one else in the world. They were two souls connected, alone on a mountaintop. It had been unlike anything he'd ever experienced in his life.

"It's not over," he said, looking into her eyes. "It's just beginning."

He took her by the hand, then, and led her away from the cabin, back toward the mountain trail. The trail was much more treacherous this time, after the heavy rains of the day before, so they took their time going down the mountain. It wasn't just the slippery mud slowing them, but also the thought of leaving the cabin behind. They were both reluctant.

About one-third of the way down, they encountered a problem. The trail was washed out where water and mud had flowed down the mountainside. A muddy slope about eight feet wide cut the trail off completely.

Jake stopped a few feet short of the mudslide, assessing the situation. They needed to get across, there were no two ways about it. If they veered off the trail even a little, it would be too easy to get lost. But the mud was slippery and there was no way they would be able to cross without slipping.

"What are we going to do?" Nora asked, looking at Jake for guidance. He'd grown up there, so surely he knew how to get across.

"Give me a second to figure it out," he said. There were a couple rocks that looked solid enough to hold their weight. Jake decided to jump across, using the rocks as footholds to bridge the gap. He made it across easily, then turned to help Nora get across.

She jumped over to the first one and stopped to get her balance. Then she prepared to make a second jump. But the rock beneath her gave way and began sliding downward. Nora lost her balance and fell to the ground.

"Nora," Jake hollered her name as he reached out and tried to grab her. But he was too late. All too quickly, she slid down the mountainside. She couldn't stop herself as she slid downward 20, 30, 40 feet.

When she came to rest, Nora lay at the base of a large tree. She didn't dare move, scared if she did, she would slide further down the mountainside. Her right ankle throbbed and even through the sock Nora could see her ankle was swollen. She must have twisted it when she fell.

Nora was in a tight spot, and she knew it. She couldn't even see the trail anymore. She couldn't walk, and even if she could, getting back to the trail would be nearly impossible with the slick mud.

"Nora," Jake hollered desperately as he left the trail and made his way through the lush undergrowth down the hillside. He couldn't see how far she'd plunged and his heart raced as he dreaded the worst. He shouldn't have let her attempt the crossing. He should have figured out a different way. He called her name again, hoping beyond hope she wasn't too badly injured.

Jake's voice echoed through the trees and even though Nora couldn't see him, she knew he was coming for her. She'd never been so happy to hear another person's voice.

"I'm here," she said, her voice creaking. Jake didn't hear her and he called out her name again. Blocking out the pain and summoning up all of her strength, Nora hollered as loud as she could. "Here," she hollered. "I'm here."

That time, Jake heard her and his heart skipped a beat. She was alive. "I hear you," he hollered back, the relief evident in his voice. He still couldn't see her, but at least he knew where she was. "Stay where you are. I'll come get you."

When he spotted her, he realized that getting her back to the trail was going to be difficult. He spent the next half hour figuring out how to get to her. First he hiked back up the slope until he found a decent path to descend. Then he slowly made his way down at an angle toward Nora. Wedging himself against a tree, Jake reached out and took her by the hand and pulled her across the mudslide toward solid ground.

"Thank God you're okay," Jake said, helping her stand up. Nora stood, placing all of her weight on her good ankle. "You are okay, right?"

Nora nodded, trying not to show her pain. "I think so."

Jake smiled as relief flooded through him. Then he grabbed her up in his arms and kissed her, long and hard. He had been so scared for her, but now he had her back in his arms. She was safe, even if she was a little battered up.

"I'm so sorry," was all Jake could say as he showered her with kisses on her cheeks, her eyelids, her mouth. "It's my fault. I shouldn't have let you try to cross like that." He couldn't stop apologizing.

"It's okay," Nora tried to reassure him. "I'm okay." But he saw her wince even as she said the words. She was obviously in pain, and the sight of her pain cut him to the core.

"What's wrong?" he asked. "Where are you hurt?"

"I sprained my ankle," Nora admitted. "I don't know if I can walk out of here."

"Don't worry," he said. "I'll get you out." Then he picked her up in his arms and carefully made his way downward, working his way back toward the trail.

In spite of the pain, Nora couldn't help but notice how strong he was or how carefully he carried her. The hike back to the trail would have been difficult for a single person. Nora couldn't imagine how hard it must have been for him to carry her over the uneven terrain and through the thick undergrowth. But he never wavered. His strong arms held her securely and his steady feet never slipped a single time.

When they reached the trail again, the going got a little easier for Jake, though he still had to be careful with each step. He didn't want Nora to suffer any more hurt, especially at his hands.

As soon as Jake reached the boardwalk, Nora insisted he put her down. Even though her ankle was still killing her, she suspected Jake was getting tired. He'd been carrying her for well over an hour, across difficult terrain.

Against his better judgment, Jake agreed to let her try walking, but he instantly regretted it. He watched as Nora limped along the long, narrow boardwalk stretching through the trees toward town.

"Let me carry you," said Jake.

"No. I can do this," Nora insisted.

Jake, who only reluctantly let her walk on her own, stayed by her side, ready to catch her at any time. They made it about 50 feet before Nora's ankle gave under her weight and she stumbled forward. Jake quickly caught her and wrapped an arm around her waist to support her. He knew she didn't want him to carry her, but that didn't mean he couldn't help. Wincing at the pain, Nora allowed Jake to steady her, grateful she hadn't fallen flat on her face.

"Enough," Jake said, getting frustrated with her. "You shouldn't be putting any pressure on your ankle, and you know it."

"I can do this on my own," she said more forcefully than she'd intended as she leaned against the railing of the boardwalk and shifted all of her weight to her good ankle.

"Well, I can't stand by and watch. You're in pain. I'm going to carry you whether you like it or not," Jake said. He could be precisely as stubborn as Nora, if he wanted to be. Without another word, he scooped Nora up into his arms again. She struggled at first, but Jake didn't give in. His strength was more than Nora could contend with. Resolutely, Jake carried Nora the rest of the way into town. Wrapping her arms around his neck, Nora settled in and enjoyed the ride. *If I have to be carried, at least I can enjoy the feel of his strong arms around me,* she thought contentedly.

Her contentment turned to embarrassment when they got into town, though, and people saw him carrying her. When Jake turned left onto the boardwalk, taking Nora in the direction opposite her skiff, Nora finally spoke.

"Where are you taking me?"

"I would think that would be obvious," Jake said, looking at her. Her face was so close to his, all he wanted to do was kiss her and make up for letting her get hurt. "I'm taking you to Len's place. Since he's the closest thing we have to a doctor, I thought he should take a look at your ankle."

"But I'm fine," Nora protested. "If you'll put me down, you'll see."

Jake didn't pay any attention. He carried her to a small, gray house squeezed in between the steep mountainside and the boardwalk. He managed to knock on the door without any problem and only set her down after Len welcomed them into his home.

Jake told Len about her fall and her ankle, then he watched closely while Len examined her ankle, refusing to leave her side. The pain returned full force when Len examined her foot, pressing on the bones to feel for a break and rotating her foot to test its mobility. To block out the pain, Nora looked out the window and tried to focus on an incoming float plane, probably bringing the mail. She watched as it descended toward the inlet and as its pontoons skimmed the surface until it settled completely in the water. She was still watching the plane slowly make its way toward the dock when Len patted her on the knee and told her he was finished. Nora's ankle was wrapped tightly and Len was handing her a crutch.

"I don't think it's broken, but you should stay off that foot for at least a day," said Len. Suspecting that Nora would try to defy his orders as soon as she stepped out the door, he turned to Jake. "You can get her home, can't you?"

Jake nodded. "I'll take care of her."

"Good," said Len as he got up and began putting his med kit away. "You two can let yourselves out. I have to take care of a few things." He quickly gathered his things and carried them into a back room.

"I don't need you to take care of me," Nora said as she slowly stood up, keeping all of her weight on her good ankle.

"You heard the man," Jake said, taking Nora by the arm and helping her to the door. "You shouldn't put any weight on the foot. Even with the crutch, you're going to need some help getting home."

"Really, I'm fine," Nora insisted, but she still let Jake help her out the door. Then he led her to a nearby bench.

"You wait here. I'll bring your skiff around to the marina."

Jake left her there, with one foot propped up on the railing of the boardwalk. It was ferry day again, Nora realized when she saw the small ship was docked at the south end of town. *Has it been another two weeks already? Time really does fly.*

She watched as a few passengers disembarked the small ship. All of them walked right past her on their way to their homes, but one man stopped. He was an older man, looked to be in his early fifties. He also looked uncomfortable in his brand new khaki pants and cotton button-down shirt. Nora had the feeling he would be more at ease in a business suit. He definitely put off the businessman vibe.

"Excuse me," he said. "Can you tell me how to find a woman named Nora Cooley?"

That took her by surprise.

"I'm Nora," she answered. "Is there something I can do for

you?"

He smiled.

"Yes, actually. I saw your ad and I've come to see the place."
He saw the shock on her face. "You haven't sold it already, have
you?"

"Umm, no." Nora responded, feeling guilty she hadn't
cancelled the ad sooner. This man had wasted a significant amount
of time and money traveling to Heron, and she wasn't even
planning to sell the place anymore. "This is a little awkward."

The sound of an outboard motor interrupted them. Jake had
returned with the skiff and docked it nearby.

"Who's this?" he asked, smiling as he approached the pair. He
held out a hand to the stranger. "I'm Jake. And you are?"

"Gerald Grainger. Just arrived on the ferry," he explained
genially.

"So what brings you to Heron? Staying at one of the lodges?
Maybe I can point you in the right direction."

"No, no. I'm only here for the day. Came to see about buying
some property from this young lady."

Whoa! That took Jake by surprise. He looked at Nora,
confused, then turned back to the man.

"What do you mean?"

"Well, I saw her ad," he explained. "If the pictures do it any
justice, I think it might be exactly what I'm looking for."

Jake turned to Nora, bewildered. "You placed an ad for the
property?"

"Yes, but..."

"You were never planning to stay." He felt numb at the
thought. It was all so overwhelming. All this time, she had been
pretending like she was going to stay. And all this time, she had
been waiting for a potential buyer to come along. Well, a buyer
was there now. Nora had the opportunity to leave, once and for

all.

He'd been right from the start, to think she wouldn't stick around. And just when he let his guard down, and let her into his life, she was leaving. As if everything they'd shared had meant nothing to her. As if he meant nothing to her.

An anger rose up in Jake as he thought it. Nora was exactly like his mother. She never would have stayed in Heron. She would have strung him along, just like his mom did with his dad, but in the end she still would have left.

The pain he felt was unbearable.

"It's good that you're leaving," he spat out, wanting to hurt Nora as much as she'd just hurt him. "You never would have survived out there, anyway. You never did belong here."

His words stung.

"Jake, it's not what you think..." She wanted to tell him she wasn't selling the property. She'd decided to stay.

But Jake wasn't sticking around to hear any excuses or explanations. Before she had a chance to explain, he left Nora and the man alone on the boardwalk. He wouldn't risk any further hurt.

Lily stopped Jake in front of the pub. He had a look in his eyes like he was ready to spill blood.

"Hey, what's going on?"

"Nora's leaving. That's what's going on."

"No, she can't be," Lily tried to reassure him. "It's probably a misunderstanding. You should go find her and talk to her."

"Not a chance. She's made her choice. She listed the cabin for sale weeks ago. I think I always knew she was going to leave eventually, just like Mom did. It's better if she leaves now."

"Jake, you're being stupid. It took Mom more than fifteen years out here before she got fed up with living in the bush. How long would it take for Nora to prove to you that she's really going to stick around? A year? Ten years? Twenty?"

"You know what it did to Dad when Mom left."

"What are you so afraid of, Jake? That she's going to leave like Mom did? Or that, just like Dad, you won't be able to get over her if she does?"

That was it, exactly. He was a one-woman man, just like his father. If he let himself fall in love with Nora, he would love her until his dying day. He would never be able to move on with his life if she left him. And that scared him more than anything.

"Dad hasn't been the same since Mom left. You know that. I don't want to make the same mistake."

"Loving someone is never a mistake," Lily said softly, laying a hand on Jake's arm. "The bigger mistake is not taking the chance that's given to you."

Lily was a hopeless romantic, but maybe she had a point. Jake looked back toward the harbor, where he'd left Nora. No, he couldn't assume Nora would be exactly like his mother. Maybe she did have what it takes to stick it out in the Alaskan bush, but she obviously wasn't willing to give it a try.

"It doesn't matter," Jake said stubbornly. "Some hot shot's already here, ready to buy the land. She's probably taking him out to see the property even as we speak." His heart was breaking at the thought of Nora leaving. "And it's a good thing, too. Better that she leaves now, before..."

"Before what? Before you fall in love with her?" Lily knew her brother better than he realized. It was already too late.

CHAPTER

18

Jake's words stung. They cut right through her, leaving nothing but pieces of a shattered dream.

Maybe he was right. Hadn't Madeline told her the same thing, that she didn't belong in Heron and that she'd never be truly happy there? All of the doubt Nora had ever felt about living in the bush rushed back into her mind.

He never thought she had it in her to live out there on her own. He never believed she could survive. He always expected her to leave.

It shouldn't have come as a surprise. Everyone in Heron thought she would fail, she'd known that right from the start. But after all the time she'd spent with Jake, she really thought she had at least one person on her side. She thought he, of all people, believed in her. Obviously she was wrong.

Maybe she was wrong about a lot of other things, too. Maybe she had been wrong to think she could build a life in that little cabin. Really, what was she doing there?

"I know I showed up unexpectedly, but I am on a bit of a time crunch. Do you think we could head out to the property? I'd like to get back before the ferry leaves," said Grainger, looking impatiently at his watch, "which I believe is about an hour and a half from now."

Jake was right. She should leave before the Alaskan wilderness swallowed her up. And now she had the opportunity standing right in front of her.

"Yeah, sorry," said Nora. "Let's go."

She left the crutch Len had given her on the bench and limped toward the skiff, her ankle still aching from the fall earlier. The man followed close behind.

"You took quite a chance coming out here," she said as she carefully climbed into the boat. "You weren't worried the property would already be off the market?"

"Not really. I was already in Juneau on business when an associate of mine told me about your ad. Figured it wasn't too much of a detour to come check it out."

"Well, you're lucky, because up until a few minutes ago, I wasn't sure about selling it."

* * *

"So, this is it. Five acres, a cabin, and two outbuildings," said Nora as they walked the property. "I know it's not much."

The torrential rain from the night before left the property littered with branches and leaves. It was a mess. Nora glanced around at the debris that would need to be picked up and the long trench now dividing the property where a mudslide had come down from the mountain. It would take days to clean it all up.

"Sorry about the mess. We had a storm come through last

night."

She felt numb as they walked the perimeter of the property. She was telling him about the tides and the run-off from the mountains, but she was only going through the motions. All she could think about was Jake. The look of disappointment on his face when he realized she had listed the property for sale. The tone of his voice when he told her it was better that she sell. His insistence that it was better if she leave Heron sooner rather than later, that she never would have stayed anyway. The anguish she felt in her heart at the thought of leaving it all behind... of leaving Jake behind.

"It's perfect." Grainger was satisfied with it. "The stream, the waterfront, the mountain views. It's exactly what I'm looking for."

"Don't you want to see the cabin? You haven't been inside any of the buildings."

"Oh, sure, sure," he said, as if the condition of the cabin was completely irrelevant. "Let's take a look."

She'd been gone for two days and a light dust had settled on everything in the cabin. The old musty smell had settled in again. No matter how many times she had scrubbed the walls, the smell always came back. At first, it had been annoying. Now, it smelled rather comforting.

The wood stove was cold and Nora winced when Grainger gave the old iron stove a little kick with his boot to see how sturdy it was.

"Will you be taking any of this... stuff... with you?" He wasn't very impressed with any of it.

"Only my personal belongings. The books and clothes. The furniture all stays."

"Hmm," he said, not sounding too satisfied with her answer. "The furniture's irrelevant. I won't be needing any of it."

They walked back outside, then, and Nora showed him the outbuildings.

"The cabin's not much, like you said. And the other buildings are pretty rustic, too. But the property itself is precisely what I need. I'll take it."

Nora almost didn't trust her ears. Had she heard him correctly? "You... want to buy it?"

"That's what I said, isn't it?" He pulled out his cell phone and held it up in the air, searching for a signal.

"That won't work," said Nora, pointing at his cell phone. "At least not until we get back into town."

"Well, that's one drawback, I guess. No matter. People come to Alaska for the peace and quiet, right? That's the beauty of this place. The remoteness. It's the perfect place to get away from everything and relax." He looked around one more time, taking in the surroundings. "Come on. We should be getting back to town so I can call my attorney and have the papers drawn up. I want the paperwork to be ready and waiting for us when we get to Juneau. I assume you can make the trip today? It shouldn't take long to get the deed and title transferred."

Nora stood there in shock. She was a little taken aback by the man's take-charge attitude. He exuded confidence, an air of importance. He was obviously a business man, someone who was used to giving orders and getting his way.

"But we haven't even discussed the purchase price."

"There will be plenty of time to talk terms on the ferry," he said abruptly, climbing into the skiff and waiting for Nora. She followed, pushing the boat out into deeper water and then climbing in as carefully as she could with her still swollen ankle.

He looked at his watch impatiently as they bounced along on the waves, heading toward town. "Can this thing go any faster?"

"Sorry," Nora hollered at him. She already had the throttle

open all the way.

"I don't know why I bothered with the ferry, anyway," he muttered. "I should have chartered a flight in and out. That's what I get for listening to my therapist. 'Take time to enjoy life,' he said. 'Don't always be in such a hurry.' So instead of flying, I took the seven-hour-long boat ride. Do you have any idea how much nothing there is between here and Juneau? Thought it would give me time to relax. All it did was remind me how much time I was wasting."

This guy's really annoying, Nora thought, trying hard not to roll her eyes whenever he spoke. It was a wonder he wanted to buy a vacation cabin so far out, considering how much he evidently hated being disconnected from the rest of the world.

He looked at his watch again. Town still wasn't in sight. "We're never going to make it before the ferry leaves. There has to be flight service out of here, right?"

"Yeah," Nora shouted back over the sound of the outboard motor. "Gus has a float plane service in town."

Not surprisingly, when they arrived in town the ferry was already gone. Nora pulled the skiff up to the dock at the store and helped the man out of the boat. Like she had been when she'd first arrived in Heron, he was a little wobbly as he stepped up onto the aluminum seat and then onto the dock. Just like Nora had, he would learn.

From the dock, Nora pointed him in the direction where he would likely find Gus. Then she went in search of Jake. She had to see him. It wasn't too late to change her mind. It wasn't too late to tell Grainger she didn't want to sell. If only Jake would be willing to hear her out.

She found him at the pub, sitting alone at a small table in the farthest corner of the restaurant. He had a cup of coffee in front of him, but he hadn't taken a single sip. He just sat there staring at the hot, black liquid.

Slowly, she approached the table. Nora had never felt this awkward around Jake before, but now, she didn't know what to say to him. She didn't know how to begin.

"Jake," she said cautiously.

He glanced up at her and then returned his attention to his cup of coffee. "What do you want?" he asked. It sounded more like an accusation than a question.

"I wanted to explain," she said, stepping closer to the table. "I didn't know Grainger was coming. I never thought anyone would be interested in buying the cabin..."

"So that makes it better? You wanted to leave, but you didn't think you'd be able to? Well, now there's nothing holding you here anymore."

Her eyes pleaded with him. *Ask me to stay. Tell me the night we shared on the mountaintop meant as much to you as it did to me.*

"Please, Jake. Don't be like that."

Jake stood up, then, and looked her in the eye.

"Why didn't you tell me you were thinking about leaving?" he asked quietly, his eyes searching hers for an answer.

Nora didn't have a good answer for his question. "I don't know," she said honestly. "I mean, I thought about selling it at first, but then I decided to stay. I just never got around to cancelling the ad. I was going to, but..."

"Ah, there you are." Grainger had returned. He stepped between Nora and Jake, ignoring the fact that he was interrupting a private conversation. "Gus refuses to fly out this afternoon, even though I offered him double. So I booked a room at the Rainforest Lodge for the night. We'll leave at 9 a.m. tomorrow. Shouldn't take more than a few hours in Juneau. I thought we could work out the details now, since I'm stuck here overnight."

"Mr. Grainger, I don't mean to be impolite, but we're in the middle of something right now," said Nora, letting her irritation with Grainger's unexpected arrival get the best of her. He had messed everything up with Jake. They'd spent an incredible night together on the mountain, and now Jake would barely even speak to her. It was all because of Grainger. Not to mention, he was just plain rude and bossy. "I'll catch up with you later. Okay?"

He wasn't accustomed to people speaking to him in such a manner. Grainger was usually the one giving orders, not the other way around. He turned, then, and glanced at Jake for a moment. "I'll let you two get back to... whatever it was you were doing."

"So you're really going through with it," Jake said after Grainger walked away, masking his disappointment with anger. "You're selling it."

"That's what I wanted to talk to you about," Nora said, hoping he would ask her to stay. Wanting him to give her a reason not to sell the cabin.

"Good," he said coldly. "It's about time you got back to civilization, as you call it. Get back to your busy schedule of highbrow social events. I'm sure you already have dozens of appointments with all the best hair salons and spa treatments. The shopping malls have missed you."

"Is that really what you think of me? You think I'm some spoiled brat who spends my time shopping?"

"That's exactly what you are. Who in the hell shows up to the Alaskan bush wearing stiletto heels? You looked more like you were ready to walk down the runway than the deck of a boat."

Who does he think he is, judging me? Sure, Nora had lived a comfortable life before she came to Heron. She'd grown accustomed to a certain standard of living. But that's not who she was anymore. She had rejected that life. She didn't need the fancy clothes and expensive jewelry.

"That's not who I am anymore, and you know it. Being out there in the cabin taught me a lot about myself, what I'm capable of. For the first time in my life, I learned how to be self-reliant. I never thought I could make it on my own before, but I've proven that I can."

Jake laughed haughtily.

"So you think you managed to survive out there for a month on your own. You really do live in a dream world. The only reason you're still alive is because you had help every step of the way."

"You're wrong," Nora said stubbornly.

"Prove it." It was the closest he could come to asking her to stay.

"No." She was almost shouting now. "I don't belong here. You know it. I know it. Everyone knows it. Everything I do reminds me of that fact. Do you know how many times I've come within inches of my life? I could have died at least three times and I've only been here a month. A month! I fell overboard into the inlet. I was charged by a bear. I slid down a landslide on the side of a mountain. How many more accidents do I need to have before I get it through my thick skull that I'm in over my head? I can't do this on my own."

But I could do it if I had you by my side.

"At least you have some sense in you." He turned to leave, but Nora grabbed him by the arm. "Let me go," he said, shaking her off. "Like you said, you don't belong here. Go home. Go back to Los Angeles."

Nora's heart broke as she watched Jake walk away. He didn't want her. The realization took her breath away, replaced it with unbearable sorrow. Tears streamed down her face as she hurried out of the pub. By the time she reached the skiff, she was sobbing, gulping for air.

Back at the cabin, the tears continued as Nora pulled her

clothes out of the dresser and packed them into suitcases.

She pulled the boxes out from under the bed, opened one of them, and took out her cell phone. Soon, she would be back in the world of cell phone service and internet access. And roads. She would be able to drive places again. Anywhere she wanted to go. Anywhere. For the life of her, Nora couldn't think of a single place she wanted to go. There was nowhere else she wanted to be, she realized as the tears started flowing again.

She hauled the boxes down the ladder and stacked them next to the door. Then she picked up the radio off the table. It was still tuned to the station she and Jake always used. As Nora packed up the radio, she thought about radioing Jake one last time. But then she remembered the look on his face earlier. No. She couldn't bear the pain of his rejection again. It would be better to make a clean break, she decided, carefully placing the radio into the box of things she would be leaving behind.

As Nora looked around the cabin, she couldn't shake the feeling she was betraying her uncle. He'd left her his home and she was going to sell it to the first person that came along, like it meant nothing.

She saw the smudge of dirt in the side of the stove where the man had kicked it earlier. He was merely checking to see how solid the stove was, but it still irritated Nora that he had so little respect for her things, for Pete's things. He would never truly appreciate the cabin the way Nora did. It would never mean anything to him.

Selling the cabin felt wrong. She didn't know what she should do. The only thing she knew for certain was that Jake didn't want her. And, knowing that, she couldn't bear to be near him. She had to sell. She had to leave.

Nora had left everything behind once before, but it hadn't felt like this. Not even close. Her face was red and puffy from crying.

Her hands were trembling. The anguish was almost unbearable.

She'd grown to love the musty smell of the wood stove and the creak of the wood floor beneath her feet. The cabin didn't seem as cramped as it had when she'd first arrived. Now, it felt just right, the perfect amount of space for a single person. Even the solitude had become something Nora appreciated.

But she couldn't survive out there on her own. She knew it. Everyone knew it. She needed to take the money and start over somewhere else.

CHAPTER

19

The plane bobbed up and down on the waves next to the dock. Gripping the door tightly, Nora cautiously stepped onto the pontoon and up the three-step ladder into the front passenger seat of the plane. The seat was narrow and uncomfortable. The dash in front of her was covered in gauges and buttons.

She turned in her seat to see the rest of the airplane. It was small, to say the least. Grainger was already seated directly behind her, looking cramped and uncomfortable in the cabin of the tiny float plane. Behind him, there was a small cargo area that was mostly empty.

Gus climbed into the pilot's seat next to Nora and picked up two headsets off the dash of the cockpit. He handed one to Nora and put the other one on himself. The headset muffled the sound of the loud engine. Through the earpiece, she heard Gus announce his departure to someone as the plane pulled away from the dock slowly, making its way out into the inlet. Satisfied he had a clear path, Gus pushed a lever forward and the plane picked up speed, skidding along the surface of the water. They bounced along for a few seconds and then Gus pulled up. Nora watched out the window as the plane lifted off from the water and began its ascent.

Below, the town of Heron was illuminated with the morning sun. As they flew overhead, Nora spotted her car, still parked in the lot next to the ferry dock. Everything she owned was packed into the car. She made two trips into town earlier, the skiff loaded down with everything she wanted from the cabin. She'd been feeling especially sentimental that morning, and she decided to bring Pete's journal and log books. Grainger wasn't going to appreciate them and Nora hated to see them tossed aside. At the last minute, she also decided to bring the radio. It was a small reminder of Jake, not that she'd need anything to remind her of him. She couldn't get him off her mind. She'd hurt him. And now he didn't want her. How could he be so unwilling to hear her out, especially after the way they connected on the mountaintop? Their night together meant the world to Nora. Surely it had meant something to Jake, too. Obviously not. He'd made it clear that he didn't want her, hadn't he? Nora might have been able to learn how to live in the wilderness, even to thrive out there on her own, but she couldn't deal with Jake rejecting her.

Through the window of the plane, she watched the car until it disappeared in the distance. She would come back for the car and all of her things on the next ferry. In the meantime, she would spend some time in Juneau trying to figure out what to do next.

They followed the inlet for a short distance as the plane climbed higher, then Gus turned them inland and they crossed over the tall mountains that lined the northeastern region of the island.

Nora shifted uneasily in her seat. The thought of traveling over land in a float plane paralyzed her with fear. She'd heard about plane crashes in Alaska, and if they were going to go down, she wanted to be over water, where Gus could hopefully land the plane safely.

When the plane hit an air pocket, the ride got a little bumpy and Nora gripped her seat.

"That's nothing," said Gus calmly. "It's usually a little bumpy around this spot, but it will smooth out." His tone was reassuring, the voice of many years of experience flying from Heron to Juneau on a regular basis.

Nora smiled uneasily at him. "If you say so," she said, even though she wasn't totally convinced. Inhaling deeply, she tried to calm her nerves.

Just as Gus said, the ride got easier a few minutes later after the plane passed over the northern tip of the island and moved back over a large expanse of water.

For the next half-hour, Nora actually did relax as she looked out over the horizon. They passed over dozens of small islands and a couple large glaciers. They flew over shipping lanes and past cruise ships. Eventually, she relaxed enough to close her eyes and attempt a short nap. She even succeeded in falling asleep, only to be awakened a few minutes later when the plane rapidly dropped in altitude. Nora gripped her seat, silently praying God would keep them safe, as the plane plunged uncontrollably downward, toward the blue, salty waters. They dropped more than a thousand feet before Gus regained control.

After Gus ascended back up to their original altitude, he looked over at Nora. "That even scared me," he said. Judging by the look on his face and the sound of his voice, Nora knew he wasn't kidding.

She let out a sigh of relief as the plane leveled off. She'd had too many close calls in the past month. Almost everything that could have gone wrong did go wrong since she arrived in Alaska. But soon enough she would be back among civilization, away from all the perils of living in a remote community.

She turned and glanced back at Grainger. His face was stark white, his lips pursed together tightly.

"Are you alright?"

"I'm perfectly fine," he snapped at her. "But tell that so-called pilot to pick up the speed and get us there. I refuse to die like this."

"He's a little rattled," Nora told Gus as she turned back in her seat. "Don't mind him."

But even as she told Gus to ignore Grainger's bad attitude, Nora couldn't help but wonder if returning to "civilization" was really a good thing. If Grainger was an example of a civilized person, he had a terrible way of showing it. He was too uptight and rigid, too focused on setting goals and achieving results. He didn't think about anyone other than himself. There were a lot of people out there like Grainger. Far too many. Wasn't that what Nora was trying to get away from when she'd left Los Angeles for Alaska? Did she really want to go back to that? When the plane touched down in Juneau a few hours later, Nora still didn't know the answer to that question.

"Want me to stick around and fly you back?" Gus asked Nora as he helped her off the plane.

"No," she said. "That won't be necessary. I'll be staying here in Juneau for a while."

"Okay. But if you change your mind, I'll be flying back in about two hours. Going to stock up on supplies and get a decent meal in me before I head back."

Nora smiled at him. "Thanks, Gus. You take care." As she said goodbye, she realized the people in Heron were far more civilized than anyone she'd ever known in her life. Sure, they lived far away from what most people considered civilization, but they were the only people she'd ever met who really understood the definition of community. Spontaneously, she stepped forward and gave him a quick hug.

"Well, now that felt like goodbye," he said.

It was, Nora thought, turning and walking up the dock after Grainger.

Two men stood waiting for them next to a shiny black car, parked illegally at the curb in front of the dock. One man opened the door for Grainger and Nora, then hurried around the car and climbed into the driver's seat. The other handed Grainger a large manila envelope, quickly summarizing its contents. Grainger pulled out the documents and reviewed them while they drove away.

A few minutes later, the car stopped in front of a title office. It was a small building tucked in between a bar and an art studio. A woman sat at the receptionist's desk, playing a game on her phone, when they walked in. When Grainger told her they had an appointment, she looked up from her game long enough to point in the direction of a small conference room, then returned her attention to the task of matching colored candies in a row.

In the conference room, Nora was directed to have a seat at the table and offered a cup of coffee. She turned down the coffee, not wanting to waste any more time there than she had to. Already, she was questioning her decision to go through with the sale. She had been questioning it all morning, throughout most of the plane ride, and half of the car ride to the title office.

Let's get this over with before I change my mind, she thought.

Then they started shoving papers in front of her, asking for her signature on each of them. With the ink pen poised over the first document, Nora hesitated and looked up at Grainger. He stood in the opposite corner of the room, talking to one of his men. She assumed it was his lawyer.

"The property is perfect," she heard him telling the lawyer. "Close enough to an authentic bush community. Far enough out to experience wild Alaska."

Nora wondered, again, why Grainger was interested in buying her property. It seemed so unlikely a man like him would want a cabin in the woods. He was so focused on business and work. When would he ever find time to vacation at the cabin? Then again, Nora hadn't exactly been an outdoors-woman when she'd arrived in Heron. She still wasn't what most people would call "outdoorsy," but she had grown to love the bush.

"You do know the ferry only comes to Heron twice a month in the summer?" she interrupted Grainger's conversation with his lawyer. *Am I trying to convince him not to buy the property*, she wondered. *No, of course not. He had a lot to learn about Alaska.* She was only making sure he was aware of the most basic obstacles he would face.

"Oh, that won't be a problem. I only rode the ferry for the experience. My pilot will bring me in next time. And once the lodge is built, I'll have at least two pilots on payroll, bringing guests in and out every week."

"A lodge?" He hadn't mentioned plans to build on the property.

"Yes, yes. The plans are for a 5,000 square foot building that will be the main lodge, plus half-a-dozen small cottages for guests who want more privacy. The primary focus is going to be fishing excursions, but once I acquire more land we'll add hunting excursions, too."

"So, you're going to tear down the cabin."

"Well, of course. Everything needs to be razed to make room for construction." He said it matter-of-factly, as if she should have known his intention from the start.

"No." The word was out of Nora's mouth before she realized she'd said it. He was going to destroy everything she'd grown to love about the place. Pete's cabin would be gone. Everything he'd worked so hard to build, everything he'd given to her, would be demolished.

She set the ink pen down next to the stack of unsigned papers.

"What do you mean?" Grainger looked at her sternly. "We have an agreement. I made all the arrangements and had all the paperwork drawn up. I paid for your airfare here. Do you have any idea how much I have invested in this already?"

She didn't waver. It didn't matter. There was no chance in hell she was going to sell her cabin to someone like Grainger... or to anyone for that matter. Heron was her home. It was the only place she wanted to be. She knew that now.

Nora had grown to love the town and its people, especially one person in particular. Maybe she wasn't cut out for living alone in the wilderness, but if she had Jake she wouldn't be alone. She could adapt. She'd learn.

"I'm not selling," she said firmly. She pushed the papers across the table, stood up, and walked out of the title office. She didn't look back to see Grainger's reaction. If she had, she would have witnessed a red-faced man throwing the papers across the room, yelling at his attorney.

On foot, Nora hurried back toward the dock nearly three miles away. Her ankle still hurt, but she pushed through the pain, determined to reach the dock before Gus left. She got there just in time to find Gus doing his pre-flight checklist. He grinned when he saw her.

"Decided to come back, after all, eh?"

"Nothing could keep me away," she said, climbing up into the cockpit.

* * *

It was dinnertime when the plane touched down in the waters of Heron. Her ankle was throbbing at that point, but she managed to hobble over to Jake's house. He was the only thing that mattered. Maybe he was unwilling to hear her out before, but she was going to make sure he listened to her now.

Pausing at the door, Nora quickly ran her fingers through her hair and inspected her reflection on the glass window. Her hair was damp from the lightly misting rain. *Oh, well. It would have to do.*

Excitedly, Nora knocked on the door. Then she waited. And waited. The curtains were drawn and Nora couldn't see inside, so she walked around the house, thinking maybe Jake hadn't heard her. At the back door, Nora knocked again. This time, she also called his name. When there was still no answer, she tried the doorknob. The door was locked.

Disappointed, Nora turned and headed toward the center of town. The pub was packed as small-time fishermen came in for a cup of coffee or an ice-cold beer after a long day out on the open waters. If Nora had been hoping to get a seat at the restaurant, she would have been out of luck. But she wasn't looking for dinner. She headed straight toward the bar, where Lily was topping off cups of coffee and taking orders for burgers and fries.

When Lily glanced up and saw Nora, her face lit up with excitement. "I knew you'd be back," Lily said, grinning. Then she noticed Nora's appearance. She was wet and tired looking. "Are you okay?"

"Do you know where Jake is?" asked Nora, ignoring Lily's question.

"Uh, no." She shook her head. "Did you check at the house?"

Nora didn't answer. She turned and hurried out of the pub. There was only one other way she could think of to find Jake. She headed for her car, still parked in the lot at the south end of town.

That's where the radio was. If there was any way to find Jake, it would be on the radio.

Nora quickly rummaged through the boxes until she found it. She sat down in the front seat, closed her eyes, and prayed Jake would be on the other end. Then she turned the power knob on and spoke.

"Jake? Are you there?"

She waited.

"Jake. Come in."

There was no answer.

"Come on, Jake. Answer me," she pleaded. *Tell me I haven't lost you for good.*

The only answer she received was the quiet crackle of radio silence on the other end.

* * *

Freezing cold, Nora hobbled toward her cabin. Getting out of the skiff had proven to be much more difficult than she'd expected. After all that walking, her ankle was throbbing again. The wobbling of the skiff in the shallow water threw her off balance. She fell into the cold water and had to drag herself up onto the shore before she was able to stand back up. She didn't bother to even try and pull the skiff up onto solid ground. Instead, she tied the rope to the nearest thing she could find, a small boulder at the edge of the water. When the tide came in, the boulder would be completely submerged and the rope would probably come loose, but Nora didn't care. The boat was the least of her worries. She'd lost Jake, probably for good. Without him, nothing else mattered.

Despondent, Nora pushed open the cabin door. She hadn't

brought any clothes back from the car. She'd left everything there, except the radio. That, she held clutched against her chest, her only connection to Jake.

It's warm in here, she realized, confused at why the stove would have a fire in it. *Someone's in here.* The cabin was dark. Only a sliver of orange glowed from the wood stove where the door didn't quite shut tight.

"Go away." It was a voice filled with anguish and pain.

It was Jake. He sat at the kitchen table, hunched over.

Nora closed the door.

Jake didn't bother to look up and when he heard the door close, he assumed whoever it was had turned and left. He figured it was Willie, checking in on him. Or maybe Lily, asking him to come home. The last person he expected was Nora. She was gone for good. She'd packed up all of her things and left.

She wasn't coming back.

That thought had been echoing in his head all day. He'd watched Nora board the float plane that morning with that Grainger guy, hoping she would change her mind. Even as he watched her leave, he knew he'd been wrong to push her away. He let his fears of rejection get the best of him. He knew that now. But being with Nora was worth the risk.

After she left, he came out to the cabin and found it empty, proof that she wasn't coming back. Not ever. He'd spent the entire day there, shut up in the dark cabin. He couldn't go home. He needed to be near her. The cabin was as close as he could get.

"So, does the offer still stand?" Nora finally found the courage to speak.

Jake looked up. His breath caught in his throat when he saw her silhouette in the darkness. Was he imagining her? Or was she really back?

"What offer?" he asked, standing up. He wanted to rush toward her and take her in his arms, but he still wasn't sure she was real.

Nora took a step toward him.

"The one to marry me," she said cautiously. "On the mountaintop, when you thought I was asleep... I believe you said you were going to marry me."

"You heard that?" His voice cracked when he spoke.

"If the offer still stands..."

That was all he needed to hear. In two steps, Jake closed the gap between them and pulled her into his arms. Nora was back. Thank God, she was back. He wasn't going to let her go ever again, not if he could help it.

"So you're not leaving? You're not selling the place?"

Nora shook her head.

"You're going to stay? For good?"

She answered him with a kiss. It was a kiss that said, "I'll never leave you again."

CHAPTER

20

"Come back to bed," Jake said in the wee hours of the morning. "A good wife wouldn't keep her husband waiting like this."

"A good husband would be a little more patient," Nora said, smiling contentedly as she grabbed some food off the shelf.

Wife, she thought, relishing the sound of the word.

The wedding had been held at the water's edge in front of the cabin. It was a short ceremony, with Lily serving as maid of honor and Willie as the best man. Samuel and Madeline watched as Jake slipped the ring onto Nora's finger, promising to love and cherish her forever.

Everyone in town, all 152 residents, watched from skiffs floating in the inlet as Jake kissed his new bride and then carried her away. The two disappeared into the cabin to begin their honeymoon. Since then, they hadn't left the loft except to eat.

Nora filled a plate with cheese and crackers to take back up into the loft. Then she grabbed a bottle of wine. From the loft above her, she heard Jake groan with impatience.

"I'll just be another second," she said.

There was one more thing she needed to do, one thought she wanted to record before she forgot. Reaching up onto the shelf, she picked up Pete's journal. She opened the worn leather cover and flipped to a blank page. Then she added one more entry.

My uncle left me everything he owned, which wasn't much. But it turns out, it was exactly what I needed. Nothing more. Nothing less.

Look for the next installment in the
Alaskan Frontier Romance series

Available February 2015 in Paperback and E-Book

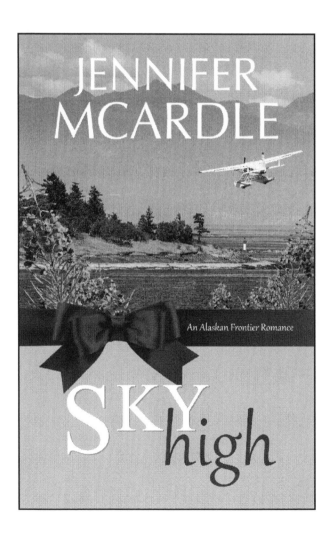

ACKNOWLEDGMENTS

Alaska is a vast and beautiful land, its regions as varied as the people who inhabit them. The short amount of time I spent in Southeast Alaska inspired me to write a story set in one of its remote locales. The people and the town depicted in *Water's Edge* are pure fiction, as are their quirky personalities and habits. The characters are in no way a reflection of real Alaskans, the men and women who choose to live their lives on the edge of the last remaining frontier. For their fortitude and resilience, I'd like to thank all Alaskans… they are a true inspiration. And to the Alaskans I know personally, I hope you won't pick apart every little bit of this book.

Water's Edge would not have been possible without the support of my husband. Thank you for giving me the opportunity to devote myself full-time to this project.

As any writer well knows, there is a lot more to writing a book than sitting down and putting the story on paper. Many hours went into revising and editing to get the story right. *Water's Edge* might not be what it is without Clara Harrand, who read the earlier draft of *Water's Edge*. You provided me with some much needed encouragement and criticism. My appreciation goes out to Susan Budzinski, as well, for proofreading.

Of course, thank you to my fans. There's nothing better than receiving a note from a fan letting me know how much you enjoyed one of my books. That's what keeps me going.

Most importantly, I thank God... for everything I have and for everything I am.

ABOUT THE AUTHOR

A former newspaper reporter, Jennifer McArdle is an award-winning writer, having earned recognition from the Michigan Press Association and Suburban Newspapers of America. Since her departure from the field of print journalism, she has focused her writing talents on fiction.

She and her husband have spent a great deal of time traveling throughout the United States, including a six month stint in Alaska. The *Alaskan Frontier Romance* series is inspired by the time she spent in Southeast Alaska's Inside Passage. *Water's Edge* is the first book in that series.

In addition to the *Alaskan Frontier Romance* series, McArdle has authored a youth novel, *Back By Dawn*.